Accolades for America's greatest hero Mack Bolan

"Very, very action-oriented.... Highly successful, today's hottest books for men."
—*The New York Times*

"Anyone who stands against the civilized forces of truth and justice will sooner or later have to face the piercing blue eyes and cold Beretta steel of Mack Bolan, the lean, mean nightstalker, civilization's avenging angel."
—*San Francisco Examiner*

"Mack Bolan is a star. The Executioner is a beacon of hope for people with a sense of American justice."
—*Las Vegas Review Journal*

"In the beginning there was the Executioner—a publishing phenomenon. Mack Bolan remains a spiritual godfather to those who have followed."
—*San Jose Mercury News*

THE
ONLY WAY

It's a tough, cruel world. The savages are winning because too many good people don't want a piece of the action. There comes a time when you simply have to survive, and the effort may ultimately involve violence. I have set myself up as judge, jury and executioner, and while I believe that is wrong, I also believe it's the only way.

—Mack Bolan

''Mack Bolan stabs right through the heart of the frustration and hopelessness the average person feels about crime running rampant in the streets.''

—*Dallas Times Herald*

DON PENDLETON's
MACK BOLAN.

Knockdown

A GOLD EAGLE BOOK FROM
WORLDWIDE.

TORONTO • NEW YORK • LONDON • PARIS
AMSTERDAM • STOCKHOLM • HAMBURG
ATHENS • MILAN • TOKYO • SYDNEY

First edition February 1990

ISBN 0-373-61418-7

Special thanks and acknowledgment to
Carl Furst for his contribution to this work.

If you prick us, do we not bleed?
... if you poison us, do we not die?
and if you wrong us, shall we
not revenge?

—William Shakespeare,
The Merchant of Venice

It takes a strong man to speak out against an
injustice, to go against the tide to right a
wrong. If another man raises a hand to still
that voice, he'll have to answer to me.

—Mack Bolan

To the men and women of the
Organized Crime Bureau

CHAPTER ONE

Occasionally a man laughed when he first met John Bear Claw. John was small. His body was square, as were his head and face, and altogether he was a squat, bowlegged little man. His complexion was swarthy, his hair black and coarse and his eyes glowered from under heavy brows. When men laughed, John pretended not to notice.

No man who laughed at him ever laughed again after he saw John work, saw him walk confidently out onto a narrow beam four hundred feet above the street with his mask and gloves, squat, pull down his mask and weld two great steel girders together.

John Claw was a Native American, a Mohawk Indian, and like so many of his tribe, he and his brother worked on the high steel. They were the fourth generation of Claws who had worked above the streets of Manhattan, riveters and welders on the huge black skeletons that eventually became skyscrapers. John's family was well-known, as were the Mohawks, for their lack of fear of heights. Maybe they needed none. No man of the Claw family had ever fallen.

This morning John Claw arrived at the Seventh Avenue construction site a little early. He usually did. He liked to stand and stare up at the steel for a few minutes before he went to the engineer's trailer to get his assignment. It was a hot, steamy morning, but like every welder, John wore a long-sleeved shirt with the collar tightly buttoned at his throat. He wore heavy shoes and high socks that covered his calves inside his pants. This was his protection, not just against the hot sparks that would fly from his welding, but more importantly against the intense ultraviolet radiation off an arc welder, radiation that would blister a man's skin like a severe sunburn.

He was proud of the building they were erecting. He'd been proud of most of them. This one would rise fifty-four stories and would provide offices for a score of big companies. Thousands of people would work there rushing in every morning like so many busy ants and rushing out again at the end of the day. John Claw was glad his job was to *build* their office building, not to work in it.

He was in a happy frame of mind. His elder daughter, Gina, had spent the weekend at home and had prolonged the visit by staying through Monday. It had been pleasant to see her, to hear the news that she was content with her life in California and was engaged to a helicopter pilot. She would live in the northern part of the state, where her young man flew for a lumber company. On his way into town that morning, John had dropped her at Kennedy International Airport.

He shook off his reverie and without reluctance walked through the gate in the wooden fence and to the trailer.

What happened next wasn't unusual. The engineer asked him to check some welds that had been done the day before by another welder—and maybe to repair them.

"The old problem, John. You know what I mean."

John only nodded. Yes, he did know what the engineer meant. Too many of the welders had just one qualification: they were members of the union. Some of them welded badly. Some of them didn't weld at all; they drew their pay and did nothing, sometimes failing even to report to the site. This was part of the cost of doing business in New York City.

As far as John was concerned, the ones who didn't show up at all were better than the ones who showed up and did their work badly. He'd said so. He'd said so at a union meeting. If no-show workers are part of the vigorish, he said, so be it. But worthless workers put weak joints in buildings and endangered every man on the job—not to mention the people who'd work in the offices later. He'd been shouted down.

Most of the time, he did his job and minded his own business. Sometimes the whole sorry mess made him mad, and he talked. Maybe his wife was right when she said he talked too much, that it was better for a man to earn his wages and bring them home and let what she called "higher-ups" worry about the way things were. The trouble was that he had begun to notice a falling-off in his calls. He wasn't getting as much work as he had a year ago, and he knew why. They were punishing him for opening his mouth.

John Claw didn't work for a contractor, per se. Each day he put in on his current site, he worked for the contractor, but next week or next month, he'd be working for a different contractor. The contractor notified the union how many men he needed and for what, and the union handed out the assignments. Technically assignments were allocated on the basis of seniority, but it was a complicated formula and a union member would be hard put to sustain his complaint that he wasn't being given all the assignments his membership and seniority entitled him to. Complaints by John Claw were in the works—in the pipeline, as they said. He had spoken to a representative of the National Labor Relations Board about it, and that, too, was in the pipeline.

On the way up in the crew elevator, John Claw watched the city retreat beneath him. Other men in the cage ignored him, which wasn't unusual. Some didn't want to speak to him. Others did, but thought it better not to be seen in friendly conversation with the squat, muscular little Mohawk who was developing a reputation as a troublemaker.

Four hundred feet above the street he picked up a heavy sledgehammer and walked out onto a girder, ten inches wide, to its junction with a vertical girder. There he planted his feet firmly and swung the hammer. He wasn't surprised when his powerful blow cracked the weld. The engineer wouldn't be surprised, either.

John Claw turned and walked back along the beam. He didn't see the foot-long hunk of scrap I-beam that hit him on the head. It glanced off his hard hat, then crunched into his shoulder. John staggered where there was no room to stagger, and his right foot came down where there was nothing but air.

He didn't scream, only grunted "Uh-oh, this is it" as he fell to his death.

As VINCE GROTTI came back across the beam ten feet above, making his way to the safety of the floored part of the structure, he spotted Burt Whittle standing where he couldn't have helped seeing Vince drop the hunk of I-beam. He stood there, staring, his mouth hanging open.

"Hey, Burt. What's up? What ya lookin' at?"

"I, uh…" The older man paused and ran his tongue over his lips. "I been watchin' those gulls, Vince. Not usual for gulls to be up this high, is it?"

Vince saw no gulls. He was a compact, dark man in his late twenties. He moved with a peculiar grace that was at the same time both beautiful and sinister.

"Yeah," Burt continued. "Been *starin'* at those gulls. Kinda fascinate me, ya know? I been starin' at 'em the last five minutes. Really starin'."

"Gotcha, Burt," Vince said. "Starin' at birds. Good man."

VINCE STOOD just inside the door of Luciano's for a full minute before his eyes made the adjustment from the bright sunshine on the street to the cool darkness of the long room. He finally spotted the man he was looking for and went over to the bar to join him.

Whitey Albanese sat on one of the three stools at the end of the bar, where they would be apart from other customers and could speak to each other in quiet confidence. He always sat there, and no one ever went near him except by invitation.

"Beer?"

Vince nodded.

"Beer," Whitey said to the bartender.

Vince lifted himself onto a stool, then he glanced around to see whether he knew anyone else in the bar. Luciano's was a favorite in its neighborhood, where the wise guys went to have a few beers and relax. The walls were paneled in dark oak, on which hung fading old photographs of boxers. The floors were laid with little octagonal tiles in a black-and-white pattern. The grime of decades filled the gaps between the tiles and the cracks in broken ones.

The bartender put a mug of cold, foaming beer in front of Vince. He stepped away quickly, knowing Whitey would tell him to scram if he didn't.

"Understand you had an accident on the job this morning," Whitey said conversationally.

"The mouth of the Mohawks did."

"What I heard. Too bad. One hell of a welder, they say."

Vince nodded.

"Any problems?"

"Well, maybe. It was a damned public place for a job like that, so a guy saw. He's scared half to death, but he saw. I thought about giving him a heave over the edge, but—"

"That would have been a mistake," Whitey said crisply.

"That's what I figured."

"So, who's the guy?"

"Burt Whittle. He's a riveter. He told me he didn't see nothin', claimed he was watchin' some sea gulls real careful, which of course meant he *did* see."

"We'll take care of him," Whitey replied.

Vince shrugged. He knew better than to ask what Whitey meant. Whitey Albanese wasn't a man to mess around with. No way. He was a Sicilian—a *real* Sicilian, from Palermo. Tough. They said he'd carried one of those Italian shotguns in the Sicilian hills and had blasted the guts out of half a dozen men—and maybe a woman, too. And the guy was smart. He'd been in New York six years and spoke the language like he was born here. But one important thing to remember was that he was treacherous. Everyone who ever trusted him had suffered from it.

Whitey was a chain smoker and looked as if it was killing him. He was thin, and his complexion was rough and pale. His lips were oddly red—*too* red, Vince thought. He looked as if he'd been sucking on a cherry Popsicle. He'd brought with him from Sicily one habit he hadn't abandoned in order to make himself a New Yorker: he always wore a black suit with a white shirt buttoned up to his throat—and no necktie. It gave him a European-peasant look, and in the end that was what he was.

Vince felt Whitey's hand on his leg, just under the bar. He reached down and touched the envelope the mobster was pressing against his knee. He grasped the envelope, and Whitey withdrew his hand. Vince slid the envelope up his leg and slipped it in his pocket. He wouldn't ask how much was in it. It would be enough.

"Anything else I can do for you, Whitey?"

"Yeah. Take what's in that envelope and blow. Take a vacation. See you, say, in a couple of months. Just go. Don't stay around to make arrangements.

We'll take care of that woman of yours, so don't be sending her any letters. Don't call her. Just go."

Vince raised his mug and nodded gravely.

"IT'S PATHETIC, Salvatore. Just pathetic. If I can't trust you and Vincenza Grotti to do a job right, who *can* I trust? Who can I trust, Salvatore?"

Whitey was nervous. It made him nervous to face Luca Barbosa in the best of circumstances, but to have to face him and confess there was a witness to a hit was scary. What was more, Barbosa allowed no man to smoke in his presence, and Whitey needed a cigarette.

The old man shook his head. "Vincenza let this man Whittle see him, then he let Whittle live. Then you let Vincenza leave town—we don't know where." He stood and glared down at Whitey. *"Have you lost your mind?"*

"Mr. Barbosa, I can almost for sure catch Vince before he gets out of town. A quick—"

"No! I don't want any quick hit. Understand me? No quick hits. That's how you get in trouble. A good hit is planned, Salvatore. *Planned.* That's how we work. We think, we make a good plan, then we get the best men we can, and we do what we planned. It's too late to run after Vince. Let him go. He won't talk. As for this man Whittle . . . Well, I'll have to think about it."

Whitey nodded. It was best to nod sagely and remain silent, especially when Barbosa was in a touchy mood.

"Now, Salvatore. I'll give you a chance to redeem yourself. Look at this."

He handed Whitey a newspaper, folded to a story about the death of John Claw. The headline screamed out at him:

MY SON DID NOT FALL!

Robert Bear Claw, father of deceased steelworker John Bear Claw, insisted to reporters today, as he has insisted to police, that his son could not have fallen from the high steel.

"All our lives, our men have worked on the high steel, and not one of us ever has fallen. We Mohawks have no fear of high places. I never fell in thirty-five years on the high steel. My father never fell, my grandfather never fell. We do not lose our balance. None of us. Ever."

Robert Claw pledged to pursue the investigation into the death of his son, however long it might take.

"This Indian," Barbosa complained. "He talks too much. What can we do about this, Salvatore?"

Whitey smiled. "I can arrange a little accident for him, Mr. Barbosa."

"Yes. But you *plan* this accident, Salvatore. Who will do this work?"

"I would like to do it myself, Mr. Barbosa, for no fee. You paid me for a job I didn't do to your satisfaction. Let me do this one in compensation."

"No, Luca. If you murder that old Mohawk, you'll create a *cause célèbre*."

Luca Barbosa glared at Giuseppe "Joe" Rossi. "I don't understand your fancy Latin," he grumbled. "Sometimes you talk like a priest."

"You understand what newspapers are, and television and radio stations. You understand that, don't you, Luca?"

"That's the point," Barbosa said stubbornly. "That old Indian—"

"Is quoted in the paper," Rossi interrupted. "One story. Maybe another two or three, the words of the grieving father. How many stories will appear if the grieving father dies? Hmm?"

The others around the table stared curiously at this tense confrontation between the sixty-seven-year-old Luca Barbosa and the forty-three-year-old Joe Rossi. Time was, some of them must have been reflecting, when a man twenty-four years junior wouldn't have dared contradict his senior, particularly if the senior was a man like Barbosa. Now... Well, things had changed.

Luca Barbosa was a slight, wizened man, gray and hunched. His huge salt-and-pepper eyebrows were wildly curly and all but interfered with his vision. He was wearing a light-gray suit in a style that wasn't just out of fashion; it was in a style that never had been in fashion. His necktie and collar were loose. He was shaved by a barber and hadn't visited his barber yet that day, so the light from behind him was caught in the bristles on his cheeks.

Joe Rossi wore a well-tailored dark blue suit with a faint gray pinstripe. He was a lawyer and looked it—in the image of the Wall Street firms.

"I want to ask a question, Joe," Barbosa said. "When did you get the authority to tell me how to run my business?"

"I have no authority to tell you how to run your business, Luca," Rossi replied smoothly.

"That's why you called a meeting," Barbosa complained. "To get the council to—"

"To *persuade* you, Don Barbosa," Rossi interjected. "To persuade you."

"These people," Barbosa continued. "You have to keep them in line. Am I supposed to let them all shoot off their mouths? Do I have to let them raise hell about the arrangements? How am I to do business if every member of every local can have his say? I mean loud, in public. How?"

"You've made your point, Luca," Alfredo Segesta said. "You made your point when the Indian had his accident. Nobody wants to tell you how to run your business, but you should hear our advice."

"We're going to sit here, then, and spend our time arguing about one hit?" Barbosa asked testily.

"There is no argument," Rossi told him. "We're giving you our advice, that's all. You will do as you see fit."

Barbosa reached for the silver carafe that sat on a tray in the middle of the table and refilled his coffee cup. "I have a little problem," he said. "The Mohawk was knocked off the high steel by Vincenza Grotti. He let a man see him. There was a witness. He's a terrified witness but, still, a witness...."

"What kind of men did you use?" Segesta asked, visibly perturbed.

"Salvatore Albanese arranged the hit," Barbosa replied. "He assigned it to Grotti. He paid Grotti and told him to take a vacation, not show up in town for two, three months."

"Whitey Albanese... You handed the responsibility to a madman," Rossi complained.

"Albanese is a madman, true," Carlo Lentini agreed. "But he's a good man. Effective. You can trust him. And, incidentally, Joe, I wouldn't let him hear you call him a madman. I would hope the word doesn't get back to him."

"Let Albanese turn his attention to the witness," Segesta suggested.

"And leave the old Mohawk alone," Lentini said. "That's our advice."

"I would put the word out," Rossi added, "that we want to know where Vince Grotti is."

"You want to hit Vincenza Grotti?" Barbosa asked.

Rossi shook his head. "I just want to know where he is. We ought to have our options as to what we do about him."

"I will carefully consider the advice of the council," Barbosa said.

SUNGLASSES COVERED Whitey Albanese's blue eyes, which was essential. In a theatrical makeup shop on the West Side, he'd bought a jar of skin color and a dull black, frizzy wig. The mobster had parked his car on Avenue U and applied the makeup to the exposed portions of his body. Then he had settled the wig firmly in place. His skin was naturally pallid, and when he'd darkened it to a walnut hue, Albanese thought it looked pretty good.

As he walked down into the subway station, girls cast him appraising, even inviting, glances. As Salvatore Albanese, he had all his life been conscious that he didn't attract women. Now, as an apparent black, he seemed actually to appeal to them. Maybe he should enroll in a tanning salon. He'd never thought of anything like that.

He banished the thoughts from his mind. He couldn't afford distractions right now. This was a chancy thing. It wasn't as well planned as Mr. Barbosa would want it to be, but it was a chance of paying his debt to the don fast and efficiently—and that was a good idea.

Robert Bear Claw was sixty-three, but he still went to the hiring hall in Brooklyn every weekday morning. He was handed a job now and then, and Whitey thought he should have had sense enough to keep his mouth shut. At any rate, he boarded the subway every morning, a man of habit, living on a regular schedule—even on the day after his son's funeral. The easiest kind of citizen to hit.

Albanese pushed his token into the turnstile slot and shouldered his way out onto the platform, earning a few hostile stares. As he jostled through the crowd, keeping Claw in view, he felt as though this were his lucky day—the job was going to be a piece of cake. Robert Bear Claw was standing near the edge of the platform.

The hit man shoved his way up behind the graying man. Why had the old bastard come into the station so early? His train wasn't due for another ten minutes. Albanese had come early to get himself in position, to be ready for him. But why was Robert Claw here so early? Albanese looked around. Was this a setup?

The man beside Claw said something to him, but it was garbled and Albanese couldn't understand. Then Claw answered him—in Greek. Albanese stepped closer to the old man and peered at him intently. Then he stepped back, shaking. It wasn't Claw. He'd almost knocked off the wrong man.

Albanese lit a cigarette. He drew the satisfying smoke deep into his lungs and calmed himself. If he'd gotten the wrong man, he just wouldn't have told Mr. Barbosa. No. If he had to confess a second mistake, the don might—Whitey's hand shook slightly as he took a drag from the cigarette and contemplated the consequences.

The second time he saw Robert Claw, he was certain this one was really the man he sought. He looked like his son. The similarity was unreal.

The hit man elbowed his way to a position directly behind Claw. He kept his place and waited. A blast of hot, stinking air rushed out of the tunnel into the station, pushed by the coming train. People began to crowd closer to the edge of the platform, staring at the lights in the tunnel. No one would clearly see what was about to happen. The setup was more perfect than Albanese had hoped.

It took only a little push. Nothing dramatic. He gave Robert Claw a hip and shoulder, and the man fell across the third rail, electrocuted even before the train ran over him.

Albanese staggered back, as if horrified by what he'd seen. Everyone's attention was fixed on the train and the track. People screamed. No one noticed the slender black man purposefully edging his way through the crowd, away from the scene and toward an exit. He walked out of the subway station and to his car.

BURT WHITTLE'S HOURS were numbered. The way he thought of it, his days were numbered. He'd gone looking for Vince Grotti to renew his assurance that he'd seen nothing, didn't know anything and wouldn't talk even if he had seen anything. Grotti usually hung out around one construction job or another. Officially he was a union rep and could come and go as he pleased. But he wasn't around, and no one had seen him. Whittle went to his apartment. He wasn't there, either. The landlady said she hadn't seen him.

That was bad. He must have figured he was in trouble, that there was a witness who could put the finger on him, and he'd gone into hiding.

Whittle couldn't think of running away. In the first place, where would he go? He didn't have the money to hide out in some hotel, not for more than a few weeks, anyway. He owned a house; he had family, responsibilities. His youngest son was still in school. The older kids still needed help from time to time. And the grandchildren . . .

"Burt! Telephone!"

The phone was in the front hall, by the door. That was where the telephone had been kept when he was a kid, and it had never occurred to Burt Whittle to have it installed anywhere else. Or to have more than one. He sat down wearily on what his family called the telephone bench.

"Yeah?"

"Don't ask who this is, Whittle. We've got that grandson of yours. Petey, he says his name is. Now you—"

"Hey! Hey, don't—"

"Naw. We're not gonna hurt the kid. Providin' you do like I tell you. You listening?"

Burt Whittle slumped. "I'm listening," he whispered hoarsely.

"Just go for a walk. A little evening walk, Grandpa. You might not come back after your walk, but Petey will. Too blocks south, then right, then south again into the alley. Got that?"

"I got it," Burt mumbled.

He didn't go to the kitchen to tell his wife. He couldn't. He glanced around the comfortable little home they had shared, where they had reared their children. He had something to show for his life, anyway. He sobbed, but walked resolutely out the front door and trudged south.

"BOTH OF THEM? You hit both of them? Today?"

"Yessir. The old Mohawk had an accident—fell off a subway platform. The story's on the radio already. Half a dozen witnesses are screaming that he was pushed. By— Get this. By a young black man. The citizen who saw Vince do the hit on the other Mohawk had a different kind of accident. Two big charges of buckshot through his ribs. 'Gangland style,' they're saying."

Luca Barbosa had been driven to Providence this morning to collect a debt. He'd returned only late in the evening. There were two dozen telephone messages—call this one, call that one—and Albanese had been waiting for him.

"This is well done, Salvatore," he said. "Killed by a young black, huh?"

Albanese grinned. "Right. If any witness really saw, that's what he saw."

Barbosa nodded gravely. "Even those meddlers on the council will approve of this. Maybe even Giuseppe Rossi will approve and stop calling you a crazy man."

"He calls me that?"

"Yes. Sometime I'll let you teach him better. Hmm?"

"Let that sometime be soon, Don Barbosa."

CHAPTER TWO

"Hear ye! Hear ye! The Honorable Superior Court for the County of Medway is now in session pursuant to adjournment, the Honorable Justice Robert Murphy presiding. All rise!"

The excited crowd raggedly struggled up as the flush-faced, white-haired, bespectacled judge strode across the front of the courtroom and mounted the bench. The crowd stood, all, that is, except for the defendant and his attorneys. They remained seated, chatting calmly, and ignored the rap of the gavel, the announcement and the arrival of the judge.

The man on trial was Harry Greene, a.k.a. Greentree, a.k.a. Groenbaum. He weighed nearly three hundred pounds and strained the near-antique wooden armchair in which he tried to sit comfortably, while leaning back. He was bald but for a fringe of black hair; his face was moon-round, with puffed-out cheeks that nearly obstructed his vision; his huge hands were clenched into a pair of hammy, hairy fists. He wore a suit stretched to cover his bulk, with a broad green necktie—a trademark—that ended six inches short of his belt buckle.

The jury was in the box—twelve small citizens acutely self-conscious, some of them manifestly afraid. The district attorney and assistant district attorney, an attractive young woman, sat glumly at the table opposite Greene and his counsel.

"Ladies and gentlemen of the jury, have you reached a verdict?"

The foreman of the jury, a slight, slope-shouldered man, rose. "We have, Your Honor," he said.

"Hand your verdict to the clerk."

The clerk of the court carried the papers to the judge, who looked them over and them handed them back to the woman to read aloud.

"The People of the State of Connecticut versus Harry Greene, case number 88-346. On the charge of premeditated murder, we the jury find the defendant not guilty."

Harry Greene smiled benignly on his jury. Some would later say he winked at them.

"The People of the State of Connecticut versus Harry Greene, case number 88-347. On the charge of conspiracy to commit murder, we the jury find the defendant not guilty."

Most of the crowd was on its feet now, cheering and whistling. Many weren't, but most of them were. The judge banged his gavel and cried for silence. The clerk read on.

"The People of the State of Connecticut versus Harry Greene, case number 88-348. On the charge of culpable homicide, we the jury find the defendant not guilty."

The man and woman quietly weeping in the rear of the courtroom were hardly noticed—except by Harry Greene, who turned in his chair and grinned at them.

The judge couldn't keep order. He tossed down his gavel, rose and walked out of the courtroom. "Bondsmen discharged!" he yelled back as he swept through the door.

The crowd broke through the rail and swarmed around Harry Greene, grabbing for his hand, pounding him on the back, whooping their congratulations. Some of them turned on the district attorney and his assistant, shaking their fists. One advanced and spit on their piled law books.

Greene elbowed people aside and approached the unhappy pair. "Okay, punk," he growled at the district attorney. "School's out. You had your shot. Now stay off my back. I mean permanently." He scowled at the assistant.

Somebody pushed a cap down on Harry's head. It bore the logo of the Teamsters. Harry reached up and squared it. He laughed.

"Okay! Party tonight! Celebration tonight! Hey-*hey!*"

"CELEBRATION..." Joan Warnicke murmured. "Yeah."

She was the assistant district attorney. With her in the sitting room of the motel suite was District Attorney Bill Fox, Richard Lincoln and the quiet, hawk-faced man from Washington who'd agreed to meet them via Hal Brognola. He was the man, Bill had told her, who would take up the Greene case from here.

Richard Lincoln, who was sixty-five years old, was the man who, with his wife, had wept in the back of the courtroom when the verdicts were announced. It was their son, Richard Lincoln, Jr., who had called for federal assistance when he came to believe his defeat as a candidate for treasurer of the local had been rigged by Greene. Harry Greene had just been acquitted of all charges resulting from the death of Dick Lincoln.

"He has held Medway in terror for ten years," Lincoln said. "No one can open a business here, not of any kind, without his consent. If you tried to open a grocery store without paying off Greene, his truckers wouldn't deliver to you. If you tried to open an insurance agency, he'd see to it that no one bought from you."

"Dick Lincoln isn't the first person he's had murdered," Joan said. "I came here from New Haven, which isn't exactly what you'd call a squeaky-clean town, but I never saw anything like this."

She was young and pretty, with a firm slender body that might have been called wiry if it had been a man's. Her eyes were dark. She wore her dark brown hair in solid bangs that hung almost to her eyebrows. She had accepted a Scotch, had finished it already and walked to the bar to pour herself another.

"She's right," Fox agreed. "I was born here, have lived here all my life. It didn't used to be this way. But the last ten years..." He sighed. "It's not just the Teamsters. The local is the base for his power, but he has other connections."

"How did he get the acquittal?" the big man asked.

"He owns the judge," Joan replied despondently. "The rulings in the trial—" She stopped, turned down the corners of her mouth, shook her head. "The jury... God knows. Bribed. Intimidated. We tried the case for six weeks, and they took two hours to come out with a verdict."

"A defendant in a case of premeditated murder was free on bond throughout," Fox added.

He, too, went to the bar without a suggestion from his host and poured himself another gin and tonic. He was a handsome, scholarly-looking man, and prematurely gray.

"Anyway," Richard Lincoln continued, "we're glad to see somebody from Washington taking an interest."

"I'm *not* from Washington," Mack Bolan told him. "Not in any official sense, anyway. I don't work for the federal government. In fact I don't work for anybody."

"You said your name is..."

"Michael Belasko." Joan supplied the name.

Lincoln frowned hard at him. "You've got a military bearing. Were you in Nam?" he asked.

The big man nodded. "When I read that Dick Lincoln had been murdered, likely because he was trying to break a corrupt racket's hold on his hometown, I remembered him. It sounded like something he'd do. There are still a few people who won't just sit back and take it.

"I don't work for the Feds," Bolan repeated emphatically. "They can't operate the way I do. Neither can you. And you shouldn't try." He glanced from one absorbed face to the next. "None of you should ever admit you met me. Something might go wrong. For you. For me."

"Just what are you going to do, Mr. Belasko?" Fox asked.

"Let's say," Bolan said, "that I'm going back to Washington in my unofficial capacity to file a report about what I saw here." Bolan continued solemnly, "I didn't come here until the case was almost finished. I wanted to give the regular processes of justice a chance. If you had succeeded in convicting Greene, I'd have gone about my business, feeling good about people who've got the guts to do something about guys like him. But—"

"But he's got it corrupted," Lincoln interrupted. "Nobody can touch him."

"Sooner or later, somebody would," Bolan corrected. "The trouble is, by that time Greene might have murdered two or three—or maybe half a dozen—other good men and women."

"Now, just a minute here," Fox said. "Just what do you plan to do?"

Bolan spoke directly to the grave, guileless district attorney. "Forget you ever met me, Mr. Fox. I'm going to pay a debt we all owe to Dick Lincoln."

"If you kill Harry Greene—or try to—and survive, I'll be obligated to indict you."

"He'll have a perfect alibi," Joan Warnicke said.

"How's that?"

"I'll testify he was in bed with me, all night, in my apartment."

HE WAS UNPACKING his equipment when he heard the rap on the door.

"Who is it?"

"Joan."

Even so, his Beretta filled his right hand when he opened the door. But it was Joan Warnicke, wearing blue jeans and a dark blue polo shirt and sneakers.

"You need help," she said simply.

Bolan shook his head curtly.

"You don't even know where they are," she persisted. "There'll be guns outside, too, and you won't know who they are. I don't propose to go in. I'll just do a little scouting for you."

Bolan studied the young lawyer's solemn face and saw determination. Joan Warnicke wasn't going to be put off, at least not easily.

"You ought to stick to your side of the law," he said to her.

"Right," she agreed. "But you and I are on the same side. You're on the side of justice. So am I."

"You show me what you have to show me, then put a big distance between us."

"I'll show you. Then I'll drive to a place where I can wait, out of sight. Than at a time we've set, I'll pick you up."

"Thanks, but I'll look after my own retreat."

"You better listen to Aunt Joan, big guy," she said. "What you have planned isn't going to be as easy as you think."

JOAN DROVE HIS RENTED CAR, a dark blue Ford. She was right about knowing where to go. He had known that Harry Greene's victory celebration would be held at a hunting and fishing club on a country road in the woods, but he hadn't known exactly where it was and he might have spent considerable time looking for it.

Harry's Club, the place was called. It was on a twisting, two-lane, pot-holed, blacktop road, six or seven miles out of town. Other clubs were located there, too: a skeet-shooting club, a target range, and a club with the name Cheetah, which suggested it was at the very least a strip joint. All of these places were one-story cinder-block buildings with unpaved parking lots. None of them was conspicuously lighted and none had garish signs. They were for men who knew where to find them. All belonged to Harry Greene, Joan informed him.

"Greene Lane," she announced. "A great place, if you're a man with a taste for beer, shooting, fishing, hunting, gambling—and you can guess what else. Harry's buddies think he's created a paradise for them. A blue-collar paradise."

She drove past Harry's Club. The parking lot was filled with cars, vans and pickup trucks. More were parked for two hundred yards along the road in each direction.

"Look at the faded blue Oldsmobile station wagon," Joan suggested. "There'll be a couple of goons in it. With heavy weapons."

Bolan looked at the old car, which was parked near the entrance to the parking lot. He could see the two hardmen.

"They're just the doormen," she said. "Look at the maroon van over by the door. More firepower in there.

Then around back. There'll be guys patrolling. I tell you, Mike, these guys expect trouble and are ready for it."

"So do I," he replied, "and so am I."

"Yeah, I can see you are."

She had watched in awe as he'd armed himself earlier. He was carrying a silenced Beretta 93-R in harness under his left arm, and a .44 Magnum Desert Eagle rode his right hip. He wore a pair of blue jeans, a black T-shirt and a black oversized nylon jacket that covered his two holsters. Anyone who looked at him up close or in good light would see a heavily armed man. Someone who gave him a casual glance at a distance or in poor light wouldn't see anything unusual.

"I'll drive you to another road," she said. "I can show you where there's only a hundred yards or so between the roads, and you can come up over a small hill and down on Harry's just by working your way through the woods. There's a fence, but it's nothing much. As I said before, there'll be a guard or two around the back of the building, but most of the heat's out front."

"When'd you do the recon?" Bolan asked.

"I've checked out this place before."

"Not from the inside, I suppose."

"No. I can't help you there. I've never been honored with an invitation. Harry's is strictly a men's club."

She turned right at the intersection of two roads. The second road followed another little valley. After a minute or so she pulled the car to the side of the road and switched off the lights.

"Right over the top of the hill," she instructed. "When you get to the top, you can see down on the place."

"Right. Give me thirty minutes. If I'm not back, go home."

"No way," she said. "Let's compare our watches. In exactly thirty minutes I'll drive past Harry's, in front. Then I'll turn and come back here. If you're out front, I'll pick you up there. If you come back here, I'll pick you up here. You're gonna have goons in pursuit. Either way, whether you're successful in there or not."

He stretched out his wrist parallel to hers, and she set her watch ahead one minute to match his.

"Thirty minutes."

Bolan leaped a shallow drainage ditch at the edge of the road, jumped over a sagging wire fence and entered the woods.

The Executioner was at home in the gliding shadows. This was what he had been trained to do, long ago—to work his way through undergrowth, silently yet quickly. He climbed the low ridge that separated the two roads, reaching the top in two or three minutes. The clubhouse was below, just as Joan Warnicke had said it would be.

The layout was simple. Harry Greene had hardmen on duty, but he had nothing in the way of a security system. The parking lot was dimly lighted. The ground around the building was grown up in weeds.

He worked his way down the slope, stopping often to scrutinize the ground ahead and below, picking his path carefully and watching for guards.

A man sauntered around the corner of the building and walked across the back. Reaching a shadow, he stopped to urinate, then he went back the way he had come.

Another man came from the opposite direction. He opened a door at the rear of the building and stood there for a minute or so, looking in. With the door open, Bolan could hear music from inside, and laughter. Then the man closed the door and walked on. Okay. He was the guard. One of them, anyway. He ambled around the building, seemingly bored, and when he could he opened a door and looked in, catching as much as he dared of whatever excitement was being offered inside.

The guard was a big fellow with his belt slung low, circling an ample belly. He wore a cap with the union logo, as well as a jacket—no doubt to cover his hardware, just as Bolan was wearing a jacket to cover his. In fact, jackets were a tip-off. The night was hot, and Harry Greene's pals wore T-shirts or undershirts with pants or shorts. A man with a jacket was hiding something.

From his vantage point on the slope, Bolan watched a car approach the gate, then saw it turned back by the pair in the light blue Olds.

Then he noticed something else. A young man and woman came out the back door of the cinder-block building. They stood there nervously, talking in low tones. The guard rounded the corner again.

"Tom . . ." the young man called.

The guard nodded and gestured for silence. The young man glanced around, then handed Tom a couple of bills. The guard glanced at the money and slipped into the youth's hand something that remained unseen. But there was no question about what it was.

The couple didn't return to the club immediately. First they went to a car and got into the back seat. Bolan could see them in there, sniffing the coke they had bought from Harry's goon.

He glanced at his watch. As long as the young couple sat in the car, they were a complicating factor. But they didn't take long. They soon climbed out of the vehicle and trotted, giggling, to the door and returned inside the club.

Now was the time to move. Bolan would wait a couple of minutes, enough time for Tom to make another stroll around the building.

He waited. When Tom didn't appear, the warrior moved closer, then stepped over a low wire fence. Now there was nothing between him and the building except ten yards of littered, weed-grown land.

So Harry Greene pushed drugs. He dominated a labor union, an organization that was supposed to promote the interests of working men and women, not exploit them. Every business in the area was the victim of his extortion, and every man, woman and child who depended on those businesses for jobs or for goods and services paid a percentage to Harry Greene.

And he'd killed a good man who tried to interfere.

"Hey, you! Where the hell you think you're goin'?"

Tom had finally shown up. Bolan shrugged. "Back in," he said. "Came out to take a leak. How's it goin', Tom?"

The guard swaggered up to Bolan. "Who the hell are you?" he demanded.

"I'm Mike. Who the hell you suppose?"

Tom thought about it a second. No more than a second. His eyes narrowed, and his ruddy face turned a little redder. Then he went for his iron.

Bolan had expected that. He drove a fist against the guy's nose, then threw a knee into his groin. Tom was stunned, but he pulled his gun. Before he could raise the muzzle, the Executioner punched him again, hard, under the chin. Tom's knees buckled, and he staggered. His gun hand fell loose, but the bulky man was still functioning, still dangerous, until Bolan slashed him across the throat with a karate chop. At last he dropped to his knees and sprawled facedown on the ground.

Bolan grabbed the revolver out of the limp hand and threw it into the woods. Then he dragged the guard a few yards away into the weeds and left him there.

In a moment Bolan was inside Harry's Club.

Most of it was one big dark room, filled with smoke and the smells of sweat and beer. A bar ran the full length of one side. Two hustling bartenders drew beer and poured whiskey for a score of men who pushed and elbowed one another to get their drinks faster. At the center of the opposite side was a sort of stage, a platform of raw lumber raised three feet above the floor. On that creaking platform, in the glare of harsh floodlights, a pair of nude girls writhed together on the floor—naked wrestlers.

Twenty-five or thirty tables filled the center of the floor. Half a dozen men sat around each one, drinking, smoking, yelling and banging their beer mugs on the tables to encourage the straining, sweating girls.

At a table front and center, Harry Greene sat smoking a cigar and watching the wrestlers with a detached, amused air. Lolling against his shoulder was a girl, probably no older than eighteen, twenty at the most—pretty, with shoulder-length blond hair—and conspicuously stoned. She was dressed in ragged cutoff jeans and a skimpy halter. As Bolan watched, she drew a finger along the side of Harry Greene's neck and whispered something in his ear. He ignored her.

Also at the table was a man whose hawklike face seemed to cry out pitiless cruelty. Bolan wondered whether he was the man who had murdered Dick Lincoln. That might be an ironic touch with an appeal to Harry: to have at his table the hit man he'd hired to commit the murder he had just been acquitted of. Bolan knew the Harry Greenes of the world. It was the kind of jeering touch many of them enjoyed.

Hawk-face had a girl, too. She was enough like the other one to be her sister, though she was older, a little more worn. She wasn't draped across Hawk-face but was sitting bolt upright, staring with contempt at the naked wrestlers, smoking a cigarette and drinking whiskey from a water glass.

Hawk-face was wearing a loose red nylon jacket. If he wasn't Harry Greene's hit man, he was definitely his bodyguard.

Bolan worked his way into the crowd as quickly as possible. He got a few curious stares, but it was the way he'd figured—the crowd was too big, too drunk, too absorbed in ogling to take much notice of one more big man.

Even so, he figured he shouldn't approach Greene immediately. That might attract attention. He worked his way toward the bar, being careful not to let anyone jostle him enough to feel his guns. With a beer in his left hand, he would look more like everyone else, less purposeful. He pushed up to the bar, asked for a beer and found that all drinks were on Harry.

Bolan worked his way toward the center table.

The two wrestlers scrambled to their feet, grinned and bowed and scampered down from the platform and out.

An amplified voice boomed from speakers overhead. "A big hand for the Wrestling Bares! And our thanks to Harry! And...now! Hey, guys! A hand for Donald and Donna!"

A youthful couple, boy and girl, trotted out and climbed onto the platform. They, too, were stark naked, and were followed by one of Harry's hardmen, who carried a mattress over his shoulder. When he heaved it to the center of the platform, the crowd hooted and yelled its approval.

The young couple stood for one awkward moment, facing the obscene congregation that had raised its collective voice to a frenzied shriek. Then they embraced, as if seeking refuge in each other.

Bolan recognized them. They were the couple who had bought coke from Tom out back and had sat down in the car and sniffed lines. Possibly they were only half-aware of what they were now doing.

What they did mesmerized the crowd, which made Bolan's job easier. He shouldered his way forward, and the men who cursed at him supposed that all he was doing was trying to get closer to the platform.

He muscled his way toward the front, drawing little attention. Among these people, rude pushing was nothing uncommon. He was too big and muscular to be challenged, particularly in a crowd of mostly jocular drunks, and he got where he wanted to be. Suddenly he was standing arm's length from Harry Greene—a little to Harry's left, and a little nearer the platform.

Harry was in an ebullient mood. He dragged deeply on his cigar and shoved it into an ashtray. "Hey, Don, Donna!" he yelled. "Louder and funnier!"

Bolan glanced at the young couple. They were down on the mattress now.

"Hey, Donna!" Harry yelled. "Smoke his cigar! C'mon, honey!"

The warrior stepped away from the crowd and into the narrow space between Harry's table and the front of the platform.

"Hello, Harry," he said.

"Down in front, you idiot!" Harry bellowed.

"I'm a friend of Dick Lincoln," Bolan said as he drew the Desert Eagle and shoved the muzzle toward Harry.

Greene screamed in terror.

The big .44 bucked and roared. The huge, high-velocity slug decapitated Harry Greene. More correctly said, it blew his skull apart, showering everyone around with brain and bone fragments, leaving the corpse sitting with no head except a nearly intact lower jaw.

Hawk-face drew a pistol from inside his jacket, but the second shot from the Desert Eagle struck him in the chest and threw him violently backward, his chair toppling and his corpse sliding across the floor behind it.

The young blonde who had been lolling against Greene screamed hysterically and slapped frantically at her face and hair, trying to flick away the bloody bits of head that were sticking to her.

The older woman stared into her whiskey, as if trying to see whether any part of Harry had corrupted her drink. "I'll be damned," she muttered to Bolan, and she raised her glass and chugged it.

It was time to get out of there. The warrior took advantage of the moment of shock and disbelief, during which no one would be able to oppose him effectively. He shoved his way authoritatively through the screaming crowd, heading toward the door at the rear.

The door was blocked. Tom, the guard, had staggered up and was standing there, his meaty hands grasping the doorframe on each side.

"You!"

"Hey, Tom," Bolan said. "Somebody's whacked Harry."

Blood was streaming from Tom's broken nose. "Harry...?" he muttered.

"Harry," Bolan repeated firmly. "So get out of the way, buddy."

"God Almighty," Tom breathed as he staggered back from the door.

Bolan brushed past him.

A window shattered, and a man scrambled through the broken glass. It was impossible to tell whether he was furious to hunt for the killer of Harry Greene or just terrified.

"Out the back!"

Some of them had seen Bolan make his way to the back. He glanced around, formed his judgment and acted. He trotted quickly to the parked cars to one side of the building, jumped on a hood and then the roof of another and from there sprang to the roof of the club. There he crouched and watched fifty men spill onto the ground behind the building.

"Tom! What the—"

"He musta come out of the woods," the big man replied.

Bolan checked his watch. He had two minutes to meet Joan Warnicke in front of the building. He crawled across the roof, toward the front, through standing water left from a recent rain.

The ground in front of the building was more crowded than that behind. Men were hurrying to their cars, anxious only to be away from the scene of a murder. Bolan slipped to one side of the roof, spotted a car parked in shadow and dropped on top of it. A moment later he was shoving his way through the milling crowd, unrecognized.

When he reached the road, Joan was there, cruising past. He stepped out into the beam of her headlights, she stopped and he grabbed open the door and threw himself inside.

"No great speed," he muttered. "Nothing conspicuous. They haven't got it figured out yet."

"I refuse to lie," she said as she drove away. "Especially under oath. And you remember what alibi I told Bill Fox I'd swear to."

"They'll be hunting for me," he said. "How long's it going to take to check the motels around this town?"

"You aren't going to be in a motel in this town. You're going to check out and—"

"Not to your place, Joan."

"You are too quick to assume, Mike. I was going to drive you to Hartford Airport."

Bolan laughed. "That's where I'm going, eventually."

"Eventually that's where I'm going to drive you. Tonight . . . I've got a better idea."

SATISFIED THAT NO ONE could possibly know where they were, Bolan still had the Beretta in hand when he responded to the discreet but firm knock on the door not long after seven in the morning.

The knock hadn't wakened Joan, so he slipped out of bed and went to the door.

"Who is it?"

"I need to talk to you," said a woman's voice, muffled by the door.

He edged away from the door; he'd already come too close. Contrary to what old movies showed, doors weren't bulletproof. He glanced toward Joan. A burst of fire coming through that door would—

"Mr. Belasko! I really need to talk to you."

How did she know who he was? How did she find him?

They were in a small country inn at West Cornwall, Connecticut, a place known to Joan and favored by her for its setting in the beautiful upper valley of the Housatonic River. Their bedroom, one of only four in the inn, overlooked the rushing stream and a covered bridge, though he had seen little of this last night when they arrived about midnight. She had telephoned ahead and reserved the room. It was antique and cozy.

"Mr. Belasko," the voice persisted. "I want you to do for me what you did for Mr. Lincoln last night. I want you to do something about the men who murdered my father and grandfather."

Joan awakened. She couldn't understand the words coming through the door, but she saw Bolan holding the Beretta and talking intently, and she rolled off the bed and grabbed the Desert Eagle from the harness hung over a chair. Staring at it, apparently wondering whether it was loaded and cocked, she crawled across the floor and took a position opposite him, with the muzzle of the big pistol aimed at the door.

Bolan shook his head at her. "Trade," he whispered, and slid the Beretta across the floor to her.

She slid the big gun to him.

"Please, Mr. Belasko."

"All right. I'm unlocking the door."

The doorknob turned, and the door swung back.

The comely young woman standing in the hall was alone. She stepped through the door and glanced to one side, then the other, astonished to be confronted by a man and a woman aiming pistols at her.

"I—"

"Close the door," Bolan ordered.

She turned and closed the door.

He leveled the muzzle of the Desert Eagle at her. "Joan will search you," he said.

Joan rose, leaving the Beretta on the floor, and patted down the dark-haired young woman. Joan looked at Bolan and shrugged.

"All right," Bolan said. "You'll excuse us while we get dressed."

Five minutes later the warrior asked, "How did you find us?"

The young woman sat in a maple chair beside the small, cold fireplace. "My name is Gina Bear Claw," she said. "Tuesday, my father was murdered. I set out looking for you as soon as I got the word. I was too late. Yesterday my grandfather was murdered. Why? Because he dared suggest publicly that my father had been murdered. I—"

"How did you find me?" Bolan demanded.

"Hal Brognola told me to mention his name. He said you would know it."

Bolan glanced at Joan, who by now had finished dressing. "Yeah. I guess I've heard the name somewhere."

"When I learned of my father's murder, I flew to Washington and went to the Justice Department. I'd heard of Mr. Brognola, and when I asked to see him, he was good enough to listen to my story. He said he knew a man who might be able to help me, and he told me a little about you. I said I wanted to see you, as soon as possible. Then he told me you had come to Medway. He didn't say why. He described you and said you would be difficult to find. He also said if I found you I should be sure to tell you to call him."

"So you found us. How?"

Gina Claw smiled. She was an extraordinarily attractive young woman. Her dark hair, evidence of her Indian ancestry, hung luxuriant and straight below her shoulders. Her face was long, her mouth narrow. Her solemn brown eyes peered at the world from under ample eyebrows. Her complexion was olive, like a Greek or southern Italian.

"Once Mr. Brognola told me where you were, it wasn't terribly difficult," she said.

"Hal—"

"Mr. Brognola heard my story, checked it out and acted decisively. He said you had gone to Connecticut on business and he had no way to contact you. I said I'd find you if he'd just tell me where in Connecticut, so he told me Medway."

Bolan frowned. If Brognola trusted this young woman with this much, he must have had reason.

"He didn't think I could find you."

Bolan glanced at Joan and could see that she shared his thought—that if Gina Claw had found them, someone else could.

"How did you do it?" he asked.

"Mr. Brognola helped me," Gina replied. "He used the power of his office to get the car-rental companies to run their computers and find out if a car was rented to a Michael Belasko. That's how I knew you rented a car in Hartford, and I found out what kind of car it was, plus the license number. I flew into Hartford, rented a car and drove to Medway. I asked for you at the motels around the town, and I found out where you were staying. I knew you weren't there, because your car wasn't there. So I took a room in the motel and—Well, I'd had a long day, so I went out to dinner. I thought I'd probably find your car in the lot when I came back, and then I'd come and knock on your door.''

"A regular Sherlock Holmes," Joan commented.

"While I was at dinner in a restaurant downtown, the word began to be passed around that someone had killed Harry Greene. I suppose you know this, Mr. Belasko, but Medway is in a state of shock. Everyone in the restaurant was talking about— They called it murder. There was a crowd on the street when I left the restaurant. I hurried back to the motel, but I was too late. You'd checked out.''

Gina Claw paused and sighed. Then she went on. "I drove back to Hartford. I was able to find out you hadn't returned the car to the rental agency. Since then, I've driven all night, from one town to another, all over northwestern Connecticut and southwestern Massachusetts, checking parking lots, looking for that Ford. I'd about given up when I found your car here. I . . .'' She looked up at Joan Warnicke. "I'm sorry to have intruded. I could have waited until you came down to check out.''

"You say Hal wants me to look into the death of your father?''

She shook her head. "I don't know. He just told me you might be able to help me. But he emphasized that you should call him."

"Okay. Tell me about your father."

CHAPTER THREE

Hal Brognola, United States Department of Justice, arrived in New York on a department Lear jet. The little jet landed at Teterboro, and Brognola was driven to the Giants Motel near the Meadowlands sports complex. Bolan was waiting for him there.

"They murdered John Claw because he was raising hell about the way his local is run," Brognola said. "They murdered his father because he told the news media his son's death was no accident. And there's been another murder, one Gina Claw doesn't know about. They murdered another construction worker. He was on the high steel the morning John Claw had his 'accident.' It's possible he was a witness. They took him out with a shotgun."

"The Families are tough."

They sat together in Bolan's room, before a window that overlooked the New Jersey flats. The towers of Manhattan were visible in the distance, their lines softened by the haze.

"Everybody who lives in New York, everybody who does business in New York, pays for the corruption in the construction industry," Brognola went on. The big Fed was chomping on a cigar, which he now pulled from his mouth and stared at for a moment. "Not only that, they're putting up unsafe buildings. One of these days there's going to be a catastrophe. Something's going to collapse.''

"What's the city doing about it? The state?''

"The Organized Crime Task Force, which is a state operation, published a report on it a year ago.'' Brognola shrugged. "But the wheels of justice grind slow.''

"So everybody knows, but nobody is doing anything,'' Bolan concluded. "Is that what you're telling me?''

Brognola bit down hard on his cigar as his face darkened. "I thought I was doing something about it right now.''

Bolan grinned. "I'll listen.''

"Okay. In the first place, let's understand that not all labor unions and not all construction companies are corrupt. A hell of a lot of guys are trying to do their jobs the honest way.''

"But it gets harder and harder for them.''

Brognola nodded emphatically. "Harder and harder. And a lot of construction companies cooperate with the Five Families because it's the only way they can stay in business. The only way. It's not because they want to.''

"Unions—''

"It starts with the unions,'' Brognola interrupted. "The Mob infiltrated some of the important locals a long time ago, muscled the honest officers out and took over. When honest union members object—''

"They get what John Claw got.''

Brognola nodded. "Construction workers are absolutely dependent on their unions, in a way most other working people aren't. Very few of them are permanently employed by any one company. They move from job to job, company to company. When a construction company needs fifty carpenters, it notifies the union and the union sends the carpenters. So the carpenters get jobs, or don't get jobs, at the whim of the union bosses."

"And they blacklist men who get out of line," Bolan concluded.

"Exactly," Brognola agreed. "A man who speaks up, complains, talks around with other union members, suddenly stops getting work. No work, no money. A man with a family to support thinks long and hard before he starts a beef about the way his union is run."

"The NLRB?"

"Can take months to get around to hearing a case. And the man who made the complaint is blacklisted. Besides, when the case does get heard, how does a man prove he should have had a particular job because of his seniority, but didn't get it?"

Brognola again pulled his cigar from his mouth and stared at it as if he had never seen it before. "Okay. So the construction companies have to hire who the unions send. Some of the electricians they send aren't electricians, some of the plumbers aren't plumbers. You get the idea."

"Some of them are enforcers."

"Right. Also, some don't show up at all. Some of the goons they send punch two or three time cards. The extra pay goes to the union bosses. And the companies put up with it to buy labor peace," Brognola said. "They figure the payoffs to the crooked locals cost them less than strikes and job actions. Anyway, they can pass the costs along to the people who work and live in the buildings they put up.

"Union racketeering isn't the half of it," Brognola continued. "The corruption is wider and deeper. The Five Families have invested the profits from old rackets into a lot of businesses that used to be legit."

"Such as building supplies," Bolan suggested.

"Yeah, building supplies. Concrete, lumber, pipe, glass, plumbing fixtures . . . You name it. The builder asks for bids on a big load of materials, and only one company bids—the Mob's company. The price? Whatever the bidder asks. Try to bring that material in from out of town, for a much lower price, and big trouble. I mean *big* trouble. The Families own many suppliers. The ones they don't own pay them for 'accident insurance' and labor peace."

"Who's doing the buildings you think are dangerous?" Bolan asked.

"Maybe that's the worst part," Brognola said. "Some construction companies are themselves Mob businesses. They're the ones who fudge on building standards. I hardly need tell you that they bribe inspectors. But, beyond that, many of the legitimate companies simply accept Mob corruption. They say it's a fact of life in New York."

"And it's not worth risking their lives to try to break the circle," Bolan added.

"More than that. Look, suppose you're a legit construction outfit. You're being nibbled to death. You're paying too much for this, too much for that. You're paying for workers who never show up. You're being deviled by small-time racketeers who demand a payoff to keep this union on the job, to get this or that delivered to the job site on time, to insure you against 'accidents.' "

"And even when you do pay off, you're not sure you'll get what you paid for," Bolan said.

"Right. Many times they don't keep their word. Besides that, some rival crook, some rival union, might show up and demand another payoff for the same thing you've already paid for. So along comes a representative of, say, the Rossi Family and he says to you, 'Hey, man, we can give you peace on all fronts. You make an alliance with us, and we'll handle all your problems. Sure, we'll overcharge you for materials. Sure, you'll pay for workers who never show. But when you pay us, we give you results, and we'll keep everybody else off your back.' It works, too. You're better off. You know you're the victim of a vicious racket, but you're *still* better off."

"Until they demand a piece of your company as part of the price," Bolan suggested.

"That's the next step," Brognola agreed. "That's how they acquire legitimate companies. Sometimes they buy in. More often they muscle in."

"How much are they raking in?"

Brognola put his cigar aside. "Nobody knows. The Organized Crime Task Force estimates that something like five billion dollars is spent on construction each year in New York City. How much of that is skimmed off by the Five Families, no one knows. No one can even make a good guess."

"I can make one good guess."

"What's that?"

"It's enough money to kill for."

THE LITTLE HOUSE where John Claw had lived with his wife was touchingly reminiscent for Mack Bolan. It reminded him of his own family home, in Pittsfield, Massachusetts, where his father and mother had reared a family and planned for a comfortable, satisfying old age, only to lose everything to the Mob.

Mrs. Claw was a Mohawk Indian, like her husband, and she said that now she would sell the house and return to their original home upstate, where she would at least have the solace of her brothers and sisters, aunts, uncles and cousins.

"Those men, Mr. Belasko," she said, "are the scum of the earth! My husband and his father were decent men. They were killed for no reason. No reason at all."

"You've mentioned the reason," Gina said. "That he was a decent man. That grandfather was a decent man. There's no room in the construction industry for decent men. There's no room, in fact, in New York."

"If people like you leave the cities, they'll become jungles," Bolan told her. "The jungles will expand and catch up with you soon enough."

"I'd already found a new home, before my father was killed."

Bolan nodded. "I didn't mean to suggest you should stay here."

"Well, I'm not leaving immediately," Gina replied. "I'm staying until I see what progress you make in doing something about my father's murder. And my grandfather's."

"If you'll take my advice, you'll leave," he said.

"Because I'm next? Or my mother?"

"Not your mother. You. If the people who killed your father get the idea you're staying in the city to make trouble for them..."

"So I should run?"

"Your father didn't."

She nodded bitterly. "I get you."

"Take my advice," Bolan said. "We're dealing with killers."

"Go home, Gina," Mrs. Claw suggested. "That's what I'm going to do. I'm going home, to where I belong. Where John belonged. Let men like this—" she nodded toward Bolan "—do what they are qualified to do. Accept it. We have been driven out of New York. Accept that, Gina."

"I don't give a damn about New York," Gina snapped. "I do give a damn about the deaths of my father and grandfather."

"You can't help," Bolan growled.

"Oh, no? Well, where do you start, Belasko? Do you have a single name, a single lead?

"I'm not leaving town," Gina continued. "Not for a while, anyway. You might need some help, whether you like it or not."

"Okay. Do you know anything?"

"Maybe. Dad used to bitch about what he called a 'dancer' who hung around the jobs. The guy was a goon, he said, an enforcer. His name was Vince. That's all I ever heard—Vince. He was my father's favorite example of what's wrong in the construction business.''

"Vince ... A dancer. I wonder what he meant by that?"

"Maybe you can find out," she said.

"A DANCER NAMED VINCE. Vincent. Mean anything to you?"

"Maybe," said Saul Stein, Assistant Director of the Organized Crime Task Force. Brognola had telephoned ahead to encourage Stein to see Bolan.

"He might be the man who killed John Claw," Bolan told him.

"Well, it would be some sort of coup if we could identify that one," Stein replied. "But, tell me, Mr. Bolan. If I were to identify this 'dancer' for you and tell you where to find him, what would happen to him?"

"Why do you ask that?"

"Your reputation precedes you. It seems as though where Mack Bolan treads, people die. The computer has spit out some interesting data. I would like to see the murderers of John Claw brought to justice, but I'm not sure that justice is effected by blowing them away."

"Neither am I," Bolan said. "I'd much rather effect it some other way."

"Understood, Mr. Bolan. Let's see what we can come up with on a man nicknamed Vince, who might also be called a dancer. Not much to go on. But let's see."

He turned to a desktop computer on the credenza behind him. As Bolan watched, he tapped a series of keys, and the computer screen went blank. After a minute or so, the screen lit up.

"Well..." Stein said quietly. "It seems our data base does have a man named Vincent who has been referred to with the word 'dancer.' Most unusual. Look. The highlighted words caused the find."

Bolan squinted at the screen.

GROTTI, VINCENZA "VINCE"

B. 3/24/51; male; Caucasian; 5'10", 185 lb., no scars or other identifying characteristics.

Arr. 4/5/73 susp. armed rob., released, lack of ev.; arr. 7/19/75 ass. & batt., probation, fine; arr. 9/21/75 burg., chg. red. brk. & ent., sent. 90 days Rikers, served; arr. 6/11/76 ass. & batt., dismissed, lack of ev.; arr. 8/23/76 armed rob., sent. 1-5, paroled 11/21/78; arr. unlicensed weapon 1/2/80, sent. 1-3; served Attica, full term, rel. 1/2/83; arr. FBI 8/11/84, poss. automatic weapon, sent. 1-2 fed. inst., served Atlanta, rel. 7/3/86.

Reputed assoc. Barbosa Family. No wife, children. No perm. address. Reput. well dressed, reput. for springy bounce in walk, which causes nickname "Dancer" to be applied. Reput. armed, dangerous.

"Grotti," Bolan murmured. "Where would I start looking for Mr. Dancer Grotti?"

Stein shrugged. "It's a big city. But if he's a soldier of the Barbosa Family, you could do worse than to check out a bar called Luciano's. Second Avenue, between Thirty-fourth and Thirty-fifth. A lot of them hang out there."

IN A WAY, Luciano's made him think of the Italian restaurant where Michael Corleone shot Sollozzo and McCluskey. It was the same kind of place: familiar, neighborhoodish, mind-your-own-business. But the clientele was not the same. In the movie, the few people in the restaurant were quiet Italian families enjoying a quiet Italian dinner.

He had dressed as a construction worker, in dirty jeans, a stained and sweaty T-shirt, boots. He carried no weapon. He swaggered in, miming the attitude affected by the wise guys, and pushed up to the bar.

"Beer," he said.

"You got it," the bartender replied.

All the stools were taken, so Bolan stood between two of them, glanced around and waited for his beer. Most of the wise guys paid him no attention. Two or three checked him out.

It was easy to see which ones were carrying heat. The same way it had been easy at Harry's Club. He looked around. In this one little bar, half a dozen guys were carrying iron.

On the other hand, they wouldn't use it—unless absolutely necessary. In the first place, they didn't need a hassle. In the second place, the soldiers of the Five Families were almost like cops: like cops, they had to explain exactly why they used their guns when they used them. A soldier who lost his cool lost his head—the Families had strict rules on that.

Things were different in New York. The Families had coordinated their control. Indiscriminate shooting that brought newspaper attention was out. Beatings, bombings, all that was out unless somebody went crazy, or unless it was important enough. He wondered which was the case in the murders of John and Robert Claw, and Burt Whittle.

The bartender put a mug of beer in front of him. "Two and a quarter," he announced.

Bolan shoved the money toward him. "Vince been in?" he asked.

"Lots of guys called Vince come in. Vince who?"

"Vince Grotti."

The bartender turned down the corners of his mouth and shook his head. "Never heard the name," he muttered.

"The one they sometimes call Dancer."

The bartender shook his head again. "Never heard of him," he repeated, with just enough emphasis to tip Bolan that he had in fact heard of him and was lying.

"He asked me to meet him here."

"When?"

"Any time. Come in and have a beer with him. Said he hangs out here."

"Not here. You must have the wrong joint."

Bolan nodded. "Guess so."

The beer was ice cold. Bolan stood at the bar and drank from the frosted glass mug, wiping the foam off his lips. It would have looked suspicious for him to walk out before he drank his beer.

The older men sitting at tables in the rear took more interest in the stranger at the bar than did the wise guys around him. He knew who they were. Retired, mostly. But rich. And some of them still powerful. Some of them could give orders to have a man killed. And they would, over small resentments. Except that now they would have to answer to the council of the Five Families.

Bolan finished his beer and walked out into the blinding sunlight of the busy, dirty street.

"FOLLOW THAT GUY, Antonio."

The bartender had spoken urgently to one of the young mobsters as soon as Bolan was out the door, and now the guy ordered another to tail him.

"Don't follow too close. Just see where he goes."

Half an hour later, Antonio returned to Luciano's.

"He caught a cab."

"Yeah. Sure," said the bartender, who had overheard. "Working stiff, just come in to have a beer with Vince. Didn't figure."

"I got the cab number," Antonio told them. "Wrote it down."

The other wise guy glanced at the paper Antonio handed him. He went to the telephone booth in the rear and made a call.

THE BAR AND LOUNGE in the Giants Motel in New Jersey was a world removed from Luciano's, but it was nothing luxurious, nothing sophisticated. Gina Claw was there at seven, as she had insisted she would be, over his protest that he might not even be back from Manhattan by seven.

"Give me ten minutes," Bolan told her. "I need to change."

"I would trust you to receive me in your room," she said playfully.

"You would. Maybe I wouldn't. Ten minutes."

"I'm more hungry than thirsty," Gina said when he returned. "I told them to give us a booth."

As they moved from the bar to the booth, she carried a glass of wine with her. When they sat down, he ordered a Scotch from the corselet-clad waitress, tipping his head and fastening an appreciative stare on her long, shapely legs.

She drained the remainder of the wine from her glass. "So, what chance is there for a family named Bear Claw?"

"I went to Luciano's," the warrior said. "I asked for Grotti. The bartender clammed up. He didn't like the question."

"I went out to see Mrs. Whittle," Gina said. She shook her head. "If she knows anything, she's afraid to tell us. I'd guess she has no idea who murdered her husband. Or why. But she didn't want to talk to me. She has children. She doesn't want to take any chances."

Bolan nodded.

"I found out something interesting, though. Whittle's local sent her a check for twenty thousand dollars. An 'advance against benefits,' they called it. Something to tide her over until her pension checks start. She thinks his local is a fine, humanitarian organization. Or so she says."

"Doesn't she have any idea why her husband was killed or who killed him?"

"I think she knows. She's afraid to talk. My grandfather talked."

The leggy waitress returned, bringing their drinks. Seeing her approach, Bolan glanced at the menu.

"I'm going to go for a big steak," he said to Gina.

"I'm for that. Rare."

He ordered rare steaks for both of them.

"Your father had a brother," Bolan said. "What's happening with him?"

"He got the message," she replied. "I talked to him today, too. He's quitting the construction trades, going back home. He'll work in a gas station or on a farm, for a third of what he was making on the high steel. His family..." She paused, shaking her head. "They don't want him taking any chances."

"You can't blame him."

"He did give me one piece of information. It's the Barbosa Family that controls Dad's local. That's who he was challenging."

"Luca Barbosa," Bolan mused. "One of the old-time mafiosi."

"One of the old-time murderers," she said bitterly. "I'm counting on you to take him out."

"It's not that simple," Bolan told her. "And not that good an idea. If I take out Luca Barbosa, another man steps into his place."

"They'll remember," she said grimly. "I want them to know it's ͻr my father. And if you don't do it—"

"Don't even think about it, Gina," Bolan interrupted. "You wouldn't have a chance. You'd only get killed. You're not going to surprise these guys. You think they'd be surprised to have some decent citizen coming after them? Forget it. They know you'd like to kill them, and that's why you don't have a chance."

"But you have a chance."

"I don't want you to stumble into something you don't know how to control and get yourself hurt."

"I'll stand aside and watch," she said. "You've got your chance. No interference. Go get 'em. If I don't misjudge you, you've got what it takes."

When they were finished, Bolan walked with Gina Claw to her rented car in the parking lot. He had no sense of impending danger or that she needed an escort, and was moved only by the notion that it was the courteous thing to do.

Night in the megalopolis is unlike night anywhere else. The old cliché is that the city never sleeps. Under the white points of stars, New York-New Jersey never slept. The air traffic was heavier now than it had been during the day. The traffic on the neighboring superhighways roared and glowed. The sky was suffused with the orange glow of the contiguous cities. Red lights blinked all around—on the tops of buildings and radio towers, on emergency vehicles, on the superstructures of ships drawn up to the wharves in the Hudson, on the wings of airplanes. It was difficult to guess where they were blinking. Bright yellow glows might be from flaming exhaust gases at the refineries. The world was burdened with a dull, ubiquitous roar, punctuated by sirens, horns, shouts, sirens.... There was an unmistakable excitement in it.

"Take my advice," Bolan said. "Move out with your mother. Go somewhere. If you don't go upstate, move into some obscure little motel like this one. Don't use your own name. Don't take chances."

"If I call you, will you return my calls?"

He nodded. "I promise. I won't be staying here. Call me tomorrow, when you have a new number where I can reach you. Then lay low. Let me—"

He saw the sudden move too late. A slug plowed into his lower left rib, spinning him around and throwing him backward onto the pavement. But the pain wasn't as strong as his sense of urgency. Gina!

She was down beside him. He hadn't heard another shot, but he wasn't certain she hadn't been hit.

"Gina..." he grunted.

She was all but on top of him, clutching at his chest, grabbing at the Beretta.

A man stepped out from behind the Buick next to where Bolan had fallen, leveling a revolver.

Gina pulled the trigger of Bolan's 93-R, no doubt astonished that she had loosed a 3-round burst. Undoubtedly she was surprised, too, that she had killed a man—for the hard guy with the revolver wasn't knocked backward by the three slugs. He simple doubled over and fell on his face, his heart and lungs scrambled.

When the second man stepped into Gina's line of sight, an automatic in hand, she loosed a second burst. This one was low and caught the wise guy in the guts. He shrieked in agony. He dropped to his knees, bent over his ripped-open belly, clutching at it while the blood oozed from between his fingers.

Gina turned her attention to her companion.

A slug had nicked his lung. He could tell because blood came up in his mouth. The pain was just bearable. His chief concern was that he had no time. He'd be useless in a few minutes.

"Can you make it into the car?" Gina asked.

Thank God she understood he couldn't sit there and wait for the emergency squad. He struggled to rise, and she helped him to her small car.

Already people were cautiously venturing out of the motel, not sure the shooting was over.

Gina helped him into the car. "Where?" she asked him. "Who?"

"Call Brognola," he muttered, then passed out.

CHAPTER FOUR

"Chicken soup," a voice coaxed. "Come on, open your mouth!"

He opened his mouth, felt the spoon shoved in and choked on the warm, oily liquid that trickled down his throat.

"I never had a baby, but they tell me they do better than that. Come on."

The voice wasn't Gina's. He opened his eyes and saw Joan Warnicke. His eyes focused. She sat beside him, holding a bowl of yellowish liquid that had to be the chicken soup.

"In and out of consciousness, in and out of this world," she said. "Time to come out once and for all. Doc says you're going to live, and—"

"Joan . . ."

"Right the first time. Wake up. The doctor says a bastard like you could take two or three more .38 slugs and—"

"How did I get here? Wherever here is."

"Where you think, big guy? You're in my apartment in Medway, Connecticut. You've been attended to by a doctor who was honored to take a slug out of the lung of the man who is rumored to have blown away Harry Greene. A man who was similarly honored cleaned your blood out of the Hondo your girlfriend rented. And Brognola took care of your motel bill and cleaned up the mess you left in New Jersey. I like the way some Feds can cool investigations. He also let it slip, in his concern, that your real name is Mack Bolan.''

Joan paused for a moment. "Who shot you?"

For the first time since he'd recovered awareness and this conversation had begun, Bolan started to remember the details of what had happened: the steak and wine with Gina, walking with her to her car, then the shot that knocked him down. And Gina had taken out the gunmen.

"Who shot you, Mack? Gina doesn't know. I'm betting you do."

"Then you lose your bet. I don't know."

"Two New York goons," she said. "I imagine Brognola knows who they were by now. He'll be here tomorrow, incidentally."

"What day is this?"

"Saturday. You lost Friday."

He pressed down with his elbows to lift himself, but the pain in his chest was too much, and he let himself back down. He became aware, too, that he lay on a bed damp with his sweat, though a window air-conditioner roared.

"How'd I get here?" he asked.

"Gina called me. She didn't know who else to turn to."

"Hal—"

"She wasn't sure of Hal, how he'd react."

"You can always be sure of Hal Brognola," Bolan replied.

"I know. He wanted to send a jet to pick you up. I told him I had taken care of getting you medical attention and had you snug in bed. Sending a Lear into Medway would have been bad judgment. Everybody'd want to know who and why."

"Harry Greene's friends—"

"This town will never be the same," she said.

"That was the idea, wasn't it?"

She nodded. "I don't promise you things are going to become idyllic here. But what you did broke the grip. They're scared. Harry's buddies are afraid to get the club going again for fear another avenger will come in out of the night and blow some guy's head all over the room."

"Joan . . ."

"It's true. It's going to make a difference."

He sighed, let his head rest on the pillow and stared at the ceiling. "What I've come up against in New York is—"

"I know," she said solemnly. "It's a bigger fight. I've joined up."

He turned his head abruptly, too abruptly. It hurt, and he glared at her. "What does that mean?"

"Thursday you met Saul Stein," she said. "He and I were at Yale together. I called him and asked him for a job. I got it. Meet the new counsel to the Assistant Director of the Organized Crime Task Force."

"Joan . . ." He sighed weakly.

She shook her head at him. "You met Fox. Not enough guts to fight back here in Connecticut. The OCTF is doing something important, as you are. Well, I'm going to do something important, too. I had a taste of it when I worked at the Justice Department. I'm going to work where something important is being done."

"Harry Greene might have killed you," Bolan said. "The Five Families sure as hell will if they see any threat in you."

"Someone tried to kill you," she replied. "And would have, except for Gina."

"They would have killed me and would have killed Gina, too, if she hadn't been so decisive and fast with a pistol. Tell me, Joan. Could you kill a man?"

"The answer is, yes. I'm quite capable of killing a man who means to kill me—or you."

Bolan let out a deep sigh. "I'm in the hands of two women...."

BOLAN STAYED with Joan Warnicke in her Medway apartment for three more days. On Wednesday she drove him back to New York. He was still stiff and sore, and movement was painful, but he insisted that he was ready to go.

When she drove into a Brooklyn garage that Brognola had specified, they were met by a Justice Department agent who introduced himself as Joe Coppolo. He drove them to an apartment building in Brooklyn, where a safehouse was ready for Bolan.

"Not fancy, but it's guarded," Coppolo said. "We've got other people in the building. Witness protection, you understand. It would be just as well, Mr. Bolan, if you didn't try to strike up an acquaintance with anyone else in the building. I'll be here, and a couple of other agents will identify themselves to you. Otherwise—''

"Understood," Bolan grunted.

The flat had some of the aspects of a prison, he thought, and he could see that Joan reacted just the same way, only more strongly. The entrance door was steel, locked with three separate locks opened by three different keys. There was a tiny kitchen, a bathroom and a fairly large sitting room furnished with a couch that folded out to make a bed, a dining table, two reclining chairs and a new and obviously expensive television set. It was a place where some people had spent many lonely days.

The generally depressing air of the place was relieved by a magnificent view of the East River and Manhattan beyond. A double glass door slid open onto a miniature balcony.

"I suggest you enjoy the view from inside. The glass is bulletproof." Coppolo had offered the advice when he noticed Bolan surveying the balcony.

The warrior turned and studied the agent with interest.

Coppolo was a small man, not more than five foot six and probably not more than a hundred forty pounds—though, if Bolan judged him right, it was a hundred forty pounds of muscle. He wore a straw hat, and when he took it off inside the flat he revealed a bald head. His eyes were small and in another man might have been called beady. He was wearing a conservatively cut summer-weight brown suit that failed to conceal from Bolan's eye the weight of a pistol in harness under his left shoulder.

"There's an apartment vacant in the building," Coppolo said. "We can arrange to make it available to you, Miss Warnicke, during the course of the investigation into the construction business. Mr. Stein suggests you accept it."

Joan looked around, then shook her head; she found the place too depressing.

"Well, I have a few things to tell you," Coppolo announced. He sat down. "In the first place, we kept protection over Gina Claw and her mother until they moved up to Plattsburgh. We've notified the New York State Police barracks there to watch out for any strangers approaching the farm where they've taken up residence temporarily. Miss Claw insists she's coming back to the city once she has her mother settled. If she does, it will be contrary to our advice."

Coppolo nodded toward two suitcases sitting in a corner of the room. "Those are from your room in New Jersey. We packed everything and got it out of there that night. That's a real cannon, that Desert Eagle of yours. You'll find your other stuff there, too. I bought you a supply of ammunition. You were a little low, maybe. It's better I bought it for you than for you to buy it. It'd be a sure tip-off, a man buying that kind of ammo. Mr. Brognola has left instructions that we're to supply anything you need."

Bolan nodded. "Good."

"Finally Mr. Brognola assigned me to you." He reached inside his pocket. "This is a letter for you, from him."

Striker:

Trust Joe Coppolo. He knows his way around
New York and has all the latest Intel on what's
going on with the Five Families. He's a good
man, too—the kind you like to work with. We
recruited him from NYPD, where he was an effective man but unhappy with their style of operation, especially the departmental politics.
Some NYPD people don't like him, but they're
all scared of him, first because he can be tough as
hell, second because he's a Fed now.

Be careful of the two women, guy. I don't
doubt their good qualities, but their enthusiasm
is apt to get them hurt—or get you hurt trying to
save them. I know you'd rather work alone, but
this is a big one.

He folded the letter and put it in his pocket.
"Okay," he said. "Where do we start?"

IF JOE ROSSI could have had his way, all meetings of
the council would have been held in his Manhattan
office. He was uncomfortable in the settings the others
chose—the back rooms of neighborhood restaurants,
private clubs in squalid neighborhoods, sometimes
their homes. Alfredo Segesta had chosen today's
meeting place, and it was in his home on Staten Island.
They sat around a table spread with dishes of food and
bottles of wine, and while they talked, Alfredo's
black-clad wife and daughter carried in platter after
platter of rich Italian food.

Besides, the savory odors that permeated the house would go home with him in his clothes and hair—the smells of garlic, tomato, meat fats and all the spices favored by Mama Segesta. The atmosphere of the house reminded Rossi of all he had escaped when he'd assumed control of the Family and shaped it to his specifications. Things here were much as they had been when his father and grandfather had ruled the Rossi Family.

Besides Joe Rossi and Al Segesta, Luca Barbosa and Carlo Lentini were at the table. Four of the Five Families were represented. The absence of Arturo Corone was silently noted. No business was discussed while Mama Segesta and her daughter Claire were serving the meal. It was only when the two women closed the door to the kitchen and the clattering of the cleanup could be heard that the men began to talk serious matters.

"Arturo..." Rossi began ominously, raising the subject.

"They say he's dying," Segesta said. He filled his own glass and passed along the wine bottle. "Cancer."

"Then who speaks for the Corones?" Barbosa asked.

"They will fight for that right," Lentini said.

"This cannot be permitted," Barbosa stated. "You agree, don't you, Joe?"

Rossi nodded. This was why he had raised the issue. They couldn't permit control of the Corone Family to be decided by a murderous confrontation.

"What do the Corones have?" Segesta asked. "I've lost track."

"The dope, mostly," Rossi said. He spat the word. "Heroin. Amphetamines. Not cocaine. Others have muscled them out of that." He meant the Colombians. "Some unions. Teamster locals, mostly. Electricians, towel services, hauling. I have the figures. Some of it's pretty rough stuff."

"You'd like to clean it up, eh, Joe?" Lentini suggested.

Carlo Lentini was a moon-faced, bald man, with heavy jowls and a thick mouth in which the unlighted stub of a cigar usually resided. His reputation was for being an easygoing man, eager to avoid conflict, content to take his profits and make concessions where concessions could be made. Those who had known him for a long time knew that he had taken out the entire Silva Family, one by one, ignoring their tardy pleas for compromise and peace, until the last Silva fled New York—fled the United States, indeed, and retired quietly to a modest villa just outside Palermo.

"I'll make you a proposition, Carlo," Rossi said calmly. "If we can settle the question of control of the Corone businesses in a quiet, reasonable way, *you* can have everything that's theirs. Or others can have shares. I won't demand a nickel's worth."

Lentini grinned. "Peace at any price, eh, Joe?"

"I'll make you another proposition, Carlo," Rossi continued. "Why don't you and I do like Hamilton and Burr?"

"Who're Hamilton and Burr?" Lentini demanded scornfully. "What businesses *they* got?"

Rossi glanced around the table to see whether the others had caught his meaning. He couldn't tell. "Old-time guys, Carlo," he said. "They couldn't settle their argument any other way, so they went across the river with a couple pistols and stood and fired at each other. Hamilton was killed. It didn't prove anything, except that both of them had the guts to do it. You want to do that? I have the guts to face you. I know you have the guts to face me. So what would it prove?"

Lentini hadn't followed the logic at all. He shrugged. "Okay, what would it prove?"

"That I want peace, not because I haven't got the stomach for war, but because scattering bloody corpses all over town is a bad idea, bad for everybody. It brings heat, Carlo. It cuts profits. That's why I want the Corone business settled around a table, not on the streets."

Lentini scratched his cheek. "What do you propose?" he asked, a subtle degree of new respect in his voice.

"I suggest we summon everybody before the council, and *tell* them, not ask them, how it's going to be."

"While Arturo is still living?" Barbosa asked incredulously. "We divide up a man's business while he's still living?"

"Do we divide it up?" Rossi asked. "Do any of us need it? I suggest one of us meets with Arturo Corone—assuming he can still meet and talk—and ask him how he wants it. Then, unless his wishes are unacceptable to us, we tell all the others it's going to be the way Arturo wants it."

"Who meets with him," Lentini asked.

"You do, Carlo."

"You and I together," Lentini suggested.

Rossi nodded. "Agreeable, Luca? Al?"

Barbosa and Segesta nodded.

"Settled, then," Rossi declared. It always surprised him how well he, the youngest member of the council, could prevail on most issues.

"We got a bigger problem," Barbosa said. The wizened little gray man nodded solemnly. "A bigger problem."

"Bolan?" Rossi asked.

"Bolan," Barbosa replied. "He's in town. Or he was."

"You think he's in town," Segesta said. "You can't be sure."

"I sent two good men to take care of him," Barbosa told them.

"Not such good men, apparently," Lentini taunted. "He whacked the two of them."

"Good men," Barbosa insisted.

"I suspect Luca is right," Rossi said. "They were good men. It takes more than two good men to take out Bolan. I sent the best hitter I know after him during the Boston business, and..." He shrugged. "Nothing. But I suspect Luca's two good men got a slug into Bolan before he cut them down with an automatic weapon."

"Why do we think that?" Lentini asked.

"A witness," Rossi replied. "A hooker working out of the Jersey motel where the man we think was Bolan was registered. She saw a man being helped into a car by a woman. And they took off before the cops got there. Naturally she reported this to us ... and not to the police.''

"Who was the woman? What'd she look like?"

"The hooker had never seen her before and has no idea who she was. She helped a wounded man—the hooker swears this—into a little red car. And she took off like a bat out of hell.''

"I still don't see why we think it was Bolan," Segesta said.

"Start with the descriptions given by the guys who saw him in Luciano's," Barbosa replied. "One of the wise guys in there had run up against Bolan once before. He swears it was him.''

"That was no ordinary citizen in that parking lot in New Jersey," Rossi said. "He was wounded. I think we can take the hooker's word on that.''

"What would he be doing in New York?" Lentini asked. "What would he be doing in Luciano's, asking after Grotti?''

Barbosa stared at Rossi, as if expecting the answer to come from him. But it came from Segesta.

"It's probably what you bought us, Luca, when you whacked three citizens. That's what we talked about in Joe's office. You said you'd think about it, then you went ahead and had Albanese hit the old Mohawk and the witness. That was bad judgment, Luca.''

"Albanese got to them before I could call him off. I meant to take your advice.''

"What's done is done," Rossi said sympathetically. "The question now is, what do we do about it?''

"Bolan hasn't been seen or heard from since he was shot. Maybe your guys really got him, Luca," Lentini suggested.

"I'll believe it when he's been missing six months," Rossi retorted.

"So, what do we do about him?" Segesta asked.

"I have a hitter who'd like to have him," Rossi replied. "To settle a score."

"Who is the guy?" Lentini asked.

Rossi shook his head. "An element of the deal is that nobody knows. But I tell you what I need. A million dollars. My hitter has to retire on this one. One million dollars, cash. I'll put up a quarter of it myself. The other four Families—"

"You're out of your mind," Barbosa grumbled. "There's no hitter worth a million."

"Agreed," Rossi said. "No hitter. But the *hit*. What's it worth to knock off Bolan?"

"Many have tried," Segesta reminded him.

"I've got a hitter who can do it," Rossi insisted. "For a million. I'm putting up a quarter."

"The Corones have to chip in," Barbosa said.

Rossi nodded. "Something more to discuss with Arturo."

"It had better work," Lentini said. "A million—"

Rossi raised his chin. "We'll put up a quarter of a million in advance," he said. "*My* quarter of a million. When Bolan's dead, I'll call on the rest of you for the balance. If it doesn't work, it costs you nothing."

Barbosa smiled thinly. "Now, that's the kind of deal I like."

JOE ROSSI had an apartment on East Fifty-sixth Street, which was unknown to all but a few of his most trusted men. It was a handy place for him when he wanted to be alone, away from the jangling telephone. Early in the evening of the day when he met with the council of the Five Families he took a young woman there.

Her name was Salina Beaudreau.

She was an unforgettable figure—an exotically beautiful black woman, well over six feet tall, with a lithe, trim figure and close-cropped hair. She was wearing skintight black leather shorts and a white silk blouse. A heavy round pendant on a thick gold chain hung between her breasts. She sipped the Scotch that Rossi had poured for her and smoked a long, thin cigarette.

"I have no complaint," he said to her.

"I'm not apologizing."

He smiled and reached for his own Scotch. "It was a dangerous assignment. But the offer stands. I want you to take out Bolan."

She jerked her chin high and sniffed. "The first thing I'll need to do is to get near him. You know where he is?"

"I'm not sure. But I think he's going to be in town, making big trouble."

"I'll have to know where he is. And when I do, it's a big contract."

"A million," Rossi told her. "I'll pay you twenty-five percent when you take the contract and the balance when you finish the job. You can retire."

She sniffed again. "If I survive."

"Well . . . Do you want the contract?"

She nodded.

"Then it's a deal. I'll call you when I'm sure Bolan is in town. The quarter million is payable then. I'll get you a lead on him, then he's all yours."

"Thanks."

A few minutes later Rossi stood at his window and watched her hail a cab. Who would guess? Who would ever guess that bizarre young woman was the most dangerous hitter in the business? But she was, and she was damned good. She rarely failed, and she never left a mess.

He tossed back his glass and drank the last of his Scotch. If anyone could knock off Mack Bolan, it was Salina Beaudreau.

CHAPTER FIVE

It was no wonder Arturo Corone hadn't gone to recent meetings of the council. He made Joe Rossi think of a building being demolished. On a sun porch at his home on Long Island, surrounded by a jungle of green houseplants and wrapped in a wool robe and blankets even on a stifling summer day, the man once known as The Giant was a pale, gray relic.

If his two visitors hadn't been Joe Rossi and Carlo Lentini, heads of two powerful Families, plainly they wouldn't have been allowed to see him. It was immediately apparent to Rossi that Don Corone was a prisoner in his own house.

The men in the house weren't the Corone Family capos. They were young wise guys—aggressive, sullen and with no respect for the authority of their elders. Lentini's suggestion to the most aggressive of them that he and Rossi wanted to talk to Don Corone alone had only drawn a smirk and the word that Don Corone was ill and didn't see anyone other than his closest friends.

"Which is you?" Lentini had asked.

"Which is me," the young wise guy had said.

"And you are...?" Rossi had asked.

"Michael Grieco," the young wise guy had answered.

Rossi had taken a moment to appraise Michael Grieco. Young, sure. *Too* damned young. And what the Anglos called a greaseball. His hair was painstakingly combed and held in place by something with a faint, sweetish odor; he had heavy-lidded eyes and a sensual mouth—a pretty boy, except for the misfortune of acne on his cheeks.

"So, who are you, Grieco?" Lentini had asked.

Grieco had nodded at Arturo Corone. "I'm his son."

Rossi and Lentini sat beside Corone, as close to him as they could. Grieco hovered over them, anxious to miss none of their conversation.

"How are you feeling, Arturo?" Lentini asked.

The wasting man shook his head.

"The council has met," Rossi told him. "We have made a decision or two and would like your concurrence."

Arturo Corone nodded. It was apparent that he understood. Weak as he was, he knew what was happening around him.

"We think Bolan might be in town, Arturo," Rossi went on. "The Families are putting up a million dollars for a contract on him. The Corone share is $187,500—payable only if the hit is made. Do you agree?"

"He agrees," Grieco replied. "You can take the money with you when you leave."

"Do *you* agree, Arturo?" Rossi repeated.

The dying man glanced past Rossi, at the menacing figure of Michael Grieco. He shrugged and nodded.

Lentini looked up at Grieco. "Leave us," he ordered. "We want to talk privately with Don Corone."

Grieco smiled scornfully and shook his head.

Carlo Lentini rose and faced Grieco. He spit out the stub of his cigar, which fell on Grieco's shoes and rolled off on the floor. "I said *out*!" he yelled in the man's face. "Now!"

"I speak for Don Arturo," Grieco said defiantly.

"You will be very, very lucky, Grieco, if you speak tomorrow," Lentini growled. "For yourself or anyone else."

Grieco fixed a long, threatening stare on Arturo Corone, then turned on his heel and marched into the house.

Rossi, who had remained seated beside Corone, bent nearer to him and asked, "Who is he?"

"My daughter is married to him," Corone whispered hoarsely.

"If... If you don't recover your health, Don Corone—and God grant that you do—who do you want to succeed you?"

The weak old man stared past the two men, at the door through which Michael Grieco had retreated, as though he were afraid the young man could hear him through the door. "Not him," he whispered.

"Then who?" Rossi asked urgently.

Corone shook his head. "Philip," he muttered. "Not my older sons... They don't have the guts. Really, my daughter Angela is the strongest one, but she's in stir. I..." His eyes shifted toward the door again. "That one... is dangerous."

"He will not survive you, Don Corone," Rossi promised coldly.

"A SMALL JOB," Rossi said to Salina Beaudreau. "Something to tide you over until you earn your million."

They were in his chauffeured car, a nondescript black Chevrolet, not an attention-attracting limo, although it was heavily armored and equipped with a powerful oversized engine.

"Fifty thou," she said. "Not much. A capo—"

"A punk," Rossi interrupted. "An overconfident punk. A piece of cake for a pro like you. Fifty thousand. If you get him within the next twenty-four hours, I'll make it sixty."

Salina Beaudreau sighed loudly. "It suppose a girl's gotta eat."

MICHAEL GRIECO FAVORED a kosher restaurant in Brighton Beach, called Leon's. He favored it so much that he and his friends had all but taken it over—partly to the delight of its guileless, devout owners, who were happy to have so much business from a group of generally quiet and respectful young Italians, but partly also to their dismay, since the subtly menacing presence of these young men had tended to drive away some of the old families who had eaten there for decades.

Grieco favored Leon's for reasons of his own. Undeniably the food was excellent. Better, the place was respectable, out-of-the-way and unknown to certain people he didn't want to see. When he ate there, he saw no one from any of the Five Families. No one knew where to look for him.

Also, when he was there, he was cock of the walk, king of the mountain, undisputed master. None of the wise guys came but those who acknowledged Michael Grieco as an unanointed don.

They did the rituals. His men kissed his hand. He greeted his special friends with a great, back-slapping hug. He drank red wine and ate the kosher food with gusto. Leon Goldish and his wife, Emma, attended him deferentially, curious as to why this young man should spend so much money in their restaurant that he and his friends all but supported it.

One of Barbosa's capos knew all about Leon's and the way Grieco lorded it over the little nieghborhood restaurant. "Where the punk keeps out of sight," was how he put it. Four hours after Rossi sent the word around that he needed to know where to find Grieco, the answer came back: look for him at Leon's in Brighton Beach.

When Salina Beaudreau arrived in Brighton Beach on Saturday evening, she concluded she had lost ten thousand dollars. Rossi had offered fifty thousand for Grieco, sixty if she got him within twenty-four hours. But the place where she'd been told he hung out was shut tight.

Sure. The Jewish Sabbath. Then she remembered—the Sabbath ended at sunset.

And when she returned a little after eight, Leon's Family Restaurant was open.

She had rented a white Cadillac convertible, using a credit card and a New Jersey driver's license she

would never use again. Even before she drove out of
the Manhattan garage, she had pulled on clear plastic
gloves, and there wasn't a fingerprint of hers anywhere in the car. Parked for two minutes on Seventy-
ninth Street, she had pulled off the silk dress and wig
that had given her a respectable appearance for the
rental agency clerk. Now, in skimpy white shorts and
halter, she had the appearance she wanted.

She pulled the Cadillac to the curb in front of
Leon's, got out and looked in through the window.
Okay. The wise guys were at their big table, as Rossi
had said. And the central figure was a man who fit the
description of Michael Grieco.

Of course, there was a chance that it wasn't Grieco.
She would find out.

Salina lowered the convertible's top and sat smoking, avoiding the eyes of the men on the street, who
stared at her with fascination.

After a quarter of an hour, she saw what she was
waiting for: a young Italian-looking male walking toward her on the street. She flipped her cigarette away,
got out of the car and stood leaning on the right front
fender.

"Hey," she called.

He stopped, cocked his head to one side and openly
appraised the golden-skinned beauty in the tight shorts
and loose halter.

"You going in there?" she asked.

"Maybe not," he said. "Maybe not . . now."

"Sure. Well, tell Mike somebody's out here to see
him. Samantha. Tell him Samantha is out here."

The wise guy grinned. "Has to be Mike, huh?"

"First Mike," she said. "Then—" She shrugged. "Who knows. What's your name?"

"Genero."

"I'll be around, Genero. Just send Mike out first."

The young man nodded, turned and strode into the little restaurant.

"Hey, Mike!"

Grieco extended his hand to be kissed. Genero took it and pressed it perfunctorily to his lips.

"Mike, you won't guess who's outside asking for you."

Grieco stiffened.

"A lady who says her name's Samantha."

"I don't know any Samantha."

Genero grinned. "Well, she knows you. And I'd *get* to know her, if I were you. Hey, man! Tall enough to play for the Knicks! Just barely dressed. And, hey man, *bee-yoot-i-ful*!"

"I don't know any Samantha," Grieco repeated.

"She asked for you by name. Sittin' right outside in a white Caddy convertible that set somebody back forty thou. Hey—"

"Awright, a-ready! Asked for me by name, you say?"

"That her?" another young man asked, pointing toward the big window at the front of the restaurant.

Michael Grieco rose. "Okay," he grunted. "I'll see what she wants."

The others grinned.

Conscious of their smirks, he set his shoulders and affected a signature swagger as he walked across the little restaurant to the door.

Salina was ready.

This was the man; she had no doubt. He swaggered, as Rossi had told her. He was wearing a gray suit of some shiny light fabric, maybe silk, with a white shirt open at the collar, no tie.

He leaned against the door on the passenger side of the white convertible and stuck his head in the window. "What do you want, honey?"

"You're Michael Grieco?"

"I'm Michael Grieco."

"I'm from the council," she said as she thrust the muzzle of a Walther PPK toward his face.

He shrieked in terror.

She let him stagger back so none of his blood would touch the car. Then, quite calmly, with a steady aim, she put a 7.65 mm slug through his forehead.

The mobsters at the table inside, staring at Grieco and the woman, saw him stagger back and fall to the sidewalk. They upset one of the tables in their rush for the door. By the time they reached the curb, the white Cadillac was turning the corner a half block away, and the corpse of Michael Grieco lay still on the pavement.

"I DON'T SEE the connection," Saul Stein said. "But I have to think there is one. Michael Grieco was Arturo Corone's son-in-law and was a contender for head of the Corone Family. Everything is interrelated. Arturo Corone is in extremis. Somebody knocked off one of the chief contenders for his authority. What does that have to do with the murders of the Claws? Or of

Whittle? Something, you may be sure, even if only remotely."

"A tall black woman, cropped hair, exotic..." Bolan mused, remembering a previous encounter he'd had with a woman who fit that description.

"As far as NYPD is concerned," Stein continued, "the idea of a tall, black, female hitter is a fantasy thought up by Grieco's friends to throw us off the track. They're not interested in any black woman in a white Cadillac."

"I've run across her before," Bolan told them. "And I'm interested in why Grieco was hit by this woman. The witnesses are right—Grieco was taken out by a black woman in a white Cadillac."

"The white Cadillac was rented, paid for with a credit card in the name of Samantha Carter. The New Jersey address matched the address on the said Samantha Carter's driver's license. And the car, abandoned on a Brooklyn street, bears no fingerprints, other than the ones of employees of the garage where the car was rented. The New Jersey license—"

"Was bogus," Joan concluded. "Needless to say."

"Let me change the subject," Stein said. "Not entirely, but a little. On the day before Grieco was killed, Arturo Corone had two visitors—Giuseppe Rossi, head of the Rossi Family, and Carlo Lentini, head of the Lentini Family. That was Friday. On Wednesday, the Five Families council met at Alfredo Segesta's home on Staten Island. We keep watch on the Corone house, and our observers photographed Rossi and Lentini arriving and leaving."

"You're thinking the council ordered the hit on Grieco," Bolan stated.

"I think that's possible."

"Fill me in on these guys," Bolan said.

"Giuseppe Rossi is often called Clean Joe," Coppolo told him, "because he's never been arrested. He's one of the new generation. He wants to run the Mafia like a business—he has a degree in business administration from Columbia University. The Rossis own two major construction companies, plus some heavy-supplies operations. They own four or five big office buildings in Manhattan, plus a hotel-casino in Atlantic City—all this through dummy corporations and so on, hiding the real ownership. They're into trash hauling, the same way. Rossi doesn't like the high-risk stuff, like narcotics. Of course, he's got gambling in Atlantic City, and he uses the Family casinos for money laundering. The Rossi Family is into money laundering in a big way. But no rough stuff. That's his style. Some of the brotherhood who call him Clean Joe don't use the term kindly."

"The State of New Jersey caught a hauler dumping filth into the Atlantic," Stein said. "Medical waste. You know, what was washing up on the beaches. We could identify the hauler as a Rossi company. But—" he shook his head "—our evidence wasn't good enough for the people in New Jersey, and they refused to go after Rossi."

"He owned them," Coppolo stated bluntly.

"Carlo Lentini," Stein went on, "has done time. Six years, for assault with intent to kill. The Lentinis used to be into narcotics, heavily. But, like the Rossis, they don't like the risk anymore, don't like the publicity. They run a thousand books and numbers games, all over the area. Legal off-track betting and state lotteries don't compete with them, because they'll let their suckers bet on credit. Then, of course, a Lentini loan shark lends the sucker the money to pay off the book. They grab two hundred percent a month as vig, and they break arms and legs to encourage people to pay. They're also into prostitution. Don't let anybody tell you the Families have gone out of that business. The Lentinis have protection, 'insurance' and a big hunk of the waterfront and airports rackets.''

"The Corone Family?'' Bolan asked.

"They're still in narcotics, though the Colombians and some of the new Oriental gangs have all but muscled them out of the coke trade. Arturo Corone was called The Giant, and it's said that when he was a well man he picked up a Colombian dealer and broke his back. Just held him and squeezed until he broke the man's spine. The Corones have some union locals, Teamsters mostly, but also some electricians. And if you want to run a restaurant in some parts of the city, you subscribe to the Corone Towel Supply Service. If you don't . . .''

"The Corones play rough,'' Coppolo said. "They've got hitters on the payroll. And headcrushers. The old man's dying, though, and there's nobody in line to take his place. That could make a war.''

"It already has. Somebody already took out Grieco,'' Bolan stated.

"I'm interested in the black woman," Coppolo said. "We don't know anything about a hitter like that. She's new in town."

"Maybe not," Bolan replied. "Not if she's good."

"She's good," Coppolo said. "She took out Michael Grieco with no trouble at all."

"Maybe she's so good that nobody knows her."

"If she is, she made a big mistake this time," Coppolo replied. "The word's around now to look out for a tall black woman—she might be a hitter."

CHAPTER SIX

When Mack Bolan left the safehouse after recovering there for three days, he felt healed and well. He had indulged in role camouflage and wore a dark blue, pin-striped suit, with white shirt and striped necktie, and looked to be a Midtown banker or a Wall Street broker. No one would have guessed that *this* banker carried a silenced Beretta in his attaché case.

He had ventured into Luciano's in search of Vince Grotti and had become the target of a pair of hit men. Now he would try again, more cautiously.

The Intel on Grotti included an address in Manhattan, on East Sixty-sixth Street. The place turned out to be an old apartment building in a neighborhood that seemed to be slipping into decay.

One of the cards on the bell array read "V. Grotti." Bolan pushed the button and waited.

After a moment a woman's voice blared out of the speaker system. "Yeah?"

"Vince in?"

"No, Vince isn't here."

"You expect him?"

"No time soon."

"I've got some money for him. Could I leave it with you?"

A moment of silence. Then, "Okay."

The door buzzed, and Bolan walked in.

The apartment was on the top floor, and the woman was standing in the door when he reached it—an aging blonde with liquid eyes, frowzy hair and smeared makeup. She was dressed in a light blue cotton nightgown that looked as if it had been picked off the rack in a dime store. It was apparent that she'd been drinking already in the midmorning—either that, or she hadn't yet stopped from the night before.

"Is it cash," she asked.

"No such luck," Bolan replied, pressing past her and into the apartment.

"Hey! Who the hell are you, anyway?"

"The name's Conti," he said. "And you are...?"

"Sara Wald," she said. "But who the hell are you?"

"A friend of the don's, and a friend of Vince's."

"Really?"

"Really."

He looked around the living room of the apartment. Unmistakably it was the living quarters of someone who drank to excess, someone whose life had fallen apart. The gin bottle was on the coffee table, a half-empty glass beside it. The room was also littered with the wrappers and cartons of fast food.

"What you lookin' for?" she asked.

"Vince. Where is he?"

Sara Wald sat down on the couch, picked up the glass and tossed back the ounce or two of straight, warm gin that remained there. She shook her head. "Walked out."

"When?"

"Two weeks ago. 'Bout—"

"You and Vince have a big argument?"

She shook her head. "Just . . . walked out."

He looked around the room once more, at accumulated newspapers, a television set that was on, with the sound turned down, an aquarium with dead fish floating on top. . . .

"The rent?" he asked.

She shrugged. "Taken care of by Vince's friends. They're taking care of things till Vince comes home."

"And you're not supposed to tell where he is, right?"

She threw out her hands. "I don't *know* where he is. He just took off."

"Are you short of money?"

She nodded.

Bolan picked up her bottle of gin—Gordon's. "Expensive," he commented.

Sara nodded. "Yeah. I don't . . . use all that much. But . . ." She sighed. "You said you had money for Vince. Hey, he wouldn't mind if I—"

"Sure." Bolan reached into his pocket, pulled out a wad of bills and peeled off two twenties. "There you go."

She seized the money gratefully. "Thanks, buddy."

"Our little secret, huh?" he said.

She nodded. "Yeah. Gotta be."

Bolan glanced around the room once more and feigned indifference. "I need to talk to Vince, sooner or later," he said. "If you see him—"

"I won't."

"Did somebody tell him to take a vacation?"

"Yeah. Whitey. Whitey told him to take a vacation. Then Whitey came by to see that he did."

"Tell me about Whitey," Bolan urged.

She shook her head. "No. I can't."

"You can talk to me."

"Who the hell are you?" she demanded, finding a little strength for her ravaged voice. "I mean, really. Just who the hell are you, that I can talk to you?"

He sat down on a vinyl-covered chair, facing her. "I'm *consiglière*," he said.

"To Barbosa?" she asked skeptically.

Bolan shrugged. "Let's not use names," he cautioned.

"Well, Vince works for the old man. The don. But he also works for Whitey Albanese. When he came home that day—I mean the day he took off—he said Whitey'd told him to take a vacation. You don't argue with Whitey. So he left, and that was it."

"What day was this?"

"About two weeks ago."

"Then Whitey came by to see you?"

"Yeah. He asked for Vince, like he didn't know the guy was gone. I told him Vince was gone for a long time. I didn't tell him I knew he'd ordered Vince to get out of town. So he hands me a C-note and tells me the rent will be paid. He says there'll be a C-note in the mail once a week. And there has been. I'm supposed to live on a lousy hundred every Friday. What you could do for me, *consiglière*, is take back the word that I need more money."

"I'll see what I can do," Bolan promised. "But don't tell anybody I was here. Whitey wouldn't like that."

"He doesn't like much of anything, does he? Whitey—"

"Wants to kill Vince," Bolan said grimly.

"No."

Bolan nodded. "Vince messed up a job."

She squinted and tried to focus her eyes on Bolan to read his expression, to see just how serious he was.

"Somebody should warn Vince," Bolan said.

Sara raised her chin, and a sly little smile flirted with her lips. "Sure. So I should tell you where he is? C'mon, buddy, I wasn't born yesterday.

"Look," she continued, "I'd like to trust you. Do you really care if Vince gets killed or not?"

"The don doesn't want Vince killed."

She sighed loudly. "I don't know where he is. Honest to God. But I did get a note from him. He said he was okay and would see me in October. No address on the envelope, but the postmark said it was mailed from Bedford Beach, New Jersey. Which kind of figures. That's as far from home as Vince has ever been. He wouldn't want to get too far from New York."

"Can I see that note?"

"I tossed it," she said. "I was mad at him for takin' off, leaving me. Hey, he could've taken me with him.... Anyway, you couldn't tell anything from seeing it. It wasn't hotel stationery or anything like that. No return address. He didn't want me to be able to come find him. Maybe he wasn't even in Bedford Beach. Maybe he just went there to mail that note."

"Possible."

She sighed again. "Hey, when Vince is around, I don't look like this. I don't drink much. Now what am I supposed to do, just sit around and wait?"

Bolan regarded her with both sympathy and skepticism.

"If you really do talk to the don," she said, "you might tell him a C-note a week isn't much."

"I'll do that."

SAUL STEIN HAD a little information on Whitey Albanese.

"An old-country Sicilian. Smart enough to keep his name and face out of the police files. The only rap against him is that he's an illegal alien. He's overstayed his visa many times over and has no green card. His name comes up from time to time, mentioned by informers, but we have no line on him."

"Got a mug shot?" Bolan asked.

"No," Stein said, "and no fingerprints."

"There's nothing official on the guy," Coppolo offered, "but I can tell you he has a rep on the streets as a sadistic killer. The other Families didn't like it when Barbosa brought him over here."

"Somebody's got a photo," Bolan told them. "Italian authorities, Interpol. Let's ask Hal to make an official inquiry."

"Done," Coppolo said. "I'll call him."

"Okay," Bolan continued. "Bedford Beach."

"Outside my jurisdiction," Stein said wryly.

"But not outside mine," Coppolo told him. "I'll go with you."

"Tomorrow morning," Bolan replied.

DURING THE DRIVE to Bedford Beach, Bolan had a chance to get better acquainted with Joe Coppolo, and he liked what he saw and heard.

He discovered in the first place that the pistol in Coppolo's shoulder holster was a 9 mm Browning Hi-Power—an odd choice, maybe, in view of what the manufacturers now offered, but a very reasonable choice when you remembered that the Browning had a fifty-year record of reliability. Better yet, the clip held thirteen rounds—potentially a nasty surprise to some character who counted your shots then jumped, figuring you had to reload. It was a workmanlike, serviceable pistol, and a man who had chosen it for his daily weapon had to be respected.

Coppolo hadn't been in the military, but he had spent his adult life protecting the innocent public. He had a very realistic view of the world. It was an us-against-them place, he figured, where a few men and fewer women had to sacrifice everything to defend humanity against the criminals.

He was an angry man.

They stopped first at police headquarters, late in the morning, where Coppolo identified himself and Bolan as federal agents on special assignment to the Department of Justice. Lawrence Milano, chief of police for Bedford Beach, received them in his office.

"Vincenza Grotti," he said thoughtfully, looking at the mug shots Coppolo had brought with him. He shook his head. "You understand, gentlemen, that we get a lot of summer people here. If you came here in

December and asked me if there was a stranger in town, I might be able to tell you. But—''

"Understood," Coppolo said. "But this one's a hit man."

"Not here to do a contract, then?" the chief asked.

"No. Hiding out until the heat cools."

Chief Milano shook his head and pushed the mug shot across his desk. "The best I can do for you is show this around. You got an extra copy?"

"I brought a supply of them. Keep that one."

"Let's show it around to whoever's in the station," the chief suggested.

They went out to the desk, where a uniformed sergeant presided. He shook his head at the photograph, as did two uniformed patrolmen.

They left the mug shot with the desk sergeant and returned to the chief's office.

"Motels..." he said. "Beach motels. Could we assume a guy like that would go for a cheap place?"

"What would it cost to stay in a good place?" Bolan asked.

The chief shrugged. "In the summer season, when people go to the beaches... Figure a hundred a night."

"I don't think our guy could handle that," Bolan replied. "He plans on staying three or four months."

The chief opened his desk drawer and took out the Yellow Pages. After staring for a moment, he stepped to a small copy machine in the corner of his office and copied two pages. Then he took a red pen and made four or five check marks on the copies.

"There," he said. "The most likely places, if your guy is staying in Bedford Beach and wants to stay cheap. You want help?"

"We can handle him," Bolan said.

Chief Milano smiled faintly and nodded. "Yeah, I bet you can. Let me know if you find him. Otherwise, I'll have all my guys look at your mug shots."

The motels the chief had suggested were all on the highway, two blocks back from the beach, interspersed with little shopping centers, automobile agencies and fast-food restaurants. The summer sun beat down on acres of treeless pavement. Still, this was the back side of a beach resort, and families trudged to and from the beach, carrying their coolers and picnic baskets.

Coppolo drove past all the motels checked off by Chief Milano, then drove back to the first one and pulled into the parking lot. They went into the office, a small room paneled in dingy knotty pine and cooled by a straining window air conditioner.

"Yeah?" said the young woman behind the desk. Even though the air conditioner kept the room uncomfortably cool, she wore a pair of shorts and a halter. She didn't rise from her chair behind the desk but knocked the ash from her cigarette and put it in her mouth to suck heavy smoke into her lungs. "I got a couple of vacancies."

"We're federal officers," Coppolo stated. "United States Department of Justice."

She frowned and reluctantly stood up to take a look at the identification he offered.

"FBI?"

"Sensitive Operations Group," he replied. "I want you to look at a picture." He handed her a mug shot of Grotti. "Ever see him?"

She shook her head. "Can't say I ever have."

"He's not registered here? Single man. Or maybe he would have a girl with him. No kids, anyway."

She shook her head again.

"No time?"

She dragged again on her cigarette. "No time. Not since I been workin' here. Say, four months. I don't think I ever saw this guy."

They left. They tried two more motels and then struck paydirt at the Ashbury.

"Two-ought-four," the desk clerk replied to their query.

"Hmm?"

"That's the guy in 204. Uh—" he jerked open a little steel card-file box and flipped a dozen cards "—Angelo's the name. Fred Angelo. On the lam, is he?"

"Not anymore," Coppolo replied.

The desk clerk was a fat man, in a white shirt and a pair of khaki pants held up by black suspenders. "Let me call the cops to help you guys out. We got good cops here. Chief Milano—"

"We can handle it," Bolan said firmly.

The man frowned skeptically. "Far as I know, he's in his room. Goes to the beach mornings, kind of early, then sleeps in the air-conditioning in the heat of the day. Prowls at night. Brings women back."

As soon as Bolan and Coppolo were out the door, the desk man grabbed the telephone and called the Bedford Beach police. Then he locked the office and hurried across the highway to a Dunkin' Donuts. That was as close as he wanted to be to what he thought was going to happen at the motel.

Bolan and Coppolo kept close to the concrete-block walls as they made their way from the office to the steel-and-concrete stairs that led to the second story of the motel. Both of them were conscious that they looked like agents, would be seen as agents by a man looking out his window.

The first-floor rooms of the motel opened on the parking lot. The second-floor rooms opened on a narrow balcony that ran the length of the building. Reaching that balcony, Bolan nudged Coppolo and nodded at the desk clerk hurrying across the highway.

There were twelve or thirteen rooms along the balcony. The room could be reached by three stairways, one at each end of the building and one in the middle—the one Bolan and Coppolo had just climbed. Room 204 would be to their right as they faced the building at the top of the stairs. It was at the east end, the third room from the end.

The curtains were pulled across all the windows, against the midday sun that otherwise would have blazed through and defeated the air conditioners, which roared and dripped at every room. They were set through sleeves in the wall, above the windows, and beneath each one the concrete floor of the balcony was wet and stained with rust.

"I'll go ahead and get on the other side of the door," Bolan said.

"I'll knock and say I'm Whitey. That ought to scare the hell out of him."

Bolan nodded. He drew the Beretta and strode out ahead of the Justice agent.

When the Executioner heard the shot and heard Coppolo scream, he spun around. The agent was down. The man who had fired on them ducked out of sight just as Bolan raised the Beretta.

"Joe!"

"In the leg," Coppolo yelled. He had the Browning in his right hand, and he dragged himself closer to the wall and leveled it at the top of the stairway. "Down!" he shouted. "The son of a bitch is underneath us."

Bolan joined the agent and knelt beside him. A slug had torn through the flesh of his leg above the knee. He was bleeding, but it was a spreading stain, not a gush of blood. He was lucky. The artery appeared to be intact.

"Listen to me," Coppolo grunted. "He's down there. He's right underneath us. If you cover the east end of the building and I cover the west, then he can't go around the ends and get away. And he can't go out in the parking lot. So he's trapped."

"If he hasn't got away already."

"*If,*" Coppolo agreed. He began to crawl toward the west end of the balcony, dragging the wounded leg, smearing blood on the concrete.

"Are you sure?"

"I'm sure," Coppolo replied. "Cover your end."

Bolan trotted to the east end of the balcony, past room 204. The door was open and he took a moment to look inside. Grotti wasn't in there, unless he was hiding under the bed or in the bathroom.

At the end, Bolan peered around the corner of the building. Coppolo was doing the same at the other end. It was as the agent had said—Grotti was very likely trapped under the balcony. Even if he broke into a room, he might still be trapped, because it looked as if the only windows in these motel rooms were on the front. Behind the bedrooms were bathrooms, with no windows.

On the other hand, this was a standoff, and Bolan didn't like standoffs. At any time, an innocent might wander into the situation and get hurt, or perhaps be taken hostage. Going down the stairs was out. The gunner would be looking for that, pistol raised.

But, if Bolan jumped from the balcony and landed on his feet, firing... Or if he jumped and landed between two parked cars...

He signaled to Coppolo who shook his head emphatically. But when he saw that Bolan meant to make the jump, whether he agreed or not, he signaled that he would distract the man below by firing a shot or two down the stairs. Bolan nodded.

Coppolo crawled to the west stairway. It was only a few feet for him, but he moved painfully. Lying on his belly on the concrete, he lowered his head and risked a look below. Then he thrust the muzzle of the Browning downward and fired two shots. As the slugs whined off the pavement below, Bolan made his leap from the balcony.

It was the kind of jump he'd made many times. He knew how to cushion the impact to his ankles and knees and how to roll away from the landing point to avoid the fire of a startled defender. He landed between two vehicles and came out of the roll with the Beretta up and ready, seeking target acquisition.

During the bare second he was plunging to the parking-lot pavement, he'd caught sight of the man beneath the balcony. The guy had been crouched, pistol aimed with two hands at the stairway from which Coppolo had fired.

Another shot rang out, but not from Coppolo's Browning. Bolan lifted his head above the hood of the station wagon and saw the crouching man topple forward. Then a slug punched through the sheet steel of the hood and passed within a few inches of his throat.

The warrior threw himself back and scrambled for the rear of the car. A bullet ricocheted off the pavement and caught the underside of the Ford. Someone was trying to catch him in the leg by spanging a slug off the parking-lot pavement—a remote chance but maybe one worth somebody's taking.

"Office, Mack!" Coppolo yelled.

Bolan stood up. A man in a white shirt and black pants had made a dash to the door of the motel office. He'd reached it, and now he frantically twisted the handle of the locked door. He turned, spotted Bolan and raised his automatic. Bolan loosed a 3-shot burst that caught the gunner squarely in the chest and slammed him back against the office door.

It was over. One man lay sprawled on the pavement in front of the door to the motel office, the other doubled over and dying, but not yet dead, on the concrete in front of room 118. Joe Coppolo sat on the balcony and clutched his leg. Bolan holstered his Beretta and stood, calmly watching the screaming approach of a Bedford Beach police car.

THE DOCTORS at Bedford Beach General Hospital insisted that Joe Coppolo should have a blood transfusion and rest for most of the afternoon. Chief Milano was with Bolan when the Justice agent was released.

The fingerprints of the two dead men had been faxed to Washington, and identifications had come back already. The man who had been shot in front of room 118, who had died before he could be put in an ambulance, was Vincenza Grotti. The man who had fallen in front of the door to the motel office was George Aristotle, reputedly a professional gambler in Atlantic City, whose fingerprints were in the FBI central files only because he had been arrested and released for want of evidence on a charge of statutory rape—eighteen years ago. An unlikely man to have been where he was, doing what he was doing.

"Somebody had to have called Grotti and told him two Feds were looking for him," the chief said. "But that's not the half of it. Somebody tipped Aristotle that Grotti had been fingered—or probably had been—and sent him to whack Grotti before you two could arrest him. I mean, that was a hit, gentlemen.

"Let me tell you what interests me about that," the chief continued. "That son of a bitch had a lot of cool. He arrives to hit Grotti. What's he see? Grotti is in trouble already, with a couple of Feds on the balcony and Grotti stuck downstairs. Most guys would have backed off, gone back to whoever sent them and said, hey, you sent me over there too late. But no.

Aristotle walks into the middle of a firefight and kills his man. Then he turns on you, Mr. Belasko."

"Any of the desk clerks could have called Grotti. But it's unlikely that George Aristotle was so close by that he came without a little notice," Bolan replied.

"He didn't drive up here from Atlantic City in an hour," Coppolo said.

"No?" the chief queried. "We keep a log. There was an hour and twenty minutes from the time you left my office until we got the call that there was a shooting at the Ashbury."

"That's about how long we took to check out all the motels on the list and get back to the Ashbury," Coppolo told him.

"If a cop in my headquarters had called Atlantic City while you were there, George Aristotle, using the Garden State Parkway, could have been here in time."

"Or somebody, say a reporter—" Bolan began to say.

Chief Milano interrupted. "Hey, thanks. But no. If a call went out from my headquarters, it was one of my men."

"Are you plagued by the Barbosas?" Coppolo asked.

"The Barbosa Family... Their influence extends to Atlantic City," the chief replied.

"Atlantic City belongs to the Five Families," Coppolo explained. "The Barbosa Family is a little more crude, a little more traditional, a little more ready to kill than others, but why should we be surprised to find a Barbosa hitter in New Jersey? It's where he's needed, that's all."

"I have my problem," the chief told them. "I'll take care of it. How would you guys take care of it for me?"

Bolan shook his head. "I don't think our methods would work too well for you."

"No. I agree. But I wish they would."

CHAPTER SEVEN

As Bolan drove the Garden State Parkway north to New York, he took no particular notice of the humming Italian sports car coming up behind him. Suddenly the Ferrari drew abreast, and a hardguy in the passenger seat fired a burst point-blank, only six or eight feet from him. Except for the unevenness of the pavement, which caused both cars to pitch and lunge, the vicious assault of 9 mm slugs from the Uzi would have taken his head off. On this road, at this speed, the shot hadn't been as easy as it looked. The slugs roared through the glass of the side window, just above Bolan's head and a little behind, and ricocheted off the roof, buzzing like insane bees and snapping out through the glass on the right side.

Bolan whipped the wheel to the left and slammed the weight of the Buick into the side of the Ferrari, using the mass of the big American car to bulldoze the lighter vehicle off the highway. He kept the fender and door of the Buick pressed hard against the other vehicle until it left the pavement, fishtailed wildly in the median and smashed against the divider guardrail.

Joe Coppolo awakened in the passenger seat and hauled out his Browning.

The Executioner pulled the Buick to the side of the road as soon as he could stop, two hundred yards beyond where the sports car had skidded into the guardrail. In an instant, Coppolo was out of the vehicle, crouched behind the open door and leveling his pistol against whoever else might be in pursuit.

On the other side, Bolan grabbed the torn metal of the Buick's left front fender and, bracing his foot against the wheel, pulled hard. The steel came away from the tire, which allowed the warrior to steer the vehicle.

"Get in!" he yelled to Coppolo.

As soon as the Justice agent complied, Bolan pulled onto the highway and accelerated. In the rearview mirror he could see cars stopping and a crowd forming around the wrecked Ferrari.

"Hey! Aren't you going back? Those guys—"

"Too many people are going to want an explanation," Bolan replied.

"Well, we're on a limited-access highway. We're apt to be stopped at the exit if somebody has a car telephone or a CB radio."

"We'll worry about that when we come to an exit."

"Two miles," Coppolo said, pointing at a sign. "Listen, I've got a solution."

He opened the glove box under the dashboard and pulled out a red emergency light. He plugged it into the cigarette-lighter socket and thrust it out the window, where strong magnets in the light's base locked it to the roof of the Buick.

"Now accelerate a little more," he directed. "Charge up to that toll booth like we're in a hell of a hurry."

Two minutes later the Buick screeched to a stop at the booth. Coppolo leaned across Bolan and flashed his identification at the startled collector. "Federal officers! You've got a red Ferrari wrecked about five miles back. Tell the police to approach it with extreme caution. The guys in it have got an Uzi, possibly other automatic weapons. And tell the police to contact Chief Milano in Bedford Beach. Got that? Tell the state police to call Chief Milano in Bedford Beach!"

"IT'S WAR!" Joe Coppolo growled. "The Barbosas have declared war."

The doctors at Bedford Beach General Hospital had told him to stay off his leg, to use crutches when he had to move, but he had tossed the crutches aside as soon as he could pick up a pair of heavy oak canes, and now he hobbled around Saul Stein's office, angered by the pain in his leg.

"When they fired on us yesterday afternoon, they knew they were firing on two federal agents—"

"*One* federal agent," Bolan corrected him dryly.

"Well, they thought they were firing on two. It comes to the same thing. I don't propose to stand for it."

"Did New Jersey come up with the makes on the guys in the Ferrari?" Bolan asked.

"Not yet, but I have something else to tell you," Saul told him. "They killed Sara Wald Monday night. She was beaten first."

"Suspects?" Bolan asked.

Stein shrugged. "*I* have a suspect in mind—Whitey Albanese. But who knows?"

"They beat her to find out where Grotti was. Monday night... So they were just a skip ahead of us when we got to Bedford Beach."

"Just a skip," Coppolo echoed. "That did give them time to get George Aristotle up from Atlantic City. But Grotti was out on the beach in the morning, so they didn't find him until just before we arrived."

"And while you were at the hospital," Bolan said, "they brought up the heavy artillery in the Ferrari."

"A rented car, incidentally," Stein informed them. "Rented in Jersey City."

"The hitters rented something fun to drive," Coppolo said. "And if that Ferrari hadn't been jerking up and down on rough pavement, that burst would have—"

"I don't want to think about it." Joan shuddered.

"*I* do," Bolan told her. "As Joe said—the Barbosas have declared war."

JOE ROSSI and Carlo Lentini confronted Luca Barbosa in a barber shop in Brooklyn. When the two men came in, the barbers and other customers respectfully slipped out for coffee so the three dons could confer in private. Rossi eased into the next barber chair, with the thought that he would let the barber trim his hair when the conference was finished. Lentini sat in one of the steel-and-vinyl waiting chairs.

"Grotti..." Lentini began. "And a Fed. Both got hit. What's goin' on, Luca?"

Barbosa was nearly hidden beneath the voluminous cloth the barber had draped over him, his hair half-cut. "Grotti knew too much," he muttered. "And he didn't have the courage to keep his mouth shut. We couldn't let him be arrested."

"You told us you didn't know where he was," Rossi said.

"I didn't. But if the Feds could find him, I could find him."

"Someone beat the information out of his girlfriend," Rossi said quietly, "then killed her."

"Yeah? Well, it was her who told the Feds where to find him."

"Who did this job for you, Luca?" Lentini asked. "Whitey Albanese?"

"I don't see how that's any business of yours," Barbosa retorted.

"Luca," Rossi began, "when Cesare Frenchi had a federal agent killed in Boston, it was the beginning of the end for him. The federal government brought in Mack Bolan."

"Bolan..." Barbosa grumbled. "You've got a million-dollar contract out on him, huh? And nothin'. *Nothin'*. Maybe the Fed who took a slug in the leg yesterday was Bolan. He wasn't FBI—some kind of special federal agent."

"Sensitive Operations Group, so they say, Department of Justice," Rossi said grimly. "Luca, you may be bringing the roof down on our heads."

"Down on *my* head," Barbosa growled. "You keep clean, Joe. I'll take the heat."

"When you catch fire, the flame spreads to *us*," Lentini shouted, angry. "To all of us."

Luca Barbosa leaned back in his barber chair and closed his eyes. "We've got other problems, gentlemen," he said. "Arturo Corone died this morning. You didn't know this? Alfredo knows. The Segestas grabbed two of his wholesalers within an hour after Don Corone passed to his reward. I don't like that. You like that, Carlo? Joe says he doesn't want a share of the Corone business, but the rest of us do, and it's being moved without the consent of the council. I think we better call a sitdown."

JOAN WARNICKE ARRIVED at the safehouse a little before seven. "I've got some news for you," she announced. "We've got the identification of the two guys in the Ferrari."

"Who are they?" Bolan probed.

"Okay. One of them, the driver, is Patrick McMahon, better known as Sandy Mac. Thirty-one years old, and he's done time for aggravated assault. Not attempted rape. Just a vicious beating that left his victim scarred for life. He's hospitalized with broken ribs."

"That all?" Coppolo asked.

She glanced at him, then went on. "The gunman is Luigi Vigaldo, better known as Louey Vig. He's thirty-four years old, and has done time for assaults, weapons possession and grand theft. He wasn't wearing his seat belt and went into the windshield. He's got a skull fracture, a cut-up face.... He'll live.

"The New Jersey State Police found the Uzi," she continued, "which is a good thing for you guys. Witnesses on the scene called it a hit-skip, probably by a drunk driver."

"Anything else?" Bolan prodded.

"Louey Vig is Barbosa's man," Coppolo told him. "McMahon, I don't know."

"Wheel man," Joan suggested. "I'm guessing. But why not? Vigaldo is sent to do a number. He hires his own driver."

"Louey Vig..." Bolan said somberly. "A Barbosa soldier involved in what?"

"The Barbosa Family makes a big buck from gambling," the Justice agent said. "They book horses, baseball, football, basketball. You name it. You know, the old deal. Bet on the cuff, pay with a loan from a Barbosa shark. Pay two hundred percent vig. The deal."

"I need to know something," Bolan said. "Where's the layoff book? The big book? Where do the proceeds and the records go when a day's action is over?"

Coppolo raised his chin. "Not until I'm well enough to go with you."

"I don't want to pull rank, but I need to know where this layoff book is...."

It was in Bensonhurst.

Each day the Barbosa books made bets, took money—or, more significantly, markers—from bettors and paid out money to winners. Because the books worked from the "line"—that is, the set of odds fixed by the pros—they couldn't lose. Mathematically, over the course of a day's business, it was impossible for a book to lose. An individual book that got too much action on one horse or one game could lay off to the bigger book up the line, the layoff book. In the long run the rigged odds would prevail.

So, at the end of a day, each book sent a large payment to the layoff book. Even allowing for skimming by the operators, each day produced a large profit that was sent to the layoff book, which then went to the don's treasury.

An important part of what each book sent to the layoff was the markers—the IOUs—collected from bettors who couldn't come up with the cash that day but had a sure tip or a firm hunch what horse was going to win. The markers were payable in a few days, and, since the bettors who had signed them were rarely luckier the next day than they had been the day they gave their markers, the markers went to enforcers—legbreakers. The legbreakers had two options: get payment or get the bettor to borrow from a Family loan shark.

The Family would rather get the borrower on a loan. A fifty-dollar bet could generate several hundred dollars in vigorish—interest—before the terrified borrower finally found some way to come up with the money before the shark's enforcer did him some harm.

The Barbosa layoff book in Bensonhurst, one of three it operated in New York, was located above a beauty parlor and beneath two floors of apartments, in a narrow, four-story brick building. The layoff book did no retail business. No bettors could place a bet there. Business was done strictly by telephone and messenger with other books, from Greenpoint to Coney Island.

The book consisted of a big telephone room, where clerks took layoffs from subordinate books, alert always to the middles and other tactics by which bettors, and sometimes other books, tried to beat the system; a countinghouse room, where other clerks received and counted money; an executive office, where the man in charge sat behind a desk, took calls, adjusted disputes and kept watch on a little empire; and a lounge for visiting wise guys, legbreakers and hardmen, where they smoked, drank coffee and waited for assignments.

The book was busy during the day, but not nearly as busy as it became during the evening, when the revenue from the retail books came in. In the evening, the hardmen were called out of the lounge to take up guard positions. It was all but unknown for Family books to be hit. Still, it did sometimes happen. Drugged-out characters, desperate for the price of the next fix, had been known to try to hit books. When one Family went to war with another, hitting the books was part of the game. No book was without a defense. Layoff books had a harder defense.

The top man at the Barbosa Bensonhurst layoff book was Emilio "Pete" Pistoia, a forty-year-old Chicagoan who had come to New York eight years ago to join the Barbosa organization. He was a smooth, tall, handsome man, a careful, quiet-spoken businessman who never misplaced a dollar. One reason why he never misplaced a dollar was the certain knowledge on the part of his subordinates that a man caught skimming more than Pistoia was willing to tolerate would never have the chance to argue his case. Pistoia used his enforcers without mercy. What was more, he carried a simple Smith & Wesson .38, and he had used it four times since he'd come from Chicago.

Bolan arrived at the address about nine, at the height of the evening action. He stood across the street and studied the site for ten minutes, watching the messengers come and go with what he took to be satchels of cash. It was perfectly apparent the precinct cops knew what happened here. There was no neon sign announcing the operation, but anyone could see what was going on. Patrol cars passing by were manned by cops who chose, for whatever reason, to ignore what they saw.

The warrior checked his equipment, then crossed the street. He trotted up the stone steps to the entrance, as if he'd often been there and knew his way confidently. At the door he met what he had expected—a belligerent hardman, with his bulk blocking the way.

"Out of the way, pal," Bolan grunted.

The hardman's hand went for the pistol inside his shabby sport coat, his anger slowing and retarding his reflexes. "Who're you, sonny?" he spit.

"Whitey sent me."

That gave the hardman pause. For an instant he hesitated, an instant in which Bolan might have taken him out. Then he lifted his chin. "Whitey who?" he demanded.

"Whitey Bust-your-Butt, smart guy," Bolan said.

The hardman's fury impeded his judgment. He reached again for his weapon, but he was slow, and Bolan chopped him hard across the throat. The guy grunted, choked and fell, gasping. Bolan relieved him of his Colt revolver, tucking it into his own waistband. He pulled the unconscious gunner to the back of the entrance hall and rolled him down the basement stairs.

The stairs to the book rose from the front hall. Bolan pressed forward, once again miming complete confidence, as if he had been there many times.

The operators relied on the man at the door, apparently. No other guards stood between Bolan and entry into the telephone room, which was now almost deserted, except for one man still on the telephone. The room was littered with scribbled slips, the discarded notes of deals made on the telephones, which would be quickly transferred to more permanent records.

A bank of fluorescent lights glared on a dozen tables, each equipped with a telephone and a notepad and pencils. The day's line—horses and baseball games—was written in big letters in chalk on blackboards across the front wall. Game and race results were posted on other boards along the side walls. The ashtrays were full of cigarette and cigar butts. Empty soda cans added to the litter on tables and floor.

The man on the telephone looked up. He didn't recognize Bolan, but he wasn't concerned. He returned to his conversation, and the warrior passed through the telephone room and into the counting room, where half a dozen men were shuffling money, separating bills by denomination, and making careful, elaborate entries into old-fashioned ledger books.

It was the kind of number-crunching that in every legitimate business was now handled by computer but was never entrusted to computers by the dons, who feared the technology they didn't attempt to understand. Numbers written on paper remained there. They could be hidden, and could be destroyed. They didn't flit around in the mysterious circuits of electrical machines, from where they might be stolen or into which they might disappear forever.

Bolan stepped into the accounting room. It was much like the telephone room: glaringly lighted, littered with butts, cans and paper, the air heavy with smoke. The men working there were no more conscious of him than had been the man on the telephone. They were confident they were protected by the hardmen in the hall below. They had no idea that an intruder had found it necessary to take out only one man to reach their sanctum.

The Executioner glanced around. Through an open door he could see a man in a white golf shirt sitting at a desk and talking to someone on the telephone. The boss. Bolan stepped into the office and closed the door behind him.

Pistoia looked up and gestured to Bolan to get out. When he didn't leave, the mobster put a hand over the mouthpiece of the telephone and barked, *"Out!"*

Bolan stood there, remaining silent.

"Back to ya, Harv. I got some smart-ass who walked in and doesn't want to blow."

Pistoia got up and walked around his desk. "When I say blow, you blow," he growled, making a grab for Bolan's jacket but moving instead into an iron fist driven into his gut. Staggering backward, Pistoia gasped for air and clawed at his .38. Bolan's fist smashed a proud, sharp nose flat. Pistoia was stunned. He loosened his fumbling grip on his revolver and clutched at the bloody wreckage of his nose.

The Executioner lifted the .38 from Pistoia's holster, flipped it open and dumped the cartridges on the floor. Then he seized the mobster's left arm and twisted it behind his back.

"Who the hell are you?" Pistoia demanded.

"Names aren't important."

"You're right about that, you son of a bitch. You're dead no matter who you are."

Bolan could sense Pistoia regaining his equilibrium. Even with his nose smashed and blood dripping onto his white shirt, the man was thinking again, calculating his escape. He could feel the guy testing the hard grip on his arm, speculating maybe on whether or not he could break loose.

"Open the door," Bolan ordered.

Pistoia did as he was told.

The Barbosa bookkeepers looked up from their stacks of bills and their ledgers, startled by the bloody apparition in the office door and the big man who held their boss from behind. Two men went for their pistols, then quickly sized up the situation and thought better of it.

Bolan glanced around the room. He spotted what he wanted.

"You," he said, nodding toward one of the bookkeepers. "Pick up that trash can and dump it."

The man looked to Pistoia for permission.

"Do it," Pistoia muttered.

The bookkeeper picked up the big round trash can and dumped a litter of trash, cigarette butts and ashes onto the floor.

"Put in your fifty-dollar bills," Bolan directed.

"Ha," Pistoia grunted. "Figures...a heist. Just another cheap heister. What do you need, pal? A fix? Ten fixes?"

Bolan nodded toward a blue-and-yellow can of lighter fluid that sat on a windowsill. "Squirt some of that in. We're going to have a little bonfire."

"The guy's nuts," the bookkeeper said ominously.

"Do what he says!"

The bookkeeper squirted a stream of lighter fluid into the trash can, coating the fifty-dollar bills.

"Light it."

The bookkeeper snapped open his cigarette lighter, set fire to a scrap of trash paper and tossed the burning paper into the can. The lighter fluid ignited with a whoosh.

"How much do you have?" Bolan asked.

"Two hundred twenty-eight thou," another bookkeeper replied glumly. "You aren't going to—"

"Start another can, boys," Bolan said.

A sweetish-smelling smoke rose from the burning money. Particles of white ash rose on the heat, then wafted down over the tables and floors. Two of the bookkeepers started a second fire and began to toss money onto the flames. The smoke began to fill the room.

Two hardmen who had been lounging in another room rushed in to see what was going on. They stopped at the door.

"Come in," Bolan snapped, leveling the muzzle of the Desert Eagle on them. "We need all the help we can get. Put your guns on the table, though, guys."

The two edged into the room and pulled their weapons from under their jackets. They laid the automatics on the table and slowly backed away.

"You'll never get out of here alive, you know," Pistoia growled.

"I'll take my chances."

It took fifteen minutes to burn a quarter of a million dollars. Other than the three men busy feeding the bills into the fire in small handfuls, the rest of the personnel stood with their backs to a wall and watched sullenly.

"All right! The fun's over." Two brawny hardmen filled the doorway, guns drawn. One had a steel-gray .357 Magnum Smith & Wesson revolver, held close to his body and leveled toward Pistoia and Bolan. The other gunner pointed here and there, around the room, with a Colt Cobra .357.

The man with the Smith & Wesson stalked across the floor and kicked the two trash cans, scattering the fire and half-burned ledger books. He began to stamp out the flames.

"Hey!" Pistoia screamed. "Don't mess around with this guy!"

The man glanced contemptuously at Pistoia and at Bolan. "So," he said. "You've got to be Mack the Bastard Bolan. Who else? Let Pete go," he growled. "Like I said, the fun and games are over."

Two more hardmen appeared in the door.

"You see," the man said to Bolan. "You don't have a chance."

Bolan sized up the four gunners.

He recognized the one with the Smith & Wesson. His name was Ruggiero Tokenese, and he was called Toke. Bolan had encountered him in Miami two years earlier. He'd regretted then that he hadn't been able to rid the world of this man, a stone killer, a person who killed without hesitation, without mercy and probably enjoyed it.

The two who had just appeared were younger and in other circumstances would have been sneering, swaggering wise guys. As things were, they were afraid of Toke, and now that they had heard who he was, they were afraid of Bolan, too.

The warrior seized Pistoia's arm again and twisted it up behind him to be sure he wouldn't lunge away from him and leave Bolan exposed.

"You can't save yourself by hiding behind Pete," Toke snarled. "Pete's not that valuable."

"Hey!" Pistoia shrieked.

"Not that valuable," Toke repeated. "If you get my meaning."

Bolan began to edge Pistoia to the door. He gestured with the muzzle of the Desert Eagle, and the two lesser hardmen slipped aside and cleared the door.

"No way, pal," Toke said. "You're not leavin'. I don't give a damn about Pete, but I give six damns about you." He gestured to his buddy to raise his pistol. "This is it for you, Bolan. Even if you get me, which you won't, it's the end of Bolan."

"No!" Pistoia screamed.

Toke fired his pistol, the .357 Magnum slug exploding Pistoia's chest. The bullet stopped just a rib short of coming out Pistoia's back and punching into Bolan, who was knocked backward with the shock and might have fallen but for the doorframe. Pistoia slumped, dead, no more a shield.

Bolan could read one thing in Toke's eyes—calculation. The gunner was taking half a second to aim a shot that would pass all the way through Pistoia's body, a shot into the belly, where a .357 slug might burst through. The delay was his death. He hadn't calculated how fast Bolan could get off a shot from his .44.

The blast from the big gun exploded in the room like a round from an artillery piece. It shook the walls. The slug threw Toke back onto one of the tables, where for one long moment he lay sprawled, until slowly he slipped off and fell heavily to the floor. His rib cage was split open, and the bloody devastation of the vital organs inside was exposed to the horrified eyes of the bookkeepers and hardmen.

Everybody froze.

Except one man. Toke's buddy raised his Cobra, and Bolan had no doubt he was good with it. There was no time to aim a shot, to place it carefully. The second slug from the Desert Eagle caught the killer on the right hip, spraying flesh and bone fragments, spinning him around and throwing him to the floor. In his agony he let his revolver fall.

Bolan finally let the inert body of Pistoia drop to the floor. He faced the two younger hardmen. "Well...?"

They shook their heads and held their hands out before them to show they weren't pulling guns.

"All right," the warrior said, then nodded at the bookkeepers. "Let's get the fire going again, boys. There's more paper to burn."

CHAPTER EIGHT

When he returned to the safehouse, Joan was still there. She blanched when she saw Pistoia's blood on his shirt, and for a moment it was plain that she thought he'd been hurt. After the warrior's assurance that he was okay, she went to the kitchen and opened two beers.

"Brognola wanted you to call him no matter when you got in."

He sat down beside the telephone and dialed the confidential number that could always be switched through to Hal Brognola, wherever he was. He waited for the call to be forwarded, probably to the big Fed's home.

"Striker?"

"What can I do for you, Hal?"

"You keep late hours. I don't think you're getting your rest."

"I had a little business to attend to."

"I know," Brognola said. "I heard already."

"Already?"

"Already. There are some unhappy people at NYPD. I had a call from a captain, complaining that my people had mounted a big operation in his jurisdiction without advising him."

"The Barbosas were running a big layoff book right under his NYPD nose," Bolan replied. "If anybody had notified the captain, it's likely someone in the department would've tipped them off."

"I know, but it doesn't make any difference. I told the captain my man Joe Coppolo had been wounded in New Jersey and was hobbling around on canes, so it couldn't have been him who shot up the Barbosa book and wasted three mafiosi."

"Wasted two, actually. The one they called Pete was killed by his own man."

"Anyway," Brognola continued, "the guys standing around heard the hit man call you Bolan. I told the captain I'd heard the name but had no idea where Bolan might be these days."

"He didn't tell you the rest of it?" Bolan asked.

"Nothing more. Only that a guy identified as Bolan had entered a big book and shot three men. Three, as he got the story. You're a wanted man, Striker."

"The rest of it is that I started a bonfire and burned almost a quarter of a million in cash, a lot more in markers and the ledgers."

Joan's mouth dropped open, and Brognola whistled.

"I figured it was a good way to let the Barbosa don know he made a big mistake when one of his hitters shot Joe Coppolo."

"There's a million-dollar contract out on you," Brognola told him. "Besides, you're on NYPD's all-time shit list."

"Figures. I've been on that list before, and it's not the first contract out on me."

"NYPD still thinks you're a complete outlaw. We can't tell them there's any relationship between you and us. NYPD is too big an organization, with too many kinds of guys. You know what I mean. Only two men in the department even know about Joe Coppolo."

"Understood."

"Listen. I've got something for you. It'll be coming up by courier. Interpol supplied a picture of Salvatore 'Whitey' Albanese. It's an old passport photo, but it'll give you an idea what the guy looks like."

"Thanks."

"What are you planning?"

"I'm going to keep the heat on the Barbosas," Bolan replied.

"Well, okay. But sooner or later you've got to turn your attention to the bigger problem."

"I PAY TWO FORTUNES into the fund for this great hitter of yours," Luca Barbosa complained angrily, "and what has he accomplished? Bolan still runs wild. Last night he cost me half a million dollars! Where's this expensive hitter? What's he doing?"

"Better than you're doing, Don Barbosa," Carlo Lentini said. "You've tried three times now to eliminate Bolan, and it's cost you six men, plus two in a hospital in New Jersey. *Under arrest* in a hospital in New Jersey, on weapons charges. What happened to you last night was retaliation for the wounding of a Fed in New Jersey. And maybe it was a warning."

"Warning! Somebody's warning me? Who?"

"Bolan, that's who," Al Segesta replied.

"In any case," Barbosa said, gathering his dignity around him, "we are free of Vincenza Grotti. That much has been accomplished."

Joe Rossi spoke. "I've had calls," he said quietly, "from Don Sestola in Baltimore and Don De-Maioribus in Providence. They want to know why we're stirring up Bolan. He was off fighting other battles. Now he's back harassing us. The Commission was ready to execute Cesare Frenchi for bringing down Bolan on our heads. Now they are talking about someone here doing the same." He turned and fixed a solemn gaze on Luca Barbosa. "I haven't mentioned your name to them, Luca. *They* do."

Barbosa frowned. He was troubled. "What am I to do?" he asked. "It's me he seems to be after. Am I to let him destroy me?"

"No," Rossi replied. "But we do ask you to stop sending out these headhunters he knocks off one after another."

"Why did Toke kill Pete?" Segesta asked gruffly.

"Bolan killed Pete," Barbosa said.

"Some say that Toke killed him," Segesta insisted. "Told him he wasn't valuable, then shot him. Which was a mistake. Toke was as wild and dangerous a man as Whitey Albanese. Why did you bring this man up from Miami, Luca? Why did you have him kill Pete? Was Pete Pistoia so inconsequential? Wasn't he valuable?"

"Valuable..." Barbosa mumbled. "Worth half a million, do you think? Half a million? Much more. They were burning the records of my biggest layoff book. When Toke called to tell me, I ordered him to stop it, whatever it cost. I was lucky he wasn't so far away."

"So you lost Toke as well as Pete, plus your cash, and markers and ledgers," Lentini said.

"How do you know this?"

"Two of your bookkeepers aren't your bookkeepers anymore," Segesta replied. "When they saw Toke shoot Pete, obviously on your orders, because he wasn't a valuable enough man, they decided they probably aren't valuable enough to you, either. You lost their respect. They've come over to me. I promise you I won't allow them to work against you in any way, but they are my men now, under my protection."

Barbosa didn't bother to conceal his resentment, but he said nothing.

"Gentlemen," Rossi said. "A new member sits at our table. We welcome Philip Corone. He would like to say a few words to us."

Arturo Corone's successor was a thin, long-faced young man with a sepulchral expression. Conspicuously nervous, he clasped his hands together on the table to stop their trembling. He was only thirty-one years old. He had two older brothers, but neither of them wanted any part in their father's Family.

"I thank you all for your assistance and support," he began. "If not for you, the Corone Family would have become the Grieco Family. Even my sister thanks you, for having relieved her of an abusive husband. As a token of my gratitude, I an transferring to your several families a substantial share of the Corone Family businesses."

The dons nodded at this young man, who hadn't yet earned—and might never earn—the title don. They had conferred on him a diminished corpus of the powers his father had held, and he was graciously bestowing on them the shares they would have taken anyway.

"We will operate a reduced, trimmed group of businesses. I venture to hope you will approve the way we run them."

The dons nodded again, pleased by the deference this young man accorded them, and Philip Corone smiled shyly and fixed his eyes very briefly on each man's eyes.

"Thank you, Phil," Rossi said. "Now...Bolan."

"What about your million-dollar contract?" Segesta asked.

"It will prove worth the million dollars," Rossi replied. "Or we won't be obligated for the million dollars."

"Would it be inappropriate for *me* to offer a suggestion?" Philip Corone asked.

All of them looked at him. Like a junior member of the United States Senate, he was supposed to listen and learn for a long time before he took part in discussions.

"Phil," Rossi said, "what is your suggestion?"

"Smoke him out, as we might say. What does he want? What does he care about? Make him come to *us*."

"'What does he care about?'" Barbosa mimicked. "All we know about the man is that he's crazy. What brings him to us?"

"Every man cares about something," Philip Corone said quietly. "I've made it a point to find out as much as I can about Mack Bolan. With every respect, Don Barbosa, the man is not crazy. He was motivated originally, a long time ago, by some very human emotions. Today...I don't know. He is unmarried and has no regular girlfriend, as far as I can discover. He has no children. His family...I mean, his parents— Well, their misfortunes seem to have been the source of the hatred that once drove Bolan. But they are long gone. He values his friends—"

"Does he work for the government or doesn't he?" Segesta interrupted.

"No," Corone replied. "There might be some kind of relationship at a very high level, but it's unofficial and secret. No. The man is independent. That could be the key to Bolan—his independence."

"What kind of key is that, Phil?" Rossi asked.

"No man," Corone replied, "can live permanently without human relationships. He cares about somebody."

"So the key to Bolan," Barbosa concluded, "is to find out who he cares about and get that person."

Corone nodded. "With all respect, Don Barbosa, the key to Bolan isn't to attack *him*, but to attack someone or something he cares about. He's one man. He can't defend everyone and everything that's important to him."

"Dammit!" Segesta snapped. "We hear Bolan, Bolan, Bolan. Who says there *is* a Bolan? Guys outsmart us sometimes. Guys—"

"There is a Bolan," Rossi interrupted. "Let's listen to Phil Corone."

The newcomer stood. They were sitting around the conference table in the Rossi's Park Avenue office. "With every respect to all of you," he began, "it's my impression that Bolan is real. He is not just a bugaboo invented by guys who've suffered losses. I don't doubt, Don Barbosa, that the man who hit your book last night was Mack Bolan. Too many good men have lost their lives—or lost what was theirs—to doubt it. Let's, then, make a rational plan to rid ourselves of him."

WHEN THE MEETING broke up, Luca Barbosa left the Pan Am Building in the company of two bodyguards. On the west ramp he entered a black Lincoln that was waiting for him. The Lincoln didn't leave the building but circled it, coming around to the east ramp and the entrance to the Hyatt Hotel, where it stopped.

Philip Corone hurried out of the hotel and entered the back seat, joining a grinning Barbosa and flashing a big grin of his own. The don extended his hand. Corone took it in his own and pressed his lips to it.

"Don Barbosa," he murmured.

"It was well spoken, Phil."

"Thank you."

"I deeply regret the loss of your two Miami men. I will pay Peter DiRenzo."

"I have already paid Don DiRenzo," Corone replied. "It's a small service, considering what you did for me."

Barbosa smiled slyly. He had told Corone that the black woman who killed Grieco was sent by him.

"I'm sorry the two Miami hitters were killed before they could do their job," Corone continued.

"So am I. But I had to try to stop what Bolan was doing to me last night. That cost me more than I admitted, Phil."

"We can find other men," Corone said sympathetically. "Maybe from Cleveland, maybe Detroit...."

Barbosa nodded. "I intend to import others," he said grimly. "This man Bolan—"

"Forgive me, Don Barbosa," Corone interrupted, "but I suggest we keep our priorities in order. First, Rossi. Then Bolan."

The mafioso shrugged. "We shall see."

THE EASTERN FLIGHT from New York arrived at Miami International a little after three, only forty minutes late. The big man in the trim business suit strode through the concourse with an air of familiarity and confidence. He *was* familiar with the airport; he'd been through it many times before.

Ruggiero Tokenese belonged to the Miami-based DiRenzo Family and had no business being in New York. Mack Bolan knew of only one way of finding out what he'd been doing up north.

At the Hertz counter he picked up the black Ford Thunderbird he had reserved, settled behind the wheel and started the engine and the air conditioner before he felt under the seat. Yeah. It was there. He felt the weight and shape of the vinyl-wrapped package and was satisfied that it contained what he had requested—a silenced Beretta 93-R.

In bright Florida sunshine he drove the Thunderbird through the interchanges, established himself on Interstate 95 and sped north out of Dade County and into Broward County. Leaving the interstate at Commercial Boulevard, he drove east to Florida Highway A1A and into the town of Pompano Beach.

He had reservations at a modest beach motel called Ocean Ranch. He checked in, carried his bag—which now held the Beretta—to his room and changed into Florida clothes: a pair of white slacks, a white polo shirt and a blue blazer. What wasn't Florida was the shoulder rig under the blazer and the snugly holstered Beretta.

It was five o'clock by now, and the Executioner went to the poolside bar and ordered a beer. Most of the men and women who lounged there were in bathing suits. They took notice of the tall, athletic-looking man in the blue blazer.

"You haven't been out on the beach yet," said a young blonde in a tiny, iridescent-blue bikini. "Anyway, you're not pink yet."

"No. Just checked in," Bolan replied.

"Alone?"

"As a matter of fact, I'm expecting some business friends," he said.

She nodded and turned her attention to her martini.

The bartender was a young bare-chested man who wore a pair of white boxer trunks. He had observed the approach by the blonde, and when she moved away, he smiled knowingly at Bolan.

"I haven't been around in a year or so," Bolan said. "Still find the action where it always was?"

The youth nodded. "Pretty much, as far as I know. I don't get around much. Depends on what kind of action you mean, I guess."

"All kinds. Anything new, that you know of?"

"I don't hear about anything."

His visit to the poolside bar had only been to reinforce his cover as a businessman-tourist. When he had finished his beer, he left the motel and drove the Thunderbird west on Atlantic Boulevard, toward the Florida Turnpike, where in past years there had been some clubs where tourists looking for relief from the beaches had gawked at strippers, spun the wheels, rolled the dice and left their money. In the parking lots of small shopping malls, white Cadillacs had waited for the customers who wanted to take little bags of white powder back to their motels.

All of this was outside the main focus of the Miami rackets, where the big action was. It was outside the battleground contested by the old Families and the new operators coming in from the south, the bloody streets where, almost nightly, men died in savage combat. In Pompano Beach, coke sold by the gram, not by the ton.

Other times, Bolan had come here to strike hard blows. Now he'd come for what might be called a surgical strike.

Maybe. If the right men were still where they used to be. If the right joints were still where they used to be. If they weren't, well, he'd have to go for a different angle.

It had been quite some time since he'd been in this part of town, but some things never changed. The Panther Lounge was still brightly lighted, and, although it had a new coat of paint, it was still, apparently, the raunchy joint it had been before.

At this time of the evening, only a few cars were in the lot, so the warrior drove on to Fort Lauderdale. He cruised past the canalfront estate of Peter DiRenzo, which was guarded by two hardmen at the gate and, doubtless, by others on the canal. Four years ago the house had been fired on from the canal. The canalside walls were reinforced by steel now, and the windows were bulletproof glass. The rumor was that Mrs. DiRenzo had wept to see her home turned into a fortress, then had moved out to live in a penthouse in Las Vegas.

Maybe DiRenzo alone knew why Tokenese and the other gunman had gone to New York. But, if Bolan understood this organization at all, the Miami don had confided in at least two men—his *consiglière*, Dominic Giancola, and his senior capo, Pablo Geraldo.

Giancola loved the Panther Lounge—or had, in years past. He could be found there almost every night, eating, drinking, and ogling the girls. If he didn't show up there tonight, then Bolan would look for Pablo Geraldo later, at his home in Deerfield Beach.

BOLAN RETURNED to the Panther Lounge at nine. The place was nothing unusual—a long bar and thirty or forty tables in a big room dimly lighted except for a garishly bright stage. When Bolan had been there years earlier, there had been live music. Now what passed for music blared from speakers. Harried waiters and waitresses scurried around the room, carrying trays of drinks. The room was smoky, and the crowd was about two-thirds male. It was about ninety percent tourist.

He stepped to the bar and ordered a beer. As his eyes adjusted to the light, he began to scan the tables and caught sight of Dominic Giancola immediately.

The mobster was in his sixties but looked older, and he had survived what would have killed a dozen lesser men. In his fifty years as a made man, Dominic Giancola had been wounded by hit men four times, had lived through the sinking of his yacht in the waters between Key West and Cuba and had served fourteen years, all told, in state and federal prisons. In his twenties he had done time on a chain gang and had been beaten by a guard and knifed by another prisoner. He drank too much, smoked too much and used cocaine. He suffered from a weak heart and reportedly from syphilis. But he survived.

His pale blue eyes watered. His sunken, wrinkled cheeks collapsed when he sucked on a cigarette. His expensive light blue silk jacket hung on him like limp clothing on a hanger. But he nibbled on shrimp, sipped from a martini and stared intently at the performance on the stage.

It was amateur night in the Panther Lounge, which had practically guaranteed that Giancola would be there. He loved to watch the girls take off their clothes.

Maybe his abused body could no longer do anything but look. He never let one of the bar girls join him at his table. He lived alone, except for a bodyguard. He came to the Panther Lounge and other clubs and looked.

Giancola was spellbound by the woman on the stage. She had been introduced as a schoolteacher from Vincennes, Indiana, and did seem genuinely embarrassed as she shuffled around the stage, out of rhythm with the pounding music, and took off her clothes. Bolan guessed she was just another stripper, maybe from some other club, stripping out of ordinary clothes instead of one of the grotesque, stiff costumes affected by the regular strippers. Anyway, it was a good act. For most of the customers, she personified a fantasy they wanted to believe, and Giancola wasn't the only man in the room who stared at her in rapt fascination.

The second man at Giancola's table was a heavyweight. He was drinking coffee, keeping sober and doing his job. An enormous, paunchy man, he, too, was interested in the performance on the stage and nodded and grinned as the "amateur" took off her bra.

"Hey? Haven't we met?"

Bolan turned to find himself being stared at quizzically by a balding man in a white golf shirt and khaki slacks. He shook his head. "I don't recall."

"Don't you play golf at Palm Aire sometimes?" the man asked.

"No. Afraid not."

"Ah. Well... Anyway, Bill Carrington," he said, extending his hand. "With West Publishing Company. You know, the law publisher? Are you a lawyer, by any chance?"

Bolan had to smile at this obviously lonely man seeking company. "I'm Mike Belasko," he said.

It was good luck to have been approached by this voluble man, who turned out to be a law-book salesman. They took a table together, and the company of the progressively drunker Carrington was a benefit to Bolan's cover. He could sit four or five tables away from Giancola and keep an eye on him while apparently in animated conversation with a buddy. Carrington also enjoyed the show and cheered and applauded as each performer stripped. When a redhead who said she was a legal secretary from Hartford, Connecticut, won the prize of one hundred dollars and an invitation to strip for money for a week, he stood up and whistled.

Giancola began to stir.

"Nice to have met you," Bolan said to Carrington. He pushed a fifty-dollar bill toward him. "That'll cover my half of the bar bill."

"Hey, more than, Mike! Too much. Let me—"

Bolan winked. "I'm on a good expense account," he said. "Gotta run, though. Big day tomorrow. See you around."

Leaving Carrington open-mouthed, Bolan strode for the exit, in a hurry to be out of the lounge ahead of Giancola and his hardman.

He reached the parking lot a minute ahead of the mobster, in time to station himself to one side and watch for the *consiglière* and his bodyguard to come out.

The men didn't have a driver, so they walked across the parking lot toward a maroon Mercedes carefully parked between the lines and apart from the spaces near the door where high-sprung pickup trucks and flamboyantly painted vans were parked in a negligent jumble. The Executioner followed.

The amateur show over, most of the crowd was leaving. Bolan wasn't conspicuous as he followed Giancola and the big hardman across the lot. When they reached their Mercedes, he simply walked around it as though he were going to the next car in the line. He edged around the hood of the Mercedes and walked up just as the bodyguard was unlocking the door for his boss.

Bolan let them see the Beretta.

Dominic Giancola shrugged and shook his head, as if being challenged with a pistol were only another disappointment in a life that had known too many disappointments. The hardman tensed but stared at the Beretta and showed his hands.

"It's silenced," Bolan said.

"Not a mugging, hmm?" Giancola asked.

"Not a hit, either. I just want a little talk with you."

Giancola shrugged again. "I can't argue with that biscuit," he replied, nodding at the Beretta.

"Good. Now I want your friend there to hunker down and let the air out of a tire. I want to see it go flat."

"Not a hit..."

"Not a hit. Let's not turn it into one."

Giancola nodded at the hardman, who then squatted by the side of the car and used the tip of a ball-point pen to push down the valve and let the air rush out of the right front tire of the car.

"Do I know you from somewhere?" Giancola asked Bolan.

The warrior shook his head. "I don't think so."

The Mercedes slumped to the right as the tire flattened.

"Okay," Bolan said to the hardman. "There's only one way your boss is going to get hurt tonight. That's if you do something stupid. You just get in the car and sit down. He and I are going for a little ride in *my* car. As soon as we're gone, you can change your tire."

"He's got us by the short hairs," Giancola said to his bodyguard. "Don't try to be a hero."

Bolan led the *consiglière* across the parking lot to the Thunderbird. When they reached the car, Bolan took a pair of handcuffs from the glove box and locked Giancola's hands behind his back. He patted him down and found a .25-caliber Baby Browning in a holster strapped to his leg. Giancola wasn't just a survivor—he was also a wily old bird.

They had no need to go far. Bolan drove only to the Pompano Air Park. They could sit there, facing the runways, almost deserted at this time of night, without attracting attention. What was more, the parking lot, also almost deserted, afforded Bolan an open view for twenty yards in all directions.

"I need a cigarette," Giancola grunted.

"We're not going to be here long. You'll survive without a cigarette for five minutes."

"If I survive, how long will you?"

"Long enough."

Giancola tugged on his handcuffs and twisted his shoulders. He said nothing.

"I came to Florida to get some information," Bolan said. "If I get it, I'll let you out, and you can walk into that airport office and call a cab. If I don't—"

"Sure, sure. I get you."

The mafioso wasn't afraid. Somehow he kept his dignity. His ravaged face, discolored by the purplish glare of the mercury lamps that lighted the parking lot, was calm. For the most part he stared through the windshield, not looking at Bolan. It was the tactic of a man who had been in this kind of trouble before— not to stare at the face of the man who had you, not to appear to be memorizing his features. Dominic Giancola had the instincts of a survivor. That was why he was one.

"I'm from New York," Bolan told him.

"So's half the population," Giancola said sarcastically.

"Peter DiRenzo sent two hitters to New York. A guy called Toke and a friend. Why? Who borrowed the killers?"

"Hell, I don't know."

"*Consiglière*, Peter DiRenzo didn't send two hitters to New York without consulting you and his chief capo. Don DiRenzo isn't a stupid man. Why should he get involved in what's going down in New York?"

"Who sent you to ask?"

Bolan shook his head. "If you had *me* handcuffed in a car in a remote, deserted parking lot, you could ask me that question."

Giancola drew a deep breath, then released it. His lungs groaned in deep wheezes. "A man in New York called for payment of a debt."

"Who?"

"Many years ago," Giancola said, "the head of one of the New York Families saved Don DiRenzo from disaster. He weighed in on the side of Don DiRenzo, in a situation where a New York Family need not have weighed in. But they are related. Their families are from the same village in Sicily. They talked the same dialect. The man from New York was overpowering in those days. Peter DiRenzo was deeply indebted to him."

"Which family?"

Giancola sighed. "When this man was dying, he was captured by a punk, a son-in-law who wanted to take over his businesses. But the old man whispered advice in his son's ear—'Call Don DiRenzo.' The son called. Don DiRenzo sent Tokenese to New York. The old man had died. More than that, someone had hit the son-in-law. The son had already captured his father's regime, but he asked Tokenese to stay, to redeem Don DiRenzo's obligation by performing another service. Don DiRenzo agreed. Then the word came that Tokenese was dead. The other hitter was dead. So..."

"Which family?" Bolan demanded.

Giancola smiled. "Corone. Don Arturo Corone, in his glory days, made Peter DiRenzo what he is. His son Philip called for payment of the debt."

"But Toke was working for Barbosa," Bolan said.

"Maybe that was the other service Philip Corone asked for," Giancola replied. "I don't know, and Don DiRenzo doesn't know."

CHAPTER NINE

Salina Beaudreau was a competitor. She liked challenge, and she liked to win. To her, Mack Bolan represented a million-dollar challenge. She wouldn't have argued that meeting the man was worth as much to her as the money. She was too realistic for that. But she did take enormous pride in herself, in her capacity for shrewd calculation and in her skills, and—apart from the money—she would take personal satisfaction in killing the man they called The Executioner.

She held no animus against him. Certainly she didn't hate him. To the contrary, she rather admired him. In her view, they were in the same business, in different ways.

He was a big man, motivated and effective. He was the only man who had ever eluded her. Joe Rossi had sent her to Los Angeles to kill Bolan months earlier, but she'd come up empty-handed. She had failed to execute her first million-dollar contract, and he had driven her into the sea off Block Island. She had barely escaped drowning.

The Bolan contract and its million-dollar payoff were her focus. Anything else was a distraction. She was unhappy that Rossi had asked her to do another fifty-thousand-dollar job before she hit Bolan.

"Where is he?" Rossi had asked. "We've got to smoke him out. You can't hit Bolan if you can't find him. I could suggest that you do another hit, to flush him, as part of the contract." He had shrugged. "I'll go along with an additional fee for—"

"Every hit is a risk," she had said. "You understand hits? I got just so many in me before I wind up dead for trying—or in the dungeons. You know where they put a chick like me? In Bedford Hills . . . for *life*. No escape through that barbed wire. *Life*. Or death. Hey, don't kid around, Joe. Hit Michael Grieco... No big deal. No great risk. Hit Bolan... I got a fifty-percent chance of getting whacked in the process. Like Toke. Like a hell of a lot of other guys who tried. I—"

"So take out the Mohawk girl for another fifty—no risk."

Now here she was. Earning her monthly living. Leaning on a young woman for no reason she understood, except that Joe Rossi would hand her fifty thou for the job.

Oh, more than that. This would grab Bolan's attention. He'd come out of the woodwork if somebody killed his friend Gina Claw.

ROSSI KNEW THINGS. For instance, he knew that Gina Claw and her fiancé would arrive at Kennedy Airport about three in the afternoon, on a Northwest Orient flight from San Francisco. That was all the information Rossi had given her, but it was enough. Salina met the flight.

She wore a wig of black hair that had been bleached to a dull, reddish brown, a style favored by a lot of black women in New York. She wore a pair of blue jeans, a yellow knit shirt and a blue denim jacket. She carried a small suitcase to make her look like a passenger. That was handy; it contained the tools of her trade.

It wasn't difficult to recognize Gina Bear Claw. Rossi had described her as a distinctive young woman, and she was: olive complexion, straight black hair halfway down her back, big solemn eyes that darted around, looking, searching for something or someone.

Her fiancé was an ordinary-looking fellow, compact and muscular. His blond hair was cut in a brush, and there was about him a sort of swagger, a suggestion of macho self-importance.

They carried some heavy luggage out onto the street. As luck would have it, they didn't look for a cab but carried their luggage to the bus stop. Salina followed, and when they got on the bus, she got on, too.

At the East Side Terminal, Gina Claw and her man did enter a cab.

Salina rushed to the next vehicle in the line. "Wake up, man. Ten bucks tip if you keep up with that cab so I can see where those people go."

The Hispanic driver said nothing, but he nodded and jerked his cab out into traffic.

The couple checked in at Loew's Summit Hotel on Lexington. By watching the elevator lights, she saw that their room was on the sixth floor.

The big question was, for fifty thousand bucks, how do you hit a young woman staying in a sixth-floor room in a prominent hotel on Lexington Avenue?

"YOU WOULD have been wise to stay in California," Bolan said to Gina Claw.

She shook her head. "My father was murdered in this town. I'm staying here until something is done about it."

"Something *is* being done about it."

They sat at breakfast in the coffee shop of the Summit Hotel—Bolan, Gina and her fiancé, Eric Kruger.

"There's no point in trying to talk her out of something once she's decided to do it," Kruger said with a smile, half-proud. "I talked till I was blue in the face against coming back to New York, and here we are."

"Gina," Bolan said, "the man who killed your father is dead."

"Vince Grotti only pulled the trigger," she said bitterly. "What about Luca Barbosa?"

Sweat suddenly beaded on Gina's forehead. "I'm sorry, I—I have to go back to the room."

"She's going to have a baby," Kruger said with obvious pride.

Bolan stood. "Let's go," he said, offering Gina an arm.

Kruger stepped to the counter. "She's sick," he told the waitress. "I'll sign the chit. We'll probably be back later."

As Kruger signed the check for their unfinished breakfasts, Bolan led the unsteady Gina toward the door, brushing past Salina Beaudreau without noticing her.

Salina reached into her purse and closed her hand around a PPK, then thought better of it. He was moving. To get the right shot into him wouldn't be easy. She'd soon have a better chance.

"TAKE HER HOME, Eric," Bolan ordered. He fixed a hard stare on Gina. "You have no right to risk the life of your child."

Gina smiled wanly. "I'll think about it."

"Okay."

His hand was on the doorknob, which he turned, then pushed the door open. "I'll call you tomorrow."

Gina screamed.

He jerked around to see what was wrong, and the shot buzzed past his shoulder and ear. He whipped around to see a gunman—*gunwoman*—kneeling on the hallway floor and holding a pistol in both hands. She was adjusting her aim for a second shot. The warrior threw himself toward her, and her second shot passed by him and hit Gina.

Gina grunted and dropped to her knees.

Bolan pulled his Beretta as Kruger screamed his anguish. The woman on the floor scrambled to her feet and ran. Bolan leveled for a shot, but didn't pull the trigger. This was a hotel corridor, and he couldn't be sure where the bullet might go.

The warrior turned to the stricken woman, who had been hit in the right armpit. The hitter had disappeared through the exit and was making good her escape.

"THE BULLET GRAZED a rib, passed just above her lung and stopped against her scapula," Bolan reported. He put down the telephone. Once he had assured himself that Gina would live, he had left the Loew's Summit. Kruger had just called from the hospital to tell him exactly what the wound was. "She was lucky."

"The tall black woman," Joe Coppolo said. "The hitter who took out Grieco."

"I didn't get a very good look at her," Bolan replied.

"Grieco did."

"Kruger told the NYPD detectives that someone knocked on their door, then shot Gina when she opened it. He didn't mention me. They know who she is, know that her father was murdered. They're putting a watch on her."

"She needs more than that," Coppolo said.

"Maybe. But *I* was the target. Not Gina."

"Not necessarily. Why would a hitter have been looking for you at the Summit?"

"All I know is, I've been fingered. Whoever that hitter was, she knows me."

"And you know her."

Bolan shook his head. "I didn't get much of a look at her. I can't flinch from every tall black woman in New York."

"And you can't go get her, because you don't know who she is."

"Right."

They were in Bolan's safehouse in Brooklyn, and Joe Coppolo strode painfully around the room, exercising his wounded leg. Joan sat on the couch, dividing her attention between the conversation and the *New York Times*.

She looked up. "Giancola," she said.

"What I want," Bolan told her, "is a rundown on Philip Corone."

"I got it from Saul. The old man, Arturo, Philip's father, was called The Giant. He was a bonecrusher. He made the Corone Family what it is. He had three sons. The other two got out of the business, out of New York. They're in legitimate enterprises in Texas and Oregon. Philip is just thirty-one, and he's the old man's illegitimate son, incidentally, born of a mistress the old man kept on the side. When his wife died, Arturo took the woman and her child in, and they lived with him after that. He gave the boy his name and treated him equally with his other two sons. Arturo also had two daughters. The elder daughter, named Angela, is serving a three-year term in the federal reformatory for women in West Virginia for filing false income tax returns. The younger daughter married Michael Grieco."

"But Philip—"

"Phil was released from the federal reformatory in Danbury only about six weeks ago. The tax problems that put Angela in jail put him in also. They took the fall for the old man, you understand. They were fronting for him when they filed the bad returns. Of course, their being out of circulation gave Grieco his chance. But Grieco was a swaggering idiot. Once Phil was out of Danbury, Grieco's days were numbered."

"You think the hitter works for Philip Corone?" Bolan asked.

"I doubt it," Coppolo replied. "I suspect Phil formed an alliance with somebody."

"Barbosa," Bolan guessed.

"It would appear so," Joan agreed. "Anyway, Philip Corone was a tough kid, the son of a tough old man who slapped him around—slapped everybody around—and the kid grew up in a brutal tradition. But he's shrewd. He kept his nose absolutely clean at Danbury, and he's out." She smiled. "Angela's played it Corone-tough in stir, and the parole board flopped her for another year. She spent two years in Bedford Hills, too—for felonious assault. The other sons are constantly watched. They're clean. Both of them have changed their names, and they don't want any identification with the Corone Family."

"Except for the tax conviction, Phil has no other criminal record," Coppolo added. "But it's widely believed in New York that he's the man who killed Campy Palermo. And Campy, incidentally, was strangled."

"'Widely believed,'" Bolan repeated. "Who believes it? NYPD?"

"They don't have evidence," Coppolo said, "so they can't do anything about it. But ... Speaking of NYPD, I've got embarrassing news for you. This place, this apartment, is no longer safe. We're going to have to move you. I got what was called a word to the wise from an old buddy, an honest detective with NYPD. It's known that this building is a safehouse, used occasionally by the Justice Department. Somebody at city hall suspects you're sanctioned, no matter how much Hal Brognola denies it, and that same somebody puts two and two together.''

"Great. A politician who can add.''

"Maybe he didn't have to," Joan suggested. "A little scenario—the Barbosas sent somebody to kill you at the motel in New Jersey. Gina shot two hit men, but there might have been other friends of the Family around. Witnesses. Maybe the Barbosas knew you were hurt. In fact, I'd say it's likely they knew it. They guess you've got a federal sanction. So, where would the Feds take a wounded man they wanted to protect?''

"They don't *know* you're here," Coppolo said. "But they suspect it.''

"You said a guy at city hall suspects it.''

"The word's spreading. Some guys at Police Plaza suspect it, according to the man who told me. They're not going to raid a federal safehouse, but..." He shrugged. "Every time you go out the door. Or come in—''

"Somebody's watching.''

"They'd like to collar you," Coppolo added. "But there's a worse problem. If the word has spread this far, then it's spread to the Families, for sure.''

"All of which means I've got to get out of here.''

"We've got another place lined up.''

Bolan shook his head. "I'll find my own place.''

Coppolo, who had continued to pace the floor, frowned hard. "Hal wants you to work with me. Put that another way—he wants you to let me work with you.''

Bolan nodded. "Will do. To start with, you can provide some cash. I'm going to have to pay my own rent, and I hear flats come high in New York."

"What about me?" Joan asked.

"I'll be in touch," Bolan promised.

IT WAS TIME for Phil Corone to feel a little heat. Unless Bolan misjudged what he had heard of Corone, the young man was a hothead who would react with blind anger to any interference in his businesses. Just out of stir, compelled to grab his turf from a pirate, undoubtedly threatened with annihilation by the other Families, who were always voracious, Corone was likely an apprehensive, uptight guy.

Bolan would find out.

He didn't shave, and by midday he had a dark shadow all around his jaw. He stopped in a store and bought a hard hat. Since he couldn't stencil on a company name, he bought an American flag sticker for it, plus a black-and-yellow happy smile. He bought a plastic lunch bucket and found that the Beretta and a couple of extra clips of ammo fit snugly inside. Lastly he bought a pair of dark sunglasses.

What the hell was going on with NYPD? He remembered something a black activist had said in Columbus, Ohio: "If my twelve-year-old can find the pushers on the streets and buy heroin or coke, why can't the cops?" Cocaine was traded on Wall Street almost as openly as stocks.

But not by the Corone Family. The warrior had made his way into the financial district, and it took only a few minutes of observation to see that. The cocaine and crack trades had been taken over by a new crowd, Latin Americans, whose reputation for viciousness overwhelmed anything known of the Mafia. The Hispanic coke dealers didn't just kill a rival—they killed him and his entire family, women and children included. They, in their turn, were being pushed back by Oriental dealers, who exceeded even them in ferocity.

The story was—according to Intel—that the Corones still controlled the less lucrative, less stylish trade in heroin, amphetamines, hash and marijuana. If you hunted, you could find these no-longer-chic substances from dealers who worked around the edges. If you wanted what the upscale crowd wanted—the Wall Street brokers and young lawyers, the showbiz hangers-on, the insecure people who would do anything to be au courant—you dealt with the Colombians.

"Got the bes', man. Got the bes'."

That was the approach.

Bolan turned toward the slight little man with the heavy accent. "Best what?"

The man grinned, showing a mouthful of black, jagged teeth. "Y' know." He laughed. "Nothin' but the bes'. The bes'. No shit, man."

"South American."

"What else?"

"I got a habit for something else," Bolan said.

The dealer shook his head. "Man, what you talkin' 'bout *kills* guys. What I got . . . pure happiness!"

Bolan had been rolling a ten-dollar bill in his pocket. He slipped it into the man's hand, still holding tightly to one end. "That's yours if you show me where I get *my* kind of happiness." Then he pulled the bill back.

"You *die* on that stuff, man."

"I'll die on yours, too. Let me die my way."

The dealer filled himself slowly with breath. "See the chick?" He nodded toward a young woman who stood in the street as if she were trying to hail a cab. "She's it."

"Who's she work for?"

The man shrank back. "What you? Narc?"

"If I was, you'd be in deep right now. No way, buddy. I just want to know how good the stuff is. Like, is she connected to the Corones?"

"Never heard the name."

"Ten bucks more. You heard the name?"

"Ten bucks more an' I heard the name Ed Koch, man."

Bolan shoved the ten back into the man's hand, then reached in his pocket for another. "I want good stuff," he said. "No powdered milk. No rat poison. The Corones sell—"

"Powdered milk and rat poison, man. When they short of the real stuff. But that chick— Gimme the other ten."

Bolan handed over the money.

"You can get the right stuff from her, most of the time. Tell her you're a friend of Hog's."

"Hog?"

The little man nodded. "Porcelino. Tell her Hog'll slice her from bottom up if she sells you powdered milk or rat poison."

"What's her name?"

The man glanced at the young woman. "They call her Rose. Never heard another name."

"Okay. Now I got a name for you."

"Huh?"

"Your name is history unless you move to another street for the next half hour. I don't want you around making signals. Understand?"

The dealer man stared briefly at Bolan, saw menace in the set of his jaw even though he couldn't see his eyes behind the sunglasses and decided to move. He waved and strode off.

Bolan approached the woman.

"Rose."

Her head jerked around. "Who?"

"Hog sent me. He told me to tell you there're Feds working the street. Narcs. Said you and I should go have a beer for a little while."

"Who the hell are you?"

"The name's Dan. I work for Phil."

He opened the red nylon jacket enough for her to see the Beretta. The sight of iron hanging in a man's armpit usually made a firm impression—in this case the impression that the man did probably work for Phil Corone—and Rose concluded that he was a coworker in the street-drugs vineyard. She accepted his suggestion that they go to a neighborhood bar for beer.

"Never saw you around before," she said when they were seated side by side at the bar in a small, dark tavern. "You don't work for Hog, do you?"

"Directly for Phil," Bolan replied. "I'm another one of the new guys. Me, I'm down from Providence.

Lucky DeMaioribus sent me down to help Phil put things together.''

''Well, I heard about that—I mean, I heard some out-of-town guys were here to help. A gal, too—the one that knocked off Mike Grieco.'' She frowned. ''Dan . . . You're kidding me.''

He grinned and shrugged.

''Hey, wait a minute! You . . . They ever call you Johnny?''

Bolan raised his beer to his lips. ''A guy gets called lots of names.''

''Hey . . . What the hell you doin'? Why the hard-hat disguise? Hog never sent you. You don't work for Phil. I know who you are. You're Johnny De-Prisco!''

Bolan didn't know who Johnny DePrisco was. He couldn't guess what she had in mind. But there might be something to be learned here. He'd play her game and see what he could find out.

''Hey, I'm right, aren't I?'' she insisted. ''You're Johnny DePrisco!''

''Drink your beer,'' he said. It wasn't a denial. Maybe it would keep her talking.

''Why you come tell me there are narcs around? Why you tell me Hog sent you?''

''How's Hog treat you?'' he asked. Marks on her face suggested that somebody didn't treat her well.

''Hey, why you wanna know?''

''Just curious.''

''You thinking of taking over Hog's turf, forget it. Even if you are DePrisco. You got a rep, but you don't know Hog. I'm not sure even Phil could—'' She jerked her chin up and stopped. "Never mind. Yeah, Phil...I mean, whatever Phil wants. Since he's back, he's the man."

Bolan studied the tracks on her arms. She used what she sold.

She saw him looking. "Sure," she said quietly. "It's my life. My whole life. I don't much care about anything else. Yeah, Hog treats me okay."

"Who broke your lip?" Bolan asked coldly, nodding at her split lip.

"Okay, the guy has a way of making his points. But he keeps me supplied. I make a little scratch, too— what pays for my room and like that. I don't know what I'd do if it wasn't for Hog."

She'd been pretty once. Now... Besides the tracks on her arms, her addiction was evident on her face, in her body. She was emaciated. She looked like a bag of jelly held in the shape of a human body by her skin. Her complexion, which had been golden brown once, was the dead color of unfinished leather. She wore tattoos on her arms, on the exposed tops of her breasts and probably other places. The swelling of her lip was ugly and had to be painful.

"How much business does Hog do?" Bolan asked.

"Hey, Johnny," she said, "take my advice. Don't mess around with Hog Porcelino. Don't even let it get told that you ask too many questions about him. The only guys he's afraid of are the Spics, and he's wasted half a dozen of them."

Bolan didn't believe that. If Porcelino had in fact wasted any of the Colombians, the turf war would have been fierce. This girl wouldn't have been working the same block with the little Hispanic who'd pointed her out; she'd be dead if she ventured near the place. No, Hog had made a truce with the Colombians. He didn't venture into their trade, and they left him alone with his. A truce like that would last until somebody got greedy. Not a minute longer.

"Tough guy, huh?" Bolan scoffed.

Rose nodded. "One tough mother. Some think he's the guy who put out the contract on Mike Grieco." She shrugged. "Figures. You know? I mean, he was the old man's guy, and it figured he'd be Phil's. Grieco's guys were punks, you know what I mean? I know Hog, and I'd take a bet he's the guy that got the gal to take out Mike Grieco. So Phil owes him one, Johnny. And so do I, and I can't change anything about my life unless... Well, unless you was to offer somethin'. You know what I mean. I mean, a different place, different—" She shook her head, a picture of hopelessness, helplessness.

"Sure," he said. "Something to think about." He shoved a five-dollar bill on the bar. "That'll take care of the beer. Give it another thirty minutes before you go back out. My best to Hog. Tell him I'll be seeing him around."

BOLAN STOOD in a doorway half a block from Rose, watching her work. Some people pulled up in cars, others approached her from the sidewalk. She took her merchandise from her voluminous purse, then she stuffed in cash.

Finally Porcelino showed up in a silver-gray BMW. He was an obese, sweating man in white pants and a loud sport jacket. He double-parked his car and got out to stand on the street to talk with Rose. When a cab driver blasted his horn in complaint about the BMW blocking the street, Porcelino shot him a finger. At the same time, a thin, pallid bodyguard got out of the car. The cabbie backed up and swung out into the left lane to get past.

Bolan walked along the sidewalk toward Porcelino. As he got closer, he could see very clearly what the man was doing—as could any cop or narc who chose to look. He took the cash from Rose's bag, then reached into the back seat of the BMW and took out a briefcase. He opened it and began to count packages and drop them in her bag.

Bolan stepped between two parked cars and paused to take the silenced Beretta from his lunch box.

The bodyguard was inside the BMW again. The raucous sound of the music he was playing on the car radio was audible on the street, even though the windows were closed for the air-conditioning.

Bolan could hear Rose pleading, but to no avail. Porcelino slapped her hard across the mouth. Her split lip broke open, and blood streamed down over her chin. She wept and shook her head.

"Whore," Porcelino grunted.

Then he noticed Bolan. What he noticed, actually, was a man who was offending him by standing too close. Hog Porcelino was territorial; he disliked having any man move within a certain, vaguely defined distance of him. When someone did, he bristled. Now he jerked his head around and glared at the idiot in the big aviator's sunglasses.

Then he saw the Beretta. His eyes bulged, and his jaw dropped. He knew. A heartbeat later he was clawing inside his jacket for hardware.

Two muffled thumps were barely audible as 9 mm slugs bored through flesh and bone. The dealer slumped back against the BMW and slowly slid to the pavement.

Rose didn't scream—she stood petrified with fear. She was already crying, and only cried a little louder.

As Bolan walked away she pounded on the car, and the bodyguard got out—irritated to have to enter the heat and dust of the street again—and came around the car. He was too late. The man he had been hired to protect lay on the street, blood streaming from his chest.

A crowd began to form.

"Hog..." someone muttered. "Too damned bad, hmm?"

The bodyguard glared at Rose.

"Johnny DePrisco," she wept.

CHAPTER TEN

"Who's Johnny DePrisco?" Bolan asked Joe Coppolo.

"One of Segesta's capos," Joe answered. "A coming man, they say. Tough, smart and good-looking, too."

"Somebody mistook me for him this afternoon."

Joe frowned, then grinned. "Okay. So maybe he's not that good-looking. He has a reputation as a guy who gives people just one demand, just one warning, then..."

"Hog Porcelino had a little accident this afternoon. Some people might think DePrisco arranged it."

The two men sat at a lunch counter on Hudson Street. Bolan had called Joe and told him he could meet him there for coffee.

"Porcelino? You get around."

"The only witness—in fact the woman who fingered Porcelino for me—got the idea I was DePrisco, and I let her think so. If Phil Corone thinks one of Segesta's capos hit Hog Porcelino, it's a bonus."

"You're right about that," Joe agreed.

"Give me a rundown on the Segesta Family."

"In some parts of town the Segestas collect a 'tax' on every shipment that moves by truck, every consignment of merchandise that's delivered. They've got books, a couple of really big crap games usually going and some prostitution. Cleaning services, trash hauling, restaurant supplies. Oh, another thing. They're big on credit cards. They've got a team of muggers that lifts them off citizens. Then they're altered and sold. The credit-card companies have gotten pretty good at making cards that can't be forged, but the Segestas are just as good at changing the names and numbers on stolen cards.''

"DePrisco?"

"On his turf, if you run a restaurant, you buy meat from DePrisco, bread from DePrisco, vegetables from DePrisco, and DePrisco's people clean your kitchen. You mightn't be able to serve the food you buy from DePrisco, but it's cheaper to buy from him, use what you can and supplement it than to pay what it's going to cost you to defy him. Also, your kitchen mightn't be particularly clean, but it will always pass city inspection. Johnny DePrisco guarantees that. Your best customers can park in front of your place, or double-park, or just abandon a car in the middle of the street. Johnny takes care of that. And you won't have a fire. He promises.''

Coppolo nodded toward a newspaper recently left on the counter by a man who had come in for a sandwich. The front page carried a large photo of the body of Hog Porcelino lying on the street. The headline read:

GANG HIT! BYE-BYE HOG!
HEROIN DROUGHT FORECAST

"Gang hit..." Coppolo mused. "You might have started a war, man."

Bolan shrugged. "Let *them* do a little of the work."

"ALL I WANT TO KNOW," Phil Corone growled, "is why you were talking to Johnny DePrisco. Why did Johnny buy you a beer?"

"Man, he just come up to me on the street. Said his name was Dan and he worked for you. Said Hog told him to get me off the street for a while 'cause some narcs was comin'. And that's the truth!"

Phil slapped Rose hard across the face. She stifled a scream, bent over and began to sob uncontrollably.

They had bound her to a chair, simply by fastening a wide belt around her and the chair back, with the buckle behind. She couldn't rise, but the belt would leave no marks on her.

Phil sat down facing her and mock-casually brandished his lighted cigarette close to her face. Her gaze followed the movements of the orange fire on the tip of the cigarette as he fluttered it back and forth in front of her, not more than an inch from her left eye.

"Rose, you're not stupid. What'd he want?"

"He said... He asked me how Hog treated me—I mean, like he wanted to take over Hog's territory. I told him, Hey, man, you can't do that. I told him Hog's a tough guy, works for you, Mr. Corone."

"You told him Hog worked for me?"

"Mr. Corone, everybody knows that. I mean, Johnny DePrisco, he didn't find that out from me!"

The mafioso put his cigarette between his lips and sucked hard on it, bringing a bright glow to the tip. He saw how she stared at it, her eyes bulging with fear. But he had no intention of burning her.

"That's right," Corone agreed. "He didn't find out from you. But what did he find out, Rose? Or, to ask the question another way, why did Johnny DePrisco buy you a beer before he hit Hog Porcelino? What was the connection?"

She drew a deep breath. "You wouldn't know he did, except that I told it. If I had somethin' to hide, why'd I finger DePrisco?"

Corone nodded. The corners of his thin lips turned down, and his eyebrows rose. "Not a bad point. Still... Still, Rose, I don't think you're telling us everything you know."

"Mr. Corone," she murmured tearfully, "I've told you everything. I was a hooker. I got a habit, and Hog was good to me. He let me earn my fixes. He's the last man in the world I'd want something bad to happen to. Where am I going to get my fixes now?"

Phil Corone smiled. "We'll take care of you. You shaking now?"

She nodded. "I need it, Mr. Corone," she said quietly. "I do need it."

He nodded to one of his men. "Augie," he said. "Give Rose a fix."

The man handed Rose a length of rubber laboratory hose to tie around her arm. She fumbled with the hose but managed to tie it and jerk it tight. He handled the syringe with a piece of tissue, careful not to leave his fingerprints.

Rose didn't notice his precaution. She accepted the syringe with a grateful glance at Corone, and with the carelessness born of experience, shoved the needle into the vein that had been raised by the tight hose around her arm.

Rose slumped in orgasmic reaction to the rush of heroin into her blood. She threw her head back and gasped for breath. Her eyes turned heavy, and she smiled languidly.

Then, "Mr. Corone..." she whispered. "How much was that?"

"More than you usually take, Rosie," he replied with a cruel smile. "And better stuff, too."

"You son of a bitch..." she breathed hoarsely. "You OD'd me!"

"What a way to go, huh, Rosie? Your life's ambition."

Rose pondered that as she slipped out of this world. For her last conscious expression, she shrugged.

JOHNNY DePRISCO sat in his favorite restaurant on the Upper West Side. He was popular there. The citizens applauded him and saw to it that he never wanted for anything.

The upper-middle-class neighborhoods of that part of Manhattan had been terrorized for a decade by a gang of young thugs who called themselves the West Siders. Some of them were the sons of old, prominent New York families. Most of them were vicious hoodlums who acknowledged neither law nor the traditions that did impose a *few* limits on the Mafia. The processes of the law had managed, after a long, laborious process, to decimate the gang. But "decimate'' meant eliminating one of ten. Nine more remained.

Until Johnny DePrisco, with the sanction of Alfredo Segesta, moved into the Upper West Side.

He had killed no one. His soldiers had, however, castrated three leading members of the West Siders and had put shotgun blasts through the kneecaps of four others. The gang had disintegrated. It was difficult to find anyone who would admit he had ever been associated with the vicious, swaggering Yuppie mob called West Siders.

Tina's was a small restaurant that had experimented over the years with a variety of cuisines—nouveau, Cajun, Vietnamese, whatever was chic. Johnny DePrisco sat over a platter of mussels, which were deliciously submerged in a buttery sauce.

His resemblance to Mack Bolan was uncanny. He was a tall man—dark of hair and complexion and solidly muscled—who held himself with an air of confident masculinity.

The Upper West Side wasn't his turf. Now that he had eliminated the West Siders, it was no one's. He accepted tribute here—and businessmen paid far more than little gifts of wines and foods—but it wasn't his turf, assigned to him, where nothing happened without his okay. It was his retreat from the hard world, where he could live and walk on the streets as a respected, welcomed citizen.

Johnny wasn't married, but he never lacked female companionship. Tonight he enjoyed the company of a bright, talented actress who didn't expect him to finance her next play, but did know that being seen with him couldn't hurt her career.

Two bodyguards sat together at a table nearer the door. They were relaxed, splitting a bottle of wine. Here in the Upper West Side, Johnny was a loved figure—and safe.

He couldn't have guessed how safe he was.

Bolan was outside. He had identified the double-parked red Maserati outside the restaurant as Johnny DePrisco's. He might take his date for a spin around the island, maybe for a run across some of the country roads in Westchester County, before he took her home.

The two bodyguards would follow in the white BMW parked just behind the Maserati.

DePrisco staggered for an instant in the door. He would drive though he was drunk, confident that he would beat any rap, anywhere, even cheat death. That was his attitude. He beat them all.

The blond actress steadied him. He was supposed to be guiding her with a gentlemanly hand, but it was she who was supporting him. Even so, in the bright light just outside the restaurant, Bolan could almost see the glint of calculation in her eyes, reflecting her willingness to do whatever this man required for whatever he could do for her.

Johnny DePrisco, drunk or not, opened the passenger door of the vehicle, assisted the actress into her seat and closed the door. He didn't fail to glance around to ensure his bodyguards were in place.

Bolan huddled in the shadows, just outside the glare of the light under the restaurant's sidewalk canopy.

Expecting to take a shot from a distance of fifty feet or more, he had fitted the Desert Eagle with a fourteen-inch, .375 Magnum barrel—a little less than maximum firepower, but maximum accuracy.

He had no intention of killing Johnny DePrisco.

Bolan's carefully aimed shot whipped past DePrisco and punched through the right rear fender and tire of the Maserati. The muzzle-flash blazed for an instant, and the blast of the big pistol was deafening.

DePrisco threw himself to the ground. A man careful of the law, he didn't carry a gun of his own. His bodyguards drew theirs, but they were cautious about facing an adversary with such a powerful weapon.

DePrisco shrieked as if he'd been hit.

Bolan shot another slug into the frame of the car, just above where DePrisco pressed himself hard into the pavement of the sidewalk.

The bodyguards ducked behind the BMW.

The warrior fired another round, this one through the front tire of the BMW. He'd be leaving on foot, and preferred to have them do the same.

He backed into the shadows and moved south, leaving DePrisco sprawled on the pavement and his bodyguards cringing behind the BMW.

"MAYBE BOLAN SHOT at you," Joe Rossi suggested. "He's in town."

Johnny DePrisco shook his head. "If it was Bolan, I'd be dead."

Rossi slammed his fist into the palm of his other hand. "Damn! In one day, somebody blows away

Porcelino and tries to blast you. Somebody trying to start a war?''

''Maybe they already started it,'' Segesta offered.

Segesta had summoned the heads of the Families to a sitdown at his home on Staten Island. So far, only Rossi had arrived. As always, Segesta served food at a sitdown. His daughter Claire brought in the platters from the kitchen. The young woman was infatuated with her father's handsome capo. DePrisco didn't even know she was alive.

''Anybody could have blasted Hog Porcelino,'' Rossi said. ''The Colombians, one of his addicts . . .''

''Well, not just anybody could have tried to drop *me*,'' DePrisco growled. ''Not only that, it's *where* he did it! I was questioned by an assistant police commissioner, no less.''

''He missed you,'' Segesta said thoughtfully. ''Why? Doesn't figure. Three shots, two disabled cars. Maybe he didn't want to hit you. Maybe it was a warning.''

''Well, if it was, it was no damn good,'' DePrisco replied. ''Since I got no idea what I was being warned about, I can hardly back off from anything.''

Rossi slapped the front pages of the morning paper. ''This is what we don't need,'' he said grimly. ''Listen to this.

'Yesterday afternoon a kingpin narcotics dealer was shot and killed in the Financial District. Last evening an attempt was made on the life of a reputed Segesta *caporegime*, on the Upper West Side. These shootings represent an alarming increase in Mob violence. Not only that, the violence has spread to neighborhoods not ordinarily visited by gang warfare. Assurances by the mayor and commissioner of a tough crackdown are for the present a hollow echo of promises made before and never kept, by this administration and its predecessors. We can hope they mean it and will follow up. The city will be watching.'"

Segesta shrugged. "Newspapers... Always bitchin'. That's their stock-in-trade, something to bitch about."

"We—"

Claire touched her father's shoulder and bent down to say something in his ear. He nodded.

"Don Barbosa has arrived," he said to Rossi and DePrisco, "with his new lapdog."

Claire opened the dining-room door, and Luca Barbosa entered, followed by Phil Corone. Segesta motioned toward chairs, and they sat down. He reached for their glasses and poured wine.

Phil Corone fixed a steady eye on Johnny DePrisco. "Rose had a little accident last night," he said. "OD'd."

DePrisco frowned. "Rose who?"

"Sweet Rosie O'Battery."

"You talk in riddles," DePrisco said. "You got somethin' to say, say it."

"She fingered you, Johnny. Maybe I did you a favor."

"This is riddles," DePrisco sneered.

"No," Rossi said coldly. "Not riddles. Maybe I understand what he's saying. I hope I don't."

"Translate," DePrisco demanded.

"Who took a shot at Johnny last night, Phil?" Rossi asked, his voice hard with anger.

"Well, not me, for damned sure." For once his pallid face colored. "Not me! So, ask *him* a question."

Rossi turned toward DePrisco. "Who killed Hog Porcelino?"

The capo slapped the table. "How the hell would I know?"

Rossi glared at Corone. "You figure he killed your man Porcelino. So it was you who had shots fired at him last night." He glanced at DePrisco but returned his eyes to Corone. "And maybe he did kill Porcelino."

"Like hell—"

Rossi stared DePrisco down. He began to tap the little pile of newspapers—a rhythmic light slap that continued as he spoke. "Luca," he began, "Alfredo. We are senior here. We must control a situation that seems to be developing. Phil suspects that Johnny killed Porcelino. That's the meaning of his riddle. And he has killed a woman—whoever she may have been—to eliminate a witness. Which was an error, Phil, because she was the witness we may now wish we could hear. A man was killed yesterday. And now this woman. Shots were fired on a street where shots ought not to be fired. This is bad for business. For everybody's business. Phil, if you believe Johnny killed Porcelino, you should have come to the council of the Five Families with it."

"That's what I'm doing now," Corone said sullenly.

Segesta spoke. "Any Family that makes war on another makes war on all the Families. Any two Families that go to war against each other have gone to war against all the other Families. That is why, Phil, neither Johnny or I will make war on you, even if you fired those shots at Johnny last night. If you did that, we will submit it to the council as to what should be done."

"I'm willing to submit everything to the council," Corone told him. "I sent no one to shoot at him last night. I was glad to hear you had called the council for a sitdown, Don Segesta, because an eyewitness told me that Johnny hit Hog. Hog Porcelino made a lot of money for the Corone Family. We're damaged by his loss."

"I didn't kill the son of a bitch," DePrisco snapped.

"Why does a witness say you did?" Corone demanded angrily.

"Why'd you kill this witness, if she was so damned convincing?"

Luca Barbosa raised his hand. "Of all of you, I am most senior. I was senior even to your father, Phil. Among some men—" he paused and cast an accusatory glance around the table "—I am accorded some respect." He paused again to let his words have their impact. "Among us," he went on, "a man's word is accepted. Otherwise there would be war always. Johnny, Phil, I ask you to stand and swear to us, by the trust we must have in one another, that you didn't do these things of which you suspect each other."

PLAY THE

LUCKY

CARNIVAL WHEEL

scratch-off game and get as many as

FIVE FREE GIFTS...

HOW TO PLAY:

1. With a coin, carefully scratch off the silver area at right. Then check your number against the chart below to see which gifts you can get. If you're lucky, you'll instantly be entitled to receive one or more books and possibly another gift, ABSOLUTELY FREE!

2. Send back this card and we'll promptly send you any Free Gifts you're entitled to. You may get brand-new, red-hot Gold Eagle® books and a terrific Surprise Mystery Gift!

3. We're betting you'll want more of these action-packed stories, so we'll send you five more high-voltage books every other month to preview (Two Mack Bolans™, and one each of Able Team®, Phoenix Force® and Vietnam: Ground Zero®). Always delivered right to your door—with the convenience of FREE home delivery—before they're available in retail stores. And always at a hefty saving off the retail price!

4. Your satisfaction is guaranteed! You may return any shipment of books, at our cost, simply by dropping it in the mail, or cancel at any time. The Free Books and Gift remain yours to keep in any case!

NO COST! NO RISK!
NO OBLIGATION TO BUY!

The old man stared at them from beneath his formidable black brows. He nodded, laboriously drawing breath.

Corone rose from his chair. "I swear, Don Barbosa. I didn't fire a shot at Johnny DePrisco. I didn't send anyone to do it. I don't know who did it." He glanced at each face, then sat down.

DePrisco glared at Corone, not believing. Even so, he stood up and swore, too. "I swear I didn't whack Hog Porcelino, or send anybody to do it, and I don't know who did."

Barbosa smiled. "Then shake hands and embrace, like two friends."

Reluctantly the two men approached each other. They extended their hands and shook. Then, with obvious distaste, they grasped each other in a traditional *abbracio*.

"How good it is," Barbosa said, not without irony, "for brethren to dwell together in peace."

ROSSI AND SEGESTA STOOD together in the vineyard behind the latter's house, sipping their final glasses of wine and looking out over the Bay.

"He's a lying son of a bitch," Segesta said, meaning Phil Corone.

Rossi nodded. His thought was that maybe Johnny DePrisco was, too. Maybe Don Segesta was lying. Maybe he had authorized DePrisco to kill Porcelino, the opening shot in a move to take over the Corone drug business. And maybe Corone had responded by giving DePrisco—and Segesta—an emphatic warning.

"A lying son of a bitch," Segesta repeated.

"Barbosa's little trick stopped us when we might have found out."

"A trick. That was what it was, too. An embrace . . . Damn!"

Rossi remained uneasy about the peace. It was as if he alone understood its value. "It was you, my friend, who said that any Family that makes war, makes it on all the Families," he reminded.

"I sometimes lie myself, when it is convenient," Segesta muttered dryly.

BOLAN STOOD looking up at the naked steel of the new office tower on Seventh Avenue. It was where John Bear Claw had died less than three weeks ago, knocked off a beam by Vince Grotti.

Bolan was wearing a hard hat, a white T-shirt and jeans. His weapons were in the plastic lunch kit—not the best carrier from which to draw them if he had to, but at least they were accessible. He walked up to the shack.

"Hey," he called. "Whitey been here?"

The foreman inside made no pretense of liking the name Whitey. He shook his head, looked back at the clipboard and made a notation.

"Whitey sent me to look around."

The man looked up again. He regarded Bolan with hostility but shrugged and tipped his head toward the inside of the construction fence.

Bolan walked in.

Some things you get used to, and some things you don't. Most kinds of danger Mack Bolan could take, with healthy respect that generated care, but without irrational fear. Heights didn't bother him, but when he came out on the high steel, forty stories above the street, he couldn't deny that this was a tough place to be. He knew he respected the men who worked up here. Now he was reminded just how much they deserved it.

"Well, don't just stand there. You got a job or don't you?"

He turned and faced a woman who looked to be about thirty. Her blond hair stuck out all around her hard hat, on which was stenciled ASMAN, the name of the construction company.

"Whitey sent me."

Her face darkened for an instant, then she turned and walked away from him as if he had said he suffered from a deadly and communicable disease.

Okay, the name Whitey produced a reaction. He wasn't surprised.

Bolan didn't walk out on a beam. He found a welder working in a corner, where planks made a platform.

"How's it going?" he asked the welder when the guy pushed up his mask.

The man looked at him. "Who asks?"

"I'm a friend of Whitey's."

The welder pushed down his mask and touched the rod to the steel. The arc flashed, and Bolan turned his eyes away.

The company woman and the union man were together in their contempt for Whitey Albanese, yet neither had said a word. They went about their business, and if they didn't like Whitey, they didn't say so.

Sure. John Claw had spoken out.

The welder raised his mask and stared hard at the joint he had just welded. He glanced around and was surprised to see Bolan still there. "You got a problem?" he asked.

"Grotti's dead," Bolan said.

"I didn't kill him."

"The people he worked for killed him."

"The people *you* work for."

"I don't work for them. I mentioned Whitey to see how you'd react."

The welder looked around to see if anyone was watching. He was a big, beefy young man, blond, with a yellowish mustache. His bushy brows rose, showing more of his pale blue eyes.

"Then who do you work for?"

"Nobody. I'm unemployed, you might say."

"How'd you get up here?"

"By saying I was sent by Whitey."

The welder grinned. "Why?" he asked. "What's the idea?"

"Like to meet me for a beer later?" Bolan asked.

"Where?"

"Your favorite place."

THE WELDER HAD CHOSEN a bar in Flushing, within sight of Shea Stadium. It was a test, probably, to see whether the stranger on the site was serious enough about having a beer to travel to Flushing. Bolan was serious enough. He entered the bar a little after seven.

"The name's Belasko," Bolan said, extending a hand toward the welder.

"O'Rourke," the man replied.

The bartender sauntered over and took their order. O'Rourke swung around on his stool. "Just what the hell you got in mind, ol' buddy?" he asked, a hint of menace in his voice.

"I was a friend of John Claw," Bolan said simply.

All that remained of the grin that had come with O'Rourke's laugh now abruptly disappeared. "I didn't know the guy."

"You know what happened to him."

O'Rourke shook his head. "I know nothin'."

Bolan stared silently for a moment at the burly Irishman. "Somebody's got to get some guts, sometime, sooner or later."

"Easy for you to say."

The bartender put a mug of beer in front of Bolan, who picked it up and took a swallow.

"All I want is information," Bolan told him. "Nobody knows me. Nobody saw us talking today."

O'Rourke drained his mug and slammed it on the bar. "John Claw talked too much. That's all he did— talk. That's not allowed. The way it is, you work when you're told, where you're told, pay your dues and keep your mouth shut. That's the way it is."

"Dues pretty high?"

O'Rourke shook his head. "Not bad. The usual thing, union dues. When I say dues, I mean the extra. Like ten percent. Ten percent of what I made today."

"Who gets it?"

"A guy named Brannigan comes around for it. If he doesn't get it—I mean, if somebody gives him an argument—Whitey comes for it."

"When does he come around for it, and where?"

"He'll be at the job tomorrow. We get paid Friday mornings, and I'll tell you, the company puts the cash in the pay envelopes so you can hand over your ten percent to Brannigan. That way, he don't have to change money. Like, this week I'll make maybe seven hundred bucks, take-home. There'll be a fifty and a twenty in there so I can pull 'em out and hand 'em over."

"What's this Brannigan look like?"

"Looks like an old union man. Know what I mean? An old fella who worked his years and then went to work for the union. Teddy Brannigan. Got white hair, red face, smokes cigars. He wears suits, like a businessman. He carries a little notebook, and he writes down what each guy hands over and drops the guys' dough into this kind of satchel, black leather. I bet he delivers every nickel he takes in. I bet he doesn't skim a cent for himself. But he knows every guy on the job and knows how much he has coming."

"Grotti?"

"Grotti worked for Whitey, and Whitey works for Barbosa. Brannigan works for the local. It doesn't make a hell of a lot of difference, to tell you the truth, but that's the way it is. Except that Brannigan's a little gentleman, like you might say, and acts like he hates to take the money. Grotti... My guess is that the

Barbosas wouldn't have trusted him to handle money.''

"What happens if you don't pay?" Bolan asked.

O'Rourke shrugged and shook his head grimly. "You don't work. Oh, sometimes you can tell 'em you got a special problem and need to keep the dough. They say okay, but they double up the next week. But you don't work."

"What happens if you complain?"

O'Rourke fixed an angry stare on Bolan, as if to suggest he was asking stupid questions. "You get worked over," he said. "But, hey, you don't complain, 'cause it's not as bad as it sounds. We cheat on the time cards. The clock is fixed. I work seven and a half hours, get paid for eight. I'm handing over six percent, really, and the company four."

"But John Claw complained."

"Some guys are nutty on some subjects. He was. He didn't just complain—he was trying to organize resistance. I mean, you know, there's more to it all than just knockin' down on hours and handing over a percentage. Work isn't done right. That sort of thing. We're putting up buildings with weaknesses in them. I don't think I even want to hear about it when one of them— Well, you know."

Bolan nodded. "I know. I've heard about it."

O'Rourke drew a deep breath and let it out in a loud sigh. "I mean, I've got some kind of pride in doin' my job right and seeing a strong building go up. Most guys feel that way—sort of, anyway. It makes me sick to think of—'' He shook his head. ''I've talked enough to get myself knocked over.''

Bolan put a hand on O'Rourke's arm. ''I never saw you. You never saw me.'' He pulled out a ten-dollar bill. ''Beer's on me.''

O'Rourke shoved the bill back at him. ''No way. I figure you might be good for something. And if so, good luck. You'll sure as hell need it.''

CHAPTER ELEVEN

Teddy Brannigan wasn't what O'Rourke thought. He wasn't an old union man, retired from some honest trade; he was an old IRA man, veteran of a British prison, veteran of a New York prison, where he'd served time for robbery in the 1960s. It had been in the tough Attica State Correctional Facility that he'd met the members of the Barbosa Family who would arrange for him to become a Barbosa collector.

Brannigan's soft, Irish-accented voice was an asset to him. It was what made men like O'Rourke mistake him for an honest man. But he wasn't an honest man, and he hadn't always left enforcement entirely to men like Grotti and Albanese. What was more, he didn't turn over every nickel he collected. He skimmed, like anybody else. Also, he carried a stubby .38 Colt revolver in a holster on his left hip, covered by the jacket of the blue or gray suit he always wore on his rounds.

It was raining Friday morning. Brannigan wore a long, black raincoat and carried a black folding umbrella. He never went up in a construction job, standing instead on the street, just at the gate. The men on the job collected their Friday-morning pay envelopes and went over to hand him his money.

He liked a job like this, where wages were paid in cash, better than jobs where men were paid with checks. Most of them couldn't hand over the money until they'd cashed their checks, so he had to come back the next day, or on Monday after a Friday pay. By then some of them had spent the money and would plead poverty. It was neat here. They got their pay in cash, handed over their dues and that was that.

Pat O'Rourke wandered over, rain streaming off his hard hat and his yellow slicker. He'd collected seven hundred and twenty, net, what with the union-arranged fudging of his time cards, and he handed over seventy-two. He said nothing. He was one of the sullen ones, who paid but resented it. Teddy Brannigan had never reported O'Rourke's attitude. He never said anything out of line, so he could make sour faces if he wanted to.

BOLAN WATCHED the little drama being played out between Brannigan and the construction workers. Only about one in four of the men went to Brannigan—only the members of the welders' local or one other union on the job. Some of them seemed to make little jokes with Brannigan, or to smile at whatever he said. Most were poker-faced, doing what they had to do but not liking it.

Something else. Teddy Brannigan would walk away with three or four thousand dollars in his satchel. Then, probably, he'd pick up as much at two or three other sites. He walked through the streets with that much money in a little black-leather case, and no one touched him. He was either shadowed by an enforcer or guys smart enough to know who he was were afraid to go near him.

The collector waved casually at whoever was looking, then turned north on Seventh Avenue. At Fifty-sixth Street he turned east. The rain slackened a little, and he lowered his umbrella. He walked at a brisk pace for a man in his late sixties. He crossed Sixth Avenue, then Fifth, and turned north again on Madison Avenue.

Bolan kept well back. These streets were too crowded for him to make a move. He followed him to Sixty-fourth Street, where Brannigan again turned east and crossed Park Avenue.

Here was a neighborhood of brownstones with hardly anyone out on the rainy sidewalks. Bolan moved up.

"Brannigan!"

The collector spun around, wary and angry. What he saw—he thought—was a construction worker. Only this one was letting him see a pistol.

"Don't be a fool, man," he cautioned in a controlled voice.

Bolan motioned for Brannigan to open the worn black satchel. The man shook his head, but he opened it. "You'll never get away with it," he muttered.

The Executioner looked down into the satchel. "All I see is money," he said. "I want the notebook, too."

For a moment Brannigan hesitated, but he frowned at the muzzle of the Beretta and undoubtedly noticed the silencer, which told him he was facing a man who knew what he was doing and probably wouldn't hesitate to drop him where he stood. He reached inside his raincoat and suit jacket and withdrew the worn notebook in which he kept track of who was supposed to pay what and who owed.

Bolan nodded, and Brannigan dropped the notebook into the satchel.

"I don't see what good that'll do you."

"More good than the money. Now, Mr. Brannigan, you go home, withdraw whatever you've got stashed, which I'm sure is plenty, and retire. Maybe to Florida. Give the word to the Barbosas that they're out of this business. Tell Whitey Albanese if he shows up on a construction site again he's a corpse."

"You're starting a war?" Brannigan asked incredulously.

Bolan shrugged. "Whatever the don wants. Just tell him he's out of this business."

Brannigan shook his head. "Man, you've just committed suicide."

"Okay, Brannigan, I want you to walk. Just keep going the way you were going, and don't turn around. If you make a sudden move of any kind, I'll have to believe you're going for your gun."

The collector kept shaking his head as he walked away.

SALINA BEAUDREAU had kept watch on the Summit Hotel since Sunday morning. Gina Claw and her boyfriend had returned. Bolan hadn't.

Her instructions had been to hit the woman, but she hadn't done it. Rossi would pay her fifty thousand for that hit, but she could very well lose the million in the process. She'd had one good look at Bolan and hadn't seen him since. She had no idea where to look for him.

If he didn't come back to the Summit Hotel to see Gina Claw, where would she look? She had no idea—nor had Rossi.

There was no way that Salina was going to hit Gina Claw and lose her only lead to Bolan. Let Gina Claw thank her lucky stars for that, because there had been plenty of opportunity.

The hitter had changed her plan. Getting close to Mack Bolan could be enormously risky. She had driven out to Wyckoff, New Jersey, where she owned a condominium that housed her arsenal. There she selected a weapon for the Bolan contract—a Savage rifle, a modified version of what had once been called a varmint rifle: barrel machined for a .22-caliber bullet, chamber expanded for a .30-caliber, center-fire cartridge case. The steel-jacket bullet tapered to a point, but the ones made specially for Salina Beaudreau were hollowed out just short of the tip and loaded with a small explosive charge. The heavy load packed in the .30-caliber cartridge drove the small bullet at an exceptionally high velocity, which gave the rifle exceptional accuracy. When it struck a target, the bullet exploded. The explosion was not much more than the bang of a big firecracker—what they called an M-80—but when it went off inside a human body, the result was deadly.

The gunsmith who had modified this rifle for Salina had shortened the barrel by an inch and a half. He'd cut the barrel from the breech and threaded the two pieces, so the barrel screwed into the breech, or could be unscrewed, allowing the rifle to be packed into an ordinary attaché case. The gunsmith had also replaced the wooden stock with a steel-loop stock, also detachable. Finally he had mounted a high-power scope on the breech.

She had paid ten thousand dollars for the rifle and two thousand for a hundred rounds of custom-loaded ammunition. It had earned her more than two hundred fifty thousand, and she had eighty rounds of ammunition left.

She had put together a variety of cases in which to carry the disassembled rifle—an attaché obviously enough, but also a duffel bag with a hard plastic cylinder inside, a bedroll she could carry affixed to a backpack and an artist's portfolio case.

For her vigil across the street from the Summit Hotel, she had chosen the briefcase. She had chosen, too, a set of conservative business suits, conservative but for the short skirts she always wore. On Lexington Avenue, in the vicinity of the Summit, she prowled every day, sometimes on the street, sometimes in the hotel itself, sitting in the lobby, sitting in the coffee shop, sometimes in neighboring stores and restaurants—but never far from the entrance to the Summit Hotel.

Her hope was to see Bolan enter the building. While he was inside, she would establish herself in one of the several vantage points she had identified across the street or up and down Lexington Avenue. When he came out, she would have a shot at him. Then she would empty the Colt into the air and make her escape while everyone on the street cowered from the heavy explosions from the revolver.

That was the advantage of revolvers—they made a hell of a lot of noise.

Wednesday to Friday. No Bolan.

Then, on Friday morning Gina Claw left the hotel with her boyfriend and another woman—and their luggage. As Salina watched from a seat in a coffee shop across the street, the three loaded themselves and their luggage into a cab.

Salina raced out onto Lexington, ducked across the street in the face of honking traffic and hailed a cab.

"Where to, honey?"

She subdued her impulse to use an obscene word in reply to his use of the word "honey," and heaved a sigh instead. "Like to make twenty bucks extra?" she asked. "Keep up with that cab that just pulled out."

"You kidding?"

"I'm not kidding," she replied, reaching into her purse and pulling out a twenty-dollar bill. She dropped it on the seat beside him. "You gotta give it back if you lose the son of a bitch."

"Plus meter."

"Plus meter, plus tip, asshole! *Go!*"

As they drove to Kennedy Airport, which turned out to be the destination, the cabdriver told her he was studying law at Brooklyn College.

"Don't look back here," she ordered as they approached the airport.

"Hey!"

She put the muzzle of the PPK to the back of his neck. "*Fifty* bucks plus meter plus tip," she said. "Maybe a hundred. Just drive and cut the conversation."

"Lady—"

"I'm no lady. I'm a killer and I got a contract on somebody. You happened to be available. Just drive and keep your mouth shut, and let's see what happens. The less you know, the less you can tell the cops and the better chance you got to make it out of this situation alive. I want you to pull up beside that cab we've been following."

She rolled down the window. The rifle would be useless here, so she had the Colt Python in her right hand, the Walther PPK in her left, held toward the back of the driver's head.

"Hey, lady, for God's sake!"

"Just take it easy, fella," she soothed. "Do what I tell you, and everything will be okay. For you. Now slow down. I want to come up beside them while they're getting their bags out of the back of the car. When I'm finished, we're going to take off out of here. That's what's going to keep you alive and well and going on to law school." She let him feel the muzzle of the Walther on the back of his neck.

The driver eased the cab up alongside the other vehicle. Gina Claw and her boyfriend stood at the back of the cab as the driver lifted their bags from the trunk. The second woman, the one Salina had never seen before, had her wallet out of her purse and was counting out money.

Salina leveled the big revolver at Gina Claw's back.

The other woman screamed. She was facing Salina and had spotted her and her pistol. She shrieked again, pointing at the cab.

The boyfriend threw himself on top of Gina Claw and wrestled her to the curb.

Furious, hindered, Salina shifted the muzzle of the Colt and fired at the screaming woman. The .357 hollowpoint threw her backward off her feet, her blood and flesh spraying a baggage porter behind her.

The cabdriver floored the accelerator. The tires spun on the pavement, but the vehicle shot forward, rolling and lurching, past the other cab, past a cop who stood stupefied, momentarily paralyzed with shock and horror.

"You *idiot*!" Salina yelled at her driver. "You, you— Oh, *Christ*!"

"You said to go when you'd done it," the driver croaked.

"I hadn't finished the job, you stupid son of a bitch!"

"How was I s'posed to know?"

"Well, move! Get us out of here!"

She turned to look back and saw chaos. The cop had now drawn his gun, but that seemed to be all he had accomplished. People were racing about, half of them toward the scene, half of them away from it, in panic. From somewhere a siren had begun to wail, and she could see a flashing emergency light.

"Hey, man, drive ordinary," she said to the cabbie. "Don't attract attention. There's a thousand cabs at the airport, and they don't know which one they're looking for. So stop for that Stop sign."

The driver threaded the cab through the complicated heavy traffic of the big airport, from the Northwest terminal, past the Pan Am terminal and along the front of the International Arrivals Building.

"Where'm I taking you?" the driver asked solemnly.

"Let me off at TWA," she said. "TWA domestic."

"Leavin' town?"

"Wouldn't you?"

She tossed two fifty-dollar bills into the front seat.

IN A WOMEN'S REST ROOM inside the TWA terminal, Salina closed herself inside a toilet stall, where she pulled off the charcoal-gray suit. Underneath it she was wearing a pair of faded blue-denim shorts—cutoff jeans—and a loose white halter. Tightly folded inside the briefcase with her weapons was a blue nylon duffel bag, twenty-four inches long and about twelve inches in diameter, with a long zipper across the top. The disassembled rifle fit nicely into this bag, as did the Colt and Walther. She wrapped them in the suit. She also had a floppy, oversized faded blue-denim cap, which she pushed down on her head.

As soon as the rest room was empty, Salina left the toilet stall, pulled twenty or thirty paper towels out of the holder and stuffed them in the duffel bag to make it soft and bulgy, leaving no hint of what might be inside. Last she pulled the silenced Walther out of the rolled clothes and let it ride under just one layer of paper towels, ready if she needed it.

There was a service room nearby. She opened the door and stashed the black briefcase behind a big box of cleaning supplies.

As she walked through the terminal toward the exit, she affected a rhythmic, rolling gait, as if she were a little high on something. People noticed her, men particularly. But neither men nor women looked at her face. They stared, approving or disapproving, at her outfit and manner.

When she walked out of the TWA terminal, the airport was teeming with police. They had begun to concentrate on the TWA domestic terminal, which meant that the cabbie had already talked. But she boarded a Carey Bus for the East Side Terminal, and it pulled away without interference. Ten minutes after that bus left Kennedy Airport, the police blocked all the exits and checked every passenger in every car and bus that left. By then the bus carrying Salina was well out on the Van Wyck Expressway, on its way to Manhattan.

"WHAT CAN I say?" Joe Coppolo asked sadly.

The newspaper lay between them.

OCTF LAWYER SHOT, KILLED AT
KENNEDY!
NEWLY HIRED WOMAN LAWYER VICTIM
OF MOB HIT!
DAUGHTER OF MURDERED UNION DIS-
SIDENT
WITNESS, MAY BE REAL TARGET

Bolan's face was stone-hard. "Somebody is going to pay for killing Joan."

"Yeah," Coppolo grunted. "But who? We don't even know who's responsible."

Bolan slapped the newspaper. "The black woman who shot Gina in the Summit Hotel. The only question is—who does she work for? Which Family?"

"Until you find out—"

"I don't have to find out," Bolan said grimly. "She works for one of them. They're all responsible."

ACROSS TOWN, Joe Rossi slapped the same edition, even more firmly. "A young woman lawyer for the Organized Crime Task Force! Have you lost your minds?"

Salina regarded Rossi with calm, heavy-lidded eyes. She'd decided how she would play this confrontation, and shrugged. "You said get Gina Claw. The first time I tried to hit Gina Claw, Bolan was there. I almost got him, too, but Bolan's a tough guy to get. The second time, this woman lawyer was there. Claw's boyfriend jumped on top of her and knocked her down, and my shot hit the lawyer."

"Salina," he said quietly, "we are lucky that the heads of the other Families don't know who you are and don't know you work for me. Each of them contributed to your million-dollar fee for the hit on Bolan. If they knew you're the one who hit that Warnicke woman, they'd switch that fee to a contract on the two of us."

"I'm going to get Bolan," she said simply. "Keep your million ready. I'll be calling on you for it very soon."

He fixed a sober stare on her. "It'd be better if you got out of town."

She shook her head. "We got a deal."

He considered that statement for a long, silent moment. "Okay, we got a deal. But, you know, the risk has doubled or tripled."

She smiled wryly. "And the fee hasn't."

MACK BOLAN and Joe Coppolo sat at the counter in a small diner on Vandam Street. Though it was early evening, Bolan was eating ham and eggs.

"Dammit, I cared for her, too."

"Joe..."

"Hal assigned me to work with you. What am I supposed to do, sit around and applaud? My leg's first-rate again. I—"

"What I'm going to do is strictly outside the law," Bolan warned.

A faint wry smile came over Coppolo's shiny face, visible more in his intent dark eyes than on his mouth. "Do tell."

"I work alone, Joe."

"You wouldn't be working alone or otherwise if Gina Claw hadn't blasted those hitters in the Meadowlands. And I thought we worked pretty well together at Bedford Beach."

Bolan closed his eyes to think for a moment. A vision of Joan filled his imagination.

"What do you want to do?"

"What do *you* want to do?"

"I want to turn up the heat," Bolan said. "I want to take out the head of a Family."

"Hey, you—"

"Barbosa, Corone, Segesta, Lentini, Rossi. Any one of them. I don't much care which."

Coppolo tipped his head to one side and raised his eyebrows. "The Lentinis are into some rough business, according to Saul Stein. Speaking of Stein, he said to tell you he'll cooperate in any way he can in avenging Joan. Since you've gone entirely off the reservation—his words—he asked me to act as liaison between the two of you. He said he hopes you'll understand that he can't work directly with you anymore, but if you need help, information or whatever, just send the word."

Bolan nodded. "Lentini—"

"Rough businesses," Coppolo continued. "His guys pick up little girls at the Port Authority bus station, for example."

"Prostitution," Bolan said.

"*Child* prostitution. They hook the kids on something, heroin usually, then literally enslave them."

"Where do we find Lentini?"

"You mean Carlo himself?"

Bolan nodded.

"You want to go after the man? Not just one of his capos?"

"The Five Families changed the character of the fight this morning. So, where do we find Carlo Lentini?"

For a long moment Coppolo sat frowning, pondering. He ran his tongue around his lips. Then he stood up and nodded toward a telephone booth. "Let me make a call or two."

"CAMPBELL."

"Hi, Alex. A voice from the past."

"Joe?"

"You got it. Can you talk?"

Detective Lieutenant Alex Campbell glanced around the squad room. All the others were intent on what they were doing—taking calls, straining over their paperwork, studying tip sheets.

"I can talk."

"I want to ask you for a big one. If you can't do it— or if you don't want to get involved—just say so."

"Lemme hear it."

"I need to know where Carlo Lentini is, where he's going to be tonight."

Instinctively the detective glanced around the squad room again. He knew no one was listening, but instinct moved him to check. He frowned at the telephone, as if wondering whether the instrument could be trusted.

"What's comin' down, Joe?"

"You don't want to know."

"Yeah. It looks like war. Or worse. I can't believe that hit at Kennedy this morning. Hey, you guys think Lentini?"

"Don't know. Hey, and there's no 'you guys' in this. The question's strictly unofficial."

"Yeah, right," Campbell replied. "Anyway, I may be able to find out. We got guys permanently assigned to Carlo. I'll have to make a call—after I think of some excuse for doing it. Where can I call you?"

"You can't. I'll call you. Half an hour?"

"Good enough. If I don't know by then, I won't ever know. But don't call me here. I'll go over to

Larry's Other Place for a drink. I'll be at the bar. You got the number?''

"I'll get it."

ALL A PERSON HAD TO DO was walk down the block to know that a big man was eating at The Palm, and a look at the two men who leaned against the big gray Mercedes suggested that the man might be mafioso. The average citizen wasn't protected by bodyguards like these.

Bolan and Coppolo walked past the Mercedes and the two mafioso guards. They were dressed like a couple of guys out for a night on the town, on their way, perhaps, to a nightclub or singles' bar. They wore white shirts, open at the collar, under summer-weight sport jackets.

Bolan's Beretta hung in its harness under his jacket. The Desert Eagle, with its six-inch .44 Magnum barrel mounted for tonight's work, was in a brown paper bag that the warrior carried as if it held a bottle from which he was sipping as he walked.

The Palm was located on Second Avenue, only two blocks from United Nations Headquarters. A little before ten o'clock the traffic on Second Avenue was moderate and fast. Not many people were on the sidewalks, though they weren't deserted. The Mercedes sat in the pool of bright light directly in front of the door to the restaurant.

"I'd guess he's got at least one more hardman inside," Bolan said. "We'll have to take them all."

Coppolo nodded, and they crossed the street and walked up the block on the opposite side.

Second Avenue was too wide, with too much traffic, for them to stay across the street until Lentini emerged from the restaurant. They'd have to be on the west side when the don came out. Their plan was to get him as he got into the car. If they couldn't, they'd run to their own car, parked on Forty-fifth Street, and tail the Mercedes to its next stop. The word from Alex Campbell was that Carlo Lentini probably wasn't dining alone but with a woman he kept now, and he'd go from The Palm to her apartment, where he would spend the night. There would be a second chance to get him there—plus a third when he left in the morning.

Half a block beyond the restaurant they ducked through traffic and returned to the west side. They separated and walked apart now, south toward the restaurant. Four doors short of the intersection, they met in a doorway where they could stand out of sight of the hardmen guarding the car.

"I'll take Lentini with my first shot," Bolan said. "That is, if I can get a shot at him. As soon as I fire, you fire at the bodyguards. The point is to panic them, send them scrambling for cover. Let them hear a lot of noise, see a lot of muzzle-flashes. When they hit the pavement, we'll get away."

They waited.

Rain began to fall. It had rained or drizzled off and on all day. Mostly it had been drizzle, and in the evening it had stopped entirely, though the skies had remained leaden and threatening. Now a sudden gust of wind seemed to shake the moisture loose from the air, and a steady, moderate rain began.

"Just as well," Bolan said. "Not so many people on the streets."

"Better yet, Lentini's bodyguards are getting inside the car."

"They won't stay in there when they see the boss coming out."

Other people left the restaurant. Cabs were scarce in the rain, and some of the former diners stood ten minutes or more under the restaurant's sidewalk canopy, trying to hail a cab. It was certain but unspoken between Bolan and Coppolo that they couldn't fire on Lentini if there were other people standing around. They watched for cabs as anxiously as the satisfied diners coming out of The Palm.

"Uh-oh," Joe muttered.

Bolan saw what he meant. The two bodyguards had scrambled out of the Mercedes, and one was hurrying to open the rear door.

"Some kind of luck," Bolan said, drawing the Desert Eagle out of the paper bag. He meant they were lucky that a cab had just pulled away with four people. The sidewalk was now clear.

A man came out. He stood under the canopy and glanced up and down the street. One of the bodyguards threw out his hands and shrugged dramatically. The man turned and nodded at someone inside the door.

Carlo Lentini stepped out onto the sidewalk, and he, too, glanced up and down the street. He paused to light a cigar. Bolan had a perfect shot at that moment, except that the woman the detective had mentioned was on his right arm.

Lentini was a squat, heavy man—bald, with a round face, thick lips, a flattened nose, maybe once badly broken. He wore a loud-checked light-blue-and-cream jacket, a cream-colored shirt with a necktie in colors vaguely matching the jacket, loose at his throat. The breast pocket of his jacket bulged with cigars.

The "woman" was a blonde, not more than seventeen years old. She was dressed in a silver lamé minidress so tight she looked about to burst out of it. The stiletto heels of her red shoes distorted her legs. A short sable jacket was carelessly draped over her shoulders. She was smoking a cigarette in a long black holder.

The man who had been inside the restaurant with Lentini moved over to the bodyguard at the car door and said something sharp to him. The man moved away, and the inside man held the door open and bowed slightly at Lentini and his companion.

Bolan stepped out of the doorway and walked casually toward the intersection, pretending to be annoyed by the rain. The big automatic hung at arm's length at his side. Coppolo stepped out behind him and slipped along close to the walls, keeping as deeply in shadow as possible.

The rain was an advantage. It began to fall harder, and the hardmen not protected by the canopy were more concerned with getting inside the car and keeping dry than with making any further survey of the vicinity.

Lentini's cigar was aflame. He shrugged the girl off his arm and nodded toward the car. She stepped ahead of him, and the man at the door offered his arm and assisted her in the somewhat awkward process—awkward because of her tight, short skirt—of climbing into the back seat of the Mercedes.

For a few seconds Carlo Lentini was alone, impatient that the girl should get in the car, not even appreciative—as far as Bolan could tell from across the street—of the display she made as she struggled into the back seat.

The range was about sixty feet—too great for accuracy for anyone not used to a big, powerful pistol and not strong enough to control it. A .44 Magnum was a small cannon. Even Bolan gripped it with two hands.

Lentini never knew what hit him. The huge, high-velocity slug happened to strike his elbow first, blowing it apart, then exploded into his chest cavity, blasting fragments of rib into his lungs, bursting every vital organ with the immense pressure generated by its invasion. The energy behind the big bullet threw him off his feet and to the side, onto the pavement beyond the canopy, halfway out of the light.

Bolan heard the sharp crack of Coppolo's Browning. The agent had taken aim on the man by the car door, and he spun around and dropped to the ground.

The Executioner looked for another target but he saw none. The surviving bodyguards were cowering, as he had expected. You couldn't shoot at one of them. They were in the car or under it.

Even so, Joe put a couple of bullet holes in the back of the Mercedes.

"It's done, Joe," Bolan grunted. "Let's go."

CHAPTER TWELVE

Eric Kruger had moved Gina Claw to a motel on the West side, registering both of them under false names. They were terrified, yet calm, and Gina still refused to leave New York.

"Don't you see?" she asked Bolan when he arrived at the motel on Sunday. "They want to kill me, too. I'm a decoy. If you had taken advantage of that—"

"*Stop*, Gina," Eric said. He turned to Bolan. "She's in shock."

"When do you take her back to California?"

"No!" Gina whispered hoarsely. "I want a gun. Get me a gun. I could have shot that woman. I saw her. I could have put a bullet right between her eyes—"

"I doubt that," Bolan said dryly. "The woman is almost certainly a cold professional killer. You almost got yourself shot. If Eric hadn't been on top of you, and if the cabbie hadn't panicked, you'd be—"

"Dead," Eric finished. "And probably me, too."

"The people who killed my father and grandfather, and now Joan, are still on the streets," Gina said bitterly. "I'm not walking away. With you or without you."

"You only make it harder."

"I'm part of this fight. I'm in it. You can't get rid of me. No way. Count on it. I'm not leaving New York."

FOUR GRIM MEN SAT at the conference table in Joe Rossi's midtown office on Monday morning: Rossi, Barbosa, Segesta and Philip Corone.

In chairs behind their dons—places carefully chosen to suggest subordination—sat a few other men. Whitey Albanese was making his first appearance at a sitdown of the council, which signified the importance of the meeting.

The Lentini Family was represented by Carmine Samenza, a capo. He sat in an armchair drawn up within two feet of the conference table, and he kept it just that far back, precisely. He was senior to any of the men in the chairs that lined the walls behind him, but he didn't head a Family. It was widely understood that Samenza would make no move to capture the position held for decades by the late don. He held his own Queens territory in so firm a grasp that no one, even a new Lentini don, would have the power to dislodge him, and at sixty-six he had no great ambition to hold anything more.

Carmine Samenza was the largest man in the room—tall, still sound and hard muscled, conservatively dressed in a black suit. His graying hair was thin, especially on his pate, but his brows were black and wiry. Because of a stroke he had suffered five or six years before, he tended to distort his mouth, unconsciously shoving his lower lip to the right. For a long time his thoughts had raced ahead of his words. It was no longer so, but he spoke slowly; it had become a habit. His words were carefully chosen and often trenchant and witty.

"We have much to discuss," Rossi began.

"Indeed," Luca Barbosa interjected belligerently. "Who's responsible for the hit on the lawyer for the OCTF? *That* was a piece of stupidity worse than anything—"

"We don't know," Rossi interrupted.

"Somebody knows," Barbosa grunted. The old man's loose cheeks fluttered. "Somebody around this table. *I* have been accused of acting intemperately. Ah. So, who whacked the young woman?"

"Who whacked Don Lentini?" Samenza asked. "I'm interested in that question."

"In the past month," Alfredo Segesta said in a ponderously solemn voice, "we have lost two of our most valued friends. May the good God rest Arturo Corone and Carlo Lentini. Don Corone, may the Lord receive him, had the good fortune to die in his bed. Don Lentini was murdered. This is not to be forgiven."

He stopped and looked around the room, directly into the eyes of each man at the table.

"May justice prevail over him who took the life of our valued friend."

"Maybe it was Bolan," Barbosa suggested.

"May a benevolent providence grant that," Segesta replied. "Better it should have been Bolan than any of us."

"I want to know who this tall black woman is," Barbosa said. "She hit Michael Grieco and now this

Warnicke woman. She's bad news." He glanced around the table. "Who's she work for?"

Rossi looked across the table at Carmine Samenza. "For the Lentini Family?" he asked.

Samenza shook his head.

"Phil? Hitting Grieco did you some good."

"No," Corone said firmly. "I had my own guy for that job. She got to Grieco first. Until she hit the OCTF woman, I supposed she had her own reasons—I mean, something Grieco did to her. But—"

"She's a hitter," Segesta said. "A pro. And whoever sent her to do that woman lawyer is a fool. I say it in front of all of you, knowing I'm probably saying it in front of the man who did it. Whoever sent her to hit that woman is an idiot."

"She is our first priority," Philip Corone said.

Barbosa turned in his chair and faced Whitey Albanese. "You take care of her. Hmm? Until you get her, nothing else. No other responsibilities. I want that woman dead."

"I agree with that," Segesta said.

Corone nodded.

Rossi nodded calmly. "Agreed. Now...the Bolan problem."

"You assumed responsibility for that," Barbosa said. "A million dollars you wanted. So? Was it Bolan who hit Don Lentini?"

"I believe so," Rossi replied. He fixed his eyes on Whitey Albanese. "I'm pleased that so skilled and determined a man is assigned to get the black woman. I had rather his skills were dedicated to the Bolan problem. With all respect to the rest of you, I suggest that Bolan is our first priority. I suggest that Bolan would laugh if he knew we are dividing our forces and sending some of our most effective people after this woman." He struck the table with a fist. "It is Bolan who threatens us most." He paused, glanced around and let out his breath, so that he seemed to diminish. "Forgive me if I dissent. But on the list of priorities, I suggest the woman isn't number one."

"You want our help with the Bolan problem?" Corone asked.

Rossi understood what that meant. Corone was suggesting that Rossi couldn't handle the Bolan problem, had in fact failed to handle it and should be relieved of responsibility for it. Rossi was threatened by a significant loss of status.

"Bolan has been a threat for many years, Phil," Rossi stated coldly. "I hate to think of the names of men of honor who lost their lives to this man, or because of him. Contadina comes to mind. Toppacardi. Battaglia. Others. Whole families have been eliminated. I suggest the extermination of Bolan is worth a cooperative effort, with honor to the Family that accomplishes it."

"This is true," Segesta rumbled.

"We agreed to pay the hitter who gets him one million dollars," Rossi went on. "I suggest we make the sum two million dollars—payable to whichever hitter gets him, mine or someone else's—and I offer half the amount myself." He turned to Whitey Albanese. "Does that seem an attractive proposition to you?"

Whitey glowered. "If it is to Don Barbosa."

Barbosa nodded at him. "Try to earn this fee, my friend. But get me the black woman, too. That should be an easy job. She shouldn't be too hard to find."

SALINA BEAUDREAU KEPT a room in Brooklyn for one purpose—to house her telephone recorder. She never went there. She could query the recorder from anywhere, just by beeping the right codes on a touch-tone phone. She and Rossi had a set of cryptic messages. He could leave one word for her, and she would be waiting for him on a specified corner at a specified hour.

His chauffeured car stopped at the corner of Forty-ninth and Amsterdam. Picking up the tall black woman in the skimpy shorts looked like a transaction that was repeated ten thousand times a day on the streets of New York.

"You ever hear the name Whitey Albanese?" he asked her.

Salina had accepted a French-fried potato from a bag he held. She shook her head.

He handed her a photograph—taken with a hidden camera during the meeting that had broken up only two hours ago. "That's Whitey Albanese. Luca Barbosa gave him a contract this morning on the black woman who hit Joan Warnicke. He hangs out around a bar called Luciano's, on Second Avenue between Thirty-fourth and Thirty-fifth. Really, I oughtn't to be asked to pay you for this one. In a sense, you ought to pay me. But, if you want to get rid of the guy who's got a contract on you, I'll pay, say, ten thousand for the effort."

Salina studied the photograph and nodded. "How'd you get the photo so quickly?"

"I have my contacts. Get a good look at that picture. You can't keep it. And don't blast away a nun or a schoolteacher this time, Salina. Let's see a hit, the kind I know you're capable of."

WHITEY ALBANESE HAD a couple of beers at Luciano's at about seven. He had work to do. These Americans had no idea where to find this man Bolan. They didn't know where to look for the black woman—though obviously one of them did—and the only one he trusted was Don Barbosa.

Interesting. The don had spoken with him after the sitdown. He'd said it might be necessary, sooner or later, to reduce the council by one. Think about it, he'd said. I don't have to tell you which one I have in mind.

Sure. Whitey trusted Don Barbosa, but he could see that the don, like all the rest of them, was falling straight into the trap being set for them by this man Bolan. Oh, he was smart, Bolan. He'd succeeded already in turning the Families against one another. Too damned smart . . .

Whitey would go to work on it. He could handle two contracts at once—the woman and Bolan. And when they faced him, they would be facing a *Sicilian*.

He wiped the beer foam off his upper lip and pushed back his stool. He looked around. No one in Luciano's approached him unless he signaled that he wanted to be approached—and tonight he hadn't given that signal. He walked toward the door.

Whitey was a man who worked the night. It was a good time. Tonight he would eat first. And then... Well, there was a fat little dark-haired girl... Tonight he'd do her a favor; he'd take her to dinner, then to her apartment.

Albanese stood for a moment on the street in front of the bar. The summer night was a soporific. For a moment he thought of spending the night with the girl, relaxing. But the time wasn't right. Everything was threatened. He set his shoulders and walked north.

"Help a poor ol' soul, would ya?"

He looked down. It was disgusting the way the city allowed vagrants—which it dignified with the word "homeless"—to foul the streets. She sat there, dirty, ugly, stoned or drunk. He sneered and drew back his foot.

Two 7.65 mm slugs punched into his chest.

Whitey Albanese staggered toward the nearest wall, grasping for support, irrationally obsessed with staying on his feet, knowing that falling was death. His right hand went instinctively to the .38 Smith & Wesson under his jacket, but he realized with horror that his hand was too weak. His chest was a barrel of pain, and he choked and spit blood.

He turned toward the woman sitting on the sidewalk, but she wasn't there. In the briefest of moments she had gathered herself up from her huddled position and walked away.

It was all too clear. Her rags lay on the pavement. Striding north on Second Avenue was a tall black woman, triumph in her posture and gait.

Whitey stared at her for a moment as his vision failed. Then he vomited blood and slipped down the wall.

JOE ROSSI'S home telephone rang. Okay. He'd told her she could call, just this once. He left his dinner table and his guests to take the call his butler said came from Detroit.

"Rossi."

"Done."

"Problems?"

"Clean."

"Okay. Original assignment. Plus one more, for half a mill."

"That big?"

"Phil Corone."

"You got it, Daddy."

JOE COPPOLO REPORTED to Bolan that Whitey Albanese was dead. "You've got them at one another's throats."

"I'd think so for sure if I knew who killed Albanese."

"There's no word around on that. Nobody knows at NYPD. Or so they say. The truth is, they don't care. I checked a couple of sources of my own—you know, old informers from my police days. I've kept in touch with them. There's no word on the street. It was professionally done."

"What kind of slugs did they dig out of Albanese?" Bolan asked.

"Uh, 7.65 mm. And yeah, I see your point."

"Grieco was killed with a 7.65 mm pistol. Gina was hit at the Summit Hotel by slugs from a 7.65 mm pistol. That one was a Walther PPK, I think."

"Our friend the tall black woman," Coppolo said.

Bolan nodded. "She's damned good," he said. "Bold. Shrewd. I want to know who she works for. We ought to be able to figure that out. Process of elimination."

"I see what you mean. If she killed Albanese, then she probably doesn't work for Barbosa. Unless he had some reason to be rid of Whitey Albanese."

"Let's figure she doesn't work for Barbosa," Bolan said. "When she hit Grieco, that smoothed the way for Phil Corone. But I doubt she works for Corone. She killed Cesare Frenchi a while back. Phil Corone was in Danbury then, serving his time. Besides, his old man was still firmly in control then."

"If you eliminate Barbosa and Corone, that leaves Segesta, Lentini and Rossi. Lentini is dead, but one of his capos may think Albanese killed him and so sent the woman hitter to take out Albanese."

"It makes more sense," Bolan said, "to think the Lentini Family is in a state of shock for the moment. Your guess could be right, but . . ."

"Segesta and Rossi."

"Segesta and Rossi," Bolan agreed. "It's speculative, but it makes a good working hypothesis. And I'll go one step more. It's Rossi. He's the only one likely to have sent a hitter to Boston. He's the only one of the five dons who has a seat on the Commission. The other four limit their operations to the New York area. I'll guess the woman works for Rossi."

Coppolo shook his head skeptically. "Why would Rossi want to kill Joan? Why Gina?"

"When she hit Gina, she was shooting at me," Bolan said. "That's her contract—to get me."

"Joan?"

"I don't know," Bolan said grimly. "Maybe they figured out that Joan was working with me. And they certainly know you're working with me."

"Yeah. Maybe I better make myself a little more difficult to find."

"I recommend it."

NICK CARAVELLA EDGED his way out on a steel girder, more stories above the street than he wanted to think about. He was three levels above the place where John Claw had fallen—some say was knocked—off the high steel.

He had heard the story of John Claw. His union local and the company that had hired him for this job said Claw had been stupid with cocaine the morning he'd fallen. They had withheld that information, they said, to avoid embarrassment to his family. Why, after all, hurt a family that has suffered tragedy enough in the death of a loved and respected father?

Nick was a building inspector, and for the past ten years he'd worked almost exclusively in Brooklyn. Over the years, he'd been promoted from the simpler jobs, with help from the City of New York, which had paid for courses in welding, riveting, foundation building and even architecture.

He carried tools—a magnifying glass to inspect welds and rivet heads, an ohmmeter to check the electrical resistance of welded or riveted joints, a Pola-roid camera to photograph suspicious structural elements and a heavy ball-peen hammer.

Today he was crawling along one girder after an-other, hitting welded joints hard. Then he examined the weld under the magnifying glass.

A welding bead isn't like glue. The melted remnant of the welding rod doesn't stick two pieces of steel to-gether; it melts and fuses with both of them, like the cement used to join two pieces of plastic. The heat of the arc melts the steel as well as the rod until two pieces of steel and the bead are one piece, one fused joint.

When Nick hit the joints with his heavy hammer, they cracked between bead and steel. The welder had moved too fast, melting the rod only, not the steel.

Time after time he whacked at joints, and they broke under the minimal shock he could give them by hitting them with a hand-held hammer.

Caravella returned to the elevator.

"How's she go, buddy?" a foreman asked.

Caravella raised his hand and joined his thumb and middle fingers in the gesture for okay. He smiled and entered the elevator. They would hear from him in writing, from his office. He'd heard too much about this job to risk telling a man up here that he'd found serious defects. Too many men fell.

He was still on the site when the accident hap-pened. He didn't see the first of it, but he saw the re-sult. The driver of a concrete mixer misjudged his distance and bumped a vertical column at about five miles an hour and with the massive force of a heavily loaded truck. A shudder went up the beam. Forty stories above, a joint broke, releasing one end of a girder. The girder swung down, breaking the joint at the other end, and suddenly the girder was falling freely. It punched through a concrete floor at the thirty-fifth level, which slowed it, and at the thirty-fourth level it broke the floor but stopped. Then it fell outward and began to turn end over end, plummeting toward the ground. It crashed into the concrete mixer, bursting the rotating barrel and spilling tons of wet concrete. Finally it smashed down the fence and crushed a car parked on the street.

No one was killed. No one was injured.

Five minutes later Nick Caravella identified himself to a police lieutenant. "Close it down," he said curtly. "Everybody out. Building's unsafe."

"Hey!" yelled a superintendent wearing a hard hat stenciled ASMAN. "An accident! Could happen anywhere. The driver could have been stoned, backed a truck—"

"*Closed*, Lieutenant," Caravella repeated. "Evacuate it."

CHARLES ASMAN SAT in a booth in a small Brooklyn restaurant, smoking a thin cigar and staring with apprehension and skepticism into the face of Natale Plumeri.

"Order something to eat," Plumeri said. "It's a modest place, but you can't find better food. Try the *polpi*—octopus. That's what I'm having. I swear it's heaven."

Plumeri frightened Asman, just by the look of evil in his lined face. He was an old man, maybe seventy, and his long, pointed jaw seemed to stretch the deeply pitted skin of his cheeks. His nose was long and sharp, yet ruddy and veined. His gray eyes were bloodshot and watery. His voice was thin and whispery.

Asman, by contrast, sought to give the impression of a conservative, deeply committed businessman. He wore big eyeglasses with silver wire frames. His sandy hair was combed severely from side to side across his head. His mouth was wide and thin, the lips white. When he withdrew the cigar from his mouth, invariably his tongue darted out as if to be sure to capture any stray crumb of tobacco that might remain there.

"Octopus . . ." Asman murmured dubiously.

"I recommend it as it is prepared here. A man must keep in mind always that life is fragile, that time may not be left to us to enjoy all that we might hope to enjoy. That's why I always take my small pleasures whenever the opportunity offers itself. What you put off until tomorrow, you may not live to experience. So I will order a wine, too, unless you see one you particularly favor."

Asman shook his head.

Plumeri looked up at the waiter, who was standing near, a respectful two paces away, where he might not accidentally overhear anything these two men might not want overheard. He stepped forward when the old man's eyes met his. After receiving their order, he hurried away.

"Now, my friend," Plumeri said to Asman. "Let us dispose of business quickly, before these fine things are brought."

Asman nodded, remembering how uneasy he was about this meeting.

"The building inspector didn't solicit a bribe," Plumeri stated firmly, "as yesterday's papers stated. You will see to it that the accusation is not repeated. Your employee who made that statement will be fired tomorrow, and you will explain to the newspapers that it was an error."

Asman flushed. "I need to talk to the don."

Plumeri put his wrinkled old hand firmly on Asman's. "My friend, do not ever again call Mr. Rossi 'the don.' Mr. Giuseppe Rossi is not a Mafia don. He is an honest businessman of Italian descent, as I am. Do you understand?"

Asman essayed a measure of indignation. "He took control of my company—" He stopped. Plumeri was shaking his head. "I—"

"You would have been out of business long ago if Mr. Rossi hadn't bolstered your company with a large infusion of capital."

"Therefore, I am his . . . underling."

Plumeri shrugged. "As you would be to the officers of a bank who let you have that much money. As you would be to the officers of a corporation who bailed you out and merged you in." He tightened his grip on Asman's hand. "The only difference is, if you say the wrong things, you may have an accident." He shrugged. "A small price to pay for what you got out of Mr. Rossi's bailout of your faltering company. All you have to do is keep your mouth firmly shut."

"Why did I falter?" Asman asked. He remembered why, vividly: the labour troubles he'd had, the accidents on job sites, the skyrocketing insurance premiums, the exorbitant increases in the cost of paying off building inspectors... "I— Well... What difference?"

Plumeri smiled. "What difference, indeed? Today you earn more income from your business than you ever earned before. We know where you are putting it, incidentally. And that's all right. Someday soon you can retire. A very comfortable retirement."

"Mr. Plumeri, the unions are killing me. Caravella was right. The building on Seventh is a mess. Welds... Hell, that's just a part of it. Barbosa—"

"Luca Barbosa killed the Mohawk."

"Murder...? My God..."

"Do not try to cope with this matter by yourself," Plumeri told him. "Forget that you are president of Asman Construction. Report your troubles to me. I will take the necessary steps."

"What happens on Seventh Avenue?" Asman asked miserably.

"Wait for your orders. Above all, keep everything quiet. Dismiss your lawsuit. Stop work. We will make you whole, one way or another."

"Who's going to pay?" asked Asman.

"That isn't your problem. It may be Don Barbosa. But not a word from you. Nothing, unless it's cleared by me. This thing is getting far too much public attention. Others will do what must be done to quiet it. And, uh, that eight million you have put away. Treasure it. Cherish it. If we have to make you the scape-goat, it will take care of you. We promise you one thing. You will not see the inside of a jail cell.''

"I—"

"Never mind. Look at the excellent food being brought to our table. Enjoy! Enjoy!''

CHAPTER THIRTEEN

Bolan had let his beard grow for several days. He stood now in front of a mirror and shaved, leaving only a mustache. When he'd finished, he grabbed a briefcase and a small leather carryon and walked out on the street—ostensibly a businessman, wearing a dark blue pin-striped suit, white shirt and striped tie.

He hailed a cab and had himself driven to the Barclay Hotel, where he checked in.

Mr. Joe Businessman wasn't Bolan, and he didn't feel comfortable in the role. But he had effectively disappeared. Whoever was looking for him—NYPD, the Mob—was searching for a man in a hard hat and red nylon jacket. In the luxurious precincts of the Barclay, Mack Bolan was a lawyer, a stockbroker, a corporate officer—anything but the Executioner. Even if he didn't much like it, he played the role well.

What was more, the new guise was a good one in which to go looking for Joe Rossi. In his executive garb, he could ride the escalators up from Grand Central Station to the elevator floor of the Pan Am Building and then go up to any floor he wanted, unchallenged. He'd fit in.

And he did. He took the elevator to the reception room of Rossi Enterprises, Incorporated. He professed to have gotten off at the wrong floor, and the—

receptionist courteously told him that Mitsubishi was to be found on the forty-second floor.

He got a good look, from the outside. Obviously Rossi Enterprises was a big deal. Offices like this rented for a fortune—solid wood paneling, paneled doors, art hanging in the reception room, leather chairs. It was a comfortable lair from which to send out orders to kill people.

Okay. He'd see it again.

THE WARRIOR HAD GIVEN his new address—the Barclay—to no one but Joe Coppolo. But when he let himself into his room, he found a man sitting in a chair by the window, sipping a drink he'd taken from Bolan's bar and reading the newspaper.

"Pull a gun on me if you want to, Bolan," the man said. "If I'd been afraid of that, there'd be one under this newspaper, and I'd drop you before you could touch it."

"Only one guy knows this address."

"Only one guy's in big trouble. Joe was picked up by a couple of NYPD lieutenants this morning and is being held on all kinds of charges."

"So, who are you?" Bolan asked.

"The name's Campbell. Alex Campbell."

"I've heard of you, Lieutenant." Campbell was the man Joe had called to find out where Lentini was last Friday night. "Joe trusts you."

"He trusts *you*," Campbell replied. "I figure it'll take the Justice Department about an hour to get him out of custody."

"Once the Justice Department knows he's in custody."

"Oh, they know. Brognola knows. I mean, Joe and I aren't amateurs. But the last time I saw Joe, say an hour ago, he was stark naked, hands cuffed behind his back—"

"It'll take more than that to break Joe Coppolo."

"If Brognola works within the hour," Campbell said. "After that, it gets sticky."

Bolan picked up a telephone. In half a minute Hal Brognola was on the line.

"I'm threatening to put the City of New York under federal martial law," he said. "Which I couldn't do in a million years, even the President couldn't do. I sent the mayor himself to the precinct station to—"

"This is big, Hal."

"Bigger than even you know," Brognola replied. "They're pulling out every stop. An assistant secretary of defense called me last night. They want your ass out of New York, Striker. Buildings... Add money laundering, cocaine bucks from the Colombian trade, through the Rossi Family. Money, the oil that lets the gears mesh. Rossi is *big*, guy. Five Families... Make it one big Family and four little ones. Word has gone to the White House, and I got a call from the Man. We've got his confidence. Don't back away from anything. I'm sorry that Joan got caught in the middle. This is a rough game."

"I'm going to have the head of the man who killed her," Bolan said quietly.

"Just don't underestimate what you're up against."

"Joe—"

"Seriously, the mayor himself has gone to the precinct station to bail him out. I'm calling him down to Washington for a day or so."

"I hope the mayor's in time."

ALEX CAMPBELL was still with Bolan in his hotel room when Joe Coppolo knocked on the door.

"Are you damned well sure nobody followed you up here?" Campbell asked, sticking his head out into the hall and looking up and down.

"Nobody followed me," Coppolo replied sullenly. He was an angry man. "I'd have dropped any stupid bastard who tried it—which they knew."

"How soon are you leaving for Washington?" Bolan asked.

"I'm not going."

"Hal—"

"I'm not going," Coppolo repeated through clenched teeth.

Bolan shrugged. "Okay. But you have to do a better job than you've so far done of making yourself invisible."

"I'm a federal officer. I don't need to be invisible."

"Listen to me, hero-boy," Campbell said. "I've got to be going, so listen for a minute. You know enough about NYPD to know what kind Ned McGrory is. He's assigned Raoul Esposito the job of tracking down Bolan. There'll be fifty men assigned to it exclusively, you can be sure. They don't know of any connection between you and Bolan, but they suspect it, so they'll be watching you. And don't forget they

know you. You've served with some of the guys assigned to you. The best thing you could do is lead
them on a merry chase. And the best way you can do
that is make your trip to Washington, the way you've
been ordered to do, then come back here and start
running purposefully around town like you were on an
important assignment. You'll draw off at least half of
Captain Esposito's detective force. You stay two miles
away from Bolan at all times, and half the guys looking for him will be two miles from him."

Joe Coppolo frowned and looked at Bolan.

"It's the best thing I can do, huh?"

"Might be," Bolan agreed.

"Too many guys know you, Joe," Campbell said.
"They remember you. A lot of them respect you, but
they'll carry out orders. Most of them will, anyway.
Plus... Some guys *don't* respect you."

Joe's shoulders slumped. "I'll go home and pack a
bag. I'll pick up a tail when I leave for the airport."

"And they'll be watching for you to come back,"
Campbell added quietly.

Coppolo nodded. "I'll run 'em all over the bor-
oughs. For a few days, anyway."

"Use Hal as a relay for anything you want to tell
me," Bolan instructed, "and I'll do the same. I'll call
you back as soon as I need you."

IT WAS TIME for the Executioner to go hunting again.
Before Campbell left the hotel, he'd given Bolan a bit
of information. Phil Corone's sister, Angela, had been
released from the federal reformatory.

"Supposed to have been flopped for another year," he'd explained, "'cause she was no model prisoner. But she got home yesterday just the same. Phil's out two months, and he gets his sister out. Stepsister, really. You know why the old man didn't get her out? He didn't care. I bet you Angela Corone has something on Phil. He pulled every string he could in Washington. The guy's a new menace. He knows how to use power. So, she's out, and so what, you might ask. They're having a coming-home party for Angela tonight. And guess where? On a yacht. Look for a boat called *Napoleon IV*. It's moored on the East River, one of the piers south of the Brooklyn Bridge."

It hadn't been difficult to find the yacht. It was a Hatteras, about fifty-eight feet long. It was big and luxurious enough to be a rich man's toy but not big enough to represent enormous wealth.

The man in the pin-striped dark blue suit stood on the pier and looked at *Napoleon IV* as if he were interested in buying a boat like it. No more than a moment was required to see that this was no ordinary rich man's toy. A fifty-eight-foot Hatteras didn't require a large crew—no more than a captain and one hand, plus maybe a cook and a steward if she was a party boat. The yacht carried a staff of at least a dozen grim guys, hanging around the decks. Hardmen.

Cases of wine and liquor were being carried aboard. Campbell's information was right. Someone was holding a big party aboard *Napoleon IV* tonight.

It was likely they'd have an uninvited guest.

BY TEN O'CLOCK, the party was in full swing. Three of the Five Families were represented by their dons— Barbosa, Segesta and Corone. Phil Corone wasn't yet called Don Corone, but it was only a matter of time. The Lentinis were represented by Carmine Samenza, which was good enough—the best the Lentini Family could do right now.

The Rossi Family was represented by Natale Plumeri. The word was that Joe Rossi was detained on a hugely important business appointment and would appear as soon as possible. In the meantime he was represented by Mr. Plumeri, the grand old man of La Cosa Nostra.

It wasn't good enough, Angela Corone noted mentally. Rossi could have been there. He wasn't kidding anybody when he said he would show up later. He wouldn't. She'd been away for a while, but she hadn't forgotten the lessons she had learned so well from her father.

She'd made her bones, as they said. And maybe she'd get rid of that damned Phil, the son her father had conceived with a hooker late in his life, and take over the Corone Family herself. How about that? One of the Five Families run by a woman! And why not?

She'd keep quiet and watch and see. The old man had let her rot in stir for his tax evasion, with never an attempt to get her out. And he'd died while she was in. Lucky for him. She'd have killed him ten seconds after her daughterly kiss if he'd survived her release. The old fool had never been smart enough to figure out how much hate she was capable of.

She looked out across the East River at the yellow lights shining on the black water. Angela Corone was filled with elation. She was back where she belonged, where opportunity waited.

IT WAITED for Mack Bolan, too.

There were several purchases he had to make: a wet suit for swimming in the East River; watertight plastic pouches for his weapons and ammo; and a duffel bag to hold his other equipment. He made the necessary purchases, and when he rode south on the subway, he wore a pair of black pants, a black T-shirt and a black baseball cap. Besides the Desert Eagle and ammo, he carried a knife, a coil of nylon rope, swim goggles and a jar of Vaseline, which he'd smear across his face to prevent the dirty oil of the river from sticking to his face.

At the end of Peck Street he vaulted over a fence and walked out on the dimly lighted pier. The guard in the house at the gate did not notice. The warrior slipped his nylon rope through a ringbolt and, without tying it, using it double, he lowered himself toward the water.

The first horizontal beam of the pier's structure was well above high tide. It was dry. He swung in and mounted it, then crawled completely out of sight under the pier. He pulled his rope down.

Now, under the pier, he looped the rope tightly between two pilings to make himself a secure place to stand. With his feet on the beam, his body between the two strands of the looped rope, he could stand without having to constantly focus his attention on his balance.

He changed out of his clothes and into the rubber wet suit. He coated his face heavily with Vaseline, then hung the Desert Eagle, still in its watertight container, in a holster at his middle. The packaged ammo and the knife went into waterproof pouches.

His street clothes were in the duffel bag. He secured it to the beam with the nylon rope so it would be waiting when he returned. Untying the loop of rope, he dropped the loose end toward the water and let himself down.

Slipping into the water of the East River was like slipping through the grease at the top of a bowl of cold vegetable soup. The layer of oil clung to him. Then he was up to his neck in urban filth.

Fighting off nausea, Bolan swam south along the sterns of yachts drawn up to the piers. The *Napoleon IV* was easy to identify. He came up under the stern of the fifty-eight footer and rested by clinging to one of the bronze propellers.

The starboard side of the yacht was moored to the pier. Between the port side and the next yacht was a space of some ten or twelve feet of water. Though the other yacht was dark, the odds were decidedly against climbing up here, anywhere, without being seen.

"WHY NOT?" Johnny DePrisco demanded of Angela Corone. "It must have been a long time. No commitment. Neither of us."

"No commitment," she said. "You wouldn't do it, you asshole, if you didn't expect a commitment."

He lifted his hands and grinned. "Honest! No commitment. Just a guy who hasn't had anything good since yesterday and a gal who—"

"Who hasn't since January 21, 1984."

Johnny shrugged. "So, no commitment. Just for fun. An alliance some time later... Who knows? Why? Why not? If we decide to talk about it, we'll know each other."

Angela Corone shrugged dramatically. "Why not?" she asked. "But you better be good."

LUCA BARBOSA NUDGED Philip Corone as Angela and Johnny went down the steep narrow stairs into the bow of the yacht, where there were two cabins and the only privacy aboard.

"She wastes no time," Barbosa observed.

"She's wasted a lot of time," Corone replied. "That's why she's in such a big hurry now."

"I was happy to use my political contacts to help arrange her release," Barbosa said, "as were Segesta and Lentini. But I'm unsure about why you wanted her out."

"She knows too much."

"That didn't trouble your father."

"What she knows is about me."

What she knew was that he had strangled Campy Palermo. She was the eyewitness that the NYPD never found. They knew the loop had been dropped over Palermo's head while he was in bed with a woman, and they'd searched for months for her. They concluded that the woman would never come forward because she'd been used as a lure. It never occurred to them, or to anyone else, that Don Arturo Corone's singularly unattractive daughter had enticed Palermo into the bed where he would die.

All she had really wanted from Phil, who was then just twenty years old, was help. She had wanted him to hit Palermo on the head or stab him, after which she would finish him. But Phil had wanted to make his bones, and he had wanted Campy Palermo to die by garroting, as befitted a traitor. He had wanted to be able to go to his father and tell him he had strangled the betrayer.

His father had respected him after that—as much as the old man was capable of respecting a son. It made Phil the heir apparent. But Angela was the witness who could destroy him. The cops would be happy to make some kind of deal with her in order to get him. He'd had to get her out of stir, and he'd written some damned big IOUs to do it, too.

Barbosa smiled and shook his head. "I'll be interested to see how you handle this one, young man."

"THERE'S ONLY one solution," Barbosa grumbled. "This damned bureaucrat—"

"No, Don Barbosa," Natale Plumeri said in the calm, authoritative voice of an aged man who no longer fears anyone. "We do not kill a city building inspector. Sometime maybe . . ." He shrugged. "Sometime that might be the solution to another problem. But not this one, and not now."

"I didn't say do it," Barbosa snapped. "I said it's the only good solution. Your man Asman has overworked his cocaine rationalization. I strongly suggest, Mr. Plumeri, that you close that man's mouth."

"It has been done. But I have a suggestion for you, Don Barbosa. Your welders' union is the source of many problems. A bit of discipline there is now in order."

"Of course," Barbosa sneered. "Let the Barbosa Family take the heat. My welders—"

"What if the goddamned building falls down, Don Barbosa? What if a hundred men, a hundred fifty, die? What heat then?"

Barbosa flared for an instant, calmed and smiled. He slapped Plumeri on the shoulder. "You and I, my friend, can remember days when no building inspector frightened us," he said in a conciliatory voice.

Plumeri nodded. "And yearn for them. But they are gone." He shook his head. "It's a different world."

"What does Joe Rossi want to do?" Barbosa asked. "His building company, my union . . ."

"The Asman company will go bankrupt," Plumeri said. "Giuseppe will lose his investment. But the damage must be contained. You must stop sending into these jobs men who cannot even begin to do the work."

Barbosa nodded. "I will look into it."

BOLAN CROUCHED on a beam in the darkness twenty feet from the hull of *Napoleon IV*. The ponderous weight of the big yacht rubbed the fenders, and the pilings and beams of the pier groaned as they took the pressure. The water lapped below, mostly dark but here and there catching a reflection from a light on the river.

The tide was going out, and the yacht was gradually sinking lower. A short gangplank had served to let guests climb to the level of the deck. Now it only covered the foot or less of space between the hull and the pier, which were now at the same level. Shortly the main deck would be below the level of the pier, and guests would go down the plank, between its handrails, to reach the deck.

Bolan settled himself on the first beam below the deck of the pier. The curve of the yacht's forward hull gave him room to stretch beyond the pilings and see the gangplank. He sat on the beam and hugged it with his legs. Then he removed the Desert Eagle from its plastic pouch. The short .44 Magnum barrel was in place. The Eagle was ready to roar.

ANGELA CORONE HAD returned to the rear deck and once again stood staring at the yellow lights of the city reflected on the black waters of the river. She held an eight-ounce tumbler in her hand, which was filled with vodka and ice.

Johnny DePrisco kept an eye on her from where he stood, near the bar just inside the main lounge. His loins ached from his experience with her. She was as tough and demanding about intimacy as she was about everything else. Some of the men grinned knowingly at him, but he kept a solemn face and was careful not to acknowledge their leers. It would be the biggest mistake of his life to let her see him joining in any kind of joke about their half-hour visit to the cabin. On the other hand, an alliance with her could be the best thing that ever happened to him.

If he could stomach her. Apart from the aggressive coarseness of her lovemaking, she had nearly choked him with the smoke from her cigarettes in that little wedge-shaped cabin. And she salted her conversation, not only with profanity, but also with slang terms from her life in prison. "Hell, I was iced before they got me unhooked," she had said, meaning she'd done something to win herself a term in an isolation cell before they had even removed the chains she had worn during the ride from jail to prison. And, from the look of things, she was going to be staggering drunk very shortly.

On the other hand, Phil Corone was afraid of her for some reason. He'd asked Segesta for political help in getting her paroled, which meant he'd asked the other dons, too. Hadn't he been better off to leave her inside?

One of Corone's hardmen was talking to her now. His name was Augie something or other, a rough sort of street hoodlum that Johnny DePrisco wouldn't have had around him.

"Nice work," Segesta commented.

Alfredo Segesta had come up behind Johnny and hadn't been noticed until he had spoken.

"She say anything interesting?" Segesta asked.

"Colorful description of life in the federal slammer," Johnny muttered.

Segesta grinned. "She any good in bed?"

"She's a woman," Johnny answered laconically.

"Well, you bought yourself a problem. Phil Corone doesn't like what you did. Be damned careful of him. I hope you get something from her that's worth making him an enemy."

"You mind if I take care of him?"

Segesta frowned, then laughed. "Such talk! But, seriously, don't even think of it. We can't have a war. Listen to me, Johnny. The Commission is looking at us. You understand me? The Commission. I don't dare think of hitting Phil, and you don't dare. We gotta keep the peace."

Johnny DePrisco nodded. He had noticed that the subjects of their conversation—Phil and Angela Corone—were talking earnestly at the rear of the yacht. They were talking so earnestly that everyone had edged away from them.

"You've been out of touch a long time," Phil said to her.

"The old man saw to that," she replied bitterly. "No help. No visitors. No letters. Nothing."

"He didn't help me, either. I helped myself. I kept my nose clean and got my release. Then, as soon as I could, I—"

"Yeah. You know, the old bastard suckered us. We did three years for him—"

"For ourselves," Phil interrupted. "Keeping him out of stir till he died, we kept the business intact. If he'd gone to Danbury instead of me, I couldn't have held it together. Neither could you."

"You almost lost it as it was," she said. "What about that Grieco character? Who hit him? They say you didn't."

"Somebody did me a favor. I had a first-class hitter here on loan to take out Grieco, and somebody did the job for me. Anyway, listen to me. DePrisco works for Segesta. He may play like he's independent, but he works for Segesta. Segesta helped me get you out of Alderson, but he's no friend."

"We got no friends, little brother," she said acidly.

"For the moment we have Barbosa. But in the long run, if it can be worked out, the key is Rossi. Rossi's got more power than any two of the rest of us. I have a suspicion—just a suspicion, mind you, but it makes sense—that it was Rossi's hitter who knocked off Michael Grieco."

"So...?"

"So, what I'm telling you is, enjoy DePrisco as a stud if you want to. But politically, the key man is Rossi. One way or the other."

"Meaning?"

"We make our alliance with Rossi, say a few months down the line. Or we have to take him out. Okay?"

Angela nodded. "If you say so, little brother."

BOLAN WAS READY. He sat securely astride the beam and would be able to take careful aim. He had established his escape route—he'd drop down into the water and swim under the pier to the opposite side, then back to the pier where he'd left his bag.

He'd promised to take out another don. He wasn't sure which ones were on board the yacht, but he thought he had recognized Barbosa and Corone. Okay, either one of them.

Barbosa had given the order to kill John Claw, then his father, then the witness, Whittle. Barbosa's men had tried to kill him in the New Jersey parking lot and again in Bedford Beach.

Corone had called Tokenese to New York, first to kill Michael Grieco—which someone else had done first—and then to stay and do another service, which almost certainly was to kill Mack Bolan. Besides, since Grieco had been killed by the black woman who then killed Joan Warnicke, it was still very possible that Corone was responsible for the murder of Joan. Even if he wasn't, he was a man who earned a living by selling heroin—hooking people, including children, on his vile poison and then exploiting their slow deaths for maximum profit.

He need have no qualms about taking out either Barbosa or Corone. Barbosa had deserved it a thousand times; Corone maybe not so many but certainly enough.

CLAIRE SEGESTA HAD watched Johnny DePrisco all evening. She knew he had gone downstairs with Angela Corone. But Claire could forgive that, easily; she understood it was business, and men did many things for the sake of business. Now he was becoming gentle from drink, and she decided to approach him.

"Johnny..."

He glanced down into her worshiping dark eyes. For the barest instant he flushed with annoyance, then abruptly allowed a warm little smile to come over his face. "Claire..."

"Can we have a drink together, Johnny?"

He glanced toward the bar. "Sure."

"I mean . . . someplace else."

His smile widened, and he tipped his head to one side. "I doubt that your father would approve our going off somewhere."

"He'd be as pleased as I would," she said simply.

A world of new ideas revolved in his drink-fogged brain like the changing color patterns in a kaleidoscope. So why not? She was small, chubby and soft, and she conspicuously adored him. Did Alfredo really . . . ? Probably. Claire wasn't devious enough to lie about a thing like that. So. Heir to Segesta. An apple to be plucked. He looked down into Claire's eyes, then took her hand.

BOLAN WATCHED AND WAITED. Some of the party goers would stay on the yacht all night, probably too drunk to stumble across the gangplank. The important ones would leave. He was counting on it.

Then he recognized Johnny DePrisco. As he'd been that night on the West Side, Johnny was a little wobbly. As he'd done that night, he let a woman steady him. This one was short, plump, dark, and clung to Johnny as if she loved him. Maybe Johnny had a wife.

Some others came up the gangplank, climbing awkwardly. Almost all of them were men. Few women had been aboard *Napoleon IV*.

A woman came on deck with a glass in one hand and a cigarette in the other. Bolan had never seen her, but he could recognize Angela Corone from her description. She walked forward, weaving, until she reached a point where the curve of the hull left open water between yacht and pier. At that point she was only five or six feet from Bolan's position.

For a moment she stood there. On deck she was still a few feet above the beam where he waited, but she could have seen him if she had peered searchingly into the darkness.

"Angela?"

It was her brother. Phil Corone walked forward, but stopped halfway to her and looked back. A hardman was following him, looking all around, searching with his eyes as Angela had not.

Bolan eased the Desert Eagle out of its holster. Phil Corone. There wouldn't be another shot as good as this. He took time to aim. No hurry.

Bolan was ready. It would be a clean shot, and he would only need to fire once. He checked the hardman out of the corner of his eye. The guy was lighting a cigarette.

A rifle shot cracked the night open. Across his sights Bolan saw Corone's head explode. The gore flew in a red spray, onto Angela, onto the cabin wall behind Corone, onto the deck. Corone was dead, the almost decapitated corpse slumping to the deck.

Angela didn't scream. "I'll be damned," she muttered as she threw herself to the deck, anticipating a second shot.

The hardman did the same.

Bolan couldn't see where the shot had come from, but it had to be from somewhere above on the pier. A marksman with a good rifle could have made the shot from a hundred yards or more—though he doubted it had been fired from that distance.

After a long moment of caution, people began to come out of the cabin. They had two anxieties: first, not to be the next victim, and second, to be far away before the police arrived. The first people out were the bodyguards. Then a hurried exodus began. The aged Natale Plumeri was the first man across the gangplank, followed quickly by Luca Barbosa.

Angela stood. She didn't so much as glance at the body of her half brother. "Augie!" she yelled.

Augie, the bodyguard who had followed Phil Corone out on deck, had scrambled up and was on his way toward the gangplank. He glanced back at her but didn't stop.

"Augie Karas, you son of a bitch! You work for me now! You're driving me out of here! You got that? You work for me now!"

Augie hesitated, then stopped and went back.

Barbosa and Plumeri had paused on the pier for a brief moment to listen and observe. They exchanged glances, and Barbosa shrugged.

Segesta, too, had heard her shout. He stood just outside the cabin door and watched her seize Augie by the arm. He nodded and pointed toward the pier where he had parked Phil's car. She led the way up the plank, and he followed her.

There was nothing more Bolan could do. He let himself slip to the water.

CHAPTER FOURTEEN

Bolan left the Barclay Hotel at ten o'clock, walked around the corner and stepped out into the street as if to hail a cab—but didn't. Even so, a cab came up fast and stopped for him. He got in. The driver turned around and grinned at him—Saul Stein.

"I've been doing it for almost a year," Stein said. "I've covered meetings with some hot guys this way. The best cover I've ever used."

He wore a white shirt, open at the collar, as well as a Mets baseball cap. His black beard was a little too luxuriant for a typical New York cabdriver—orthodox Jews didn't tend to drive cabs—but he wasn't atypical.

"I speak English too well to drive a cab in New York. But what the hell? The guys I drive around don't worry about that."

Bolan was dressed in his Joe Businessman suit. He relaxed in the back seat of the cab. Stein did something else very few New York drivers would do—he turned on the air-conditioning.

"You get no congratulations," Stein told him.

"You don't owe me any. I didn't do it."

"I didn't think you did. The word on the street is that you didn't. Not your style. They think it was done by one of their own, but they can't imagine who."

Bolan had decided to withhold, at least for the time being, the information that he had witnessed the death of Philip Corone. He'd been wondering during the night if it had been DePrisco, since Johnny had hurried away from the yacht five minutes before the hitter struck.

"The chief suspect is Angela," Stein said. "She took command of the Corone Family on the spot. Conventional wisdom is, she can't hold it, no woman could. I wouldn't make book on that."

"Home a few days, she hired a hitter and had her brother taken out?" Bolan asked. "I wouldn't make book on that, either."

"She's her father's daughter, though. The old man was a Sicilian, in both the best and worst senses of the word."

Stein pulled the cab up to a hot dog vendor's cart. The water wasn't boiling yet at this hour. The vendor was pushing his heavy cart down Third Avenue, on his way to his day's work. As the cab pulled up, the man abandoned the cart, opened the door and got in beside Bolan. He waved at the real hot dog man, who'd been following along on the sidewalk, and turned to grin at Bolan.

"Nice work last night," Joe Coppolo said.

Bolan shook his head. "Wasn't me."

"We've been talking about that," Stein said. "But it's the wrong subject. We've got real problems to talk about. Problems? Maybe I should say opportunities."

Stein turned east and down onto FDR Drive. He headed the cab toward the Triborough Bridge and

Kennedy Airport. He could drive there, circle through the traffic complex and return to Midtown, giving them an hour to talk without interruption.

"They've shut down construction on the Seventh Avenue building. A swarm of inspectors is all over it this morning. The building will be condemned. It's in danger of falling down. Asman is screaming about shoddy work by union people. The welders' local issued a statement at eight o'clock this morning that it wouldn't let its men on the steel again until the foundations are strengthened."

"Who's Asman?" Bolan asked. "I know the name, but what's the affiliation?"

"At the top of three or four levels of corporate structure, it probably comes to Rossi," Stein informed him. "That's what we suspect. We can't prove it—yet."

"Somebody's going to lose a bundle," Coppolo said.

"The Seventh Avenue job is only the tip of an iceberg. Every building inspector who's been on the take is suddenly meticulously honest. Two district attorneys have suddenly discovered that building inspectors can be bribed and are talking about indictments."

"In other words," Coppolo began, "what our friend came here to do—"

"Yeah," Stein interrupted. "You've rattled them. To what I've just said, add the real possibility of a war among the Families. They know you're in town, but they know you didn't kill Grieco and they don't think you killed Corone. They also know you didn't kill

Joan, which most of them think is the stupidest thing that's been done in this town in many, many years. What's more, they're upset because they can't get you. There's a million-dollar contract out, payable to anybody who gets you. That's a hell of a big danger, man. Remember how Corone got his last night—with a small explosive bullet fired from God knows how far away, with a powerful telescopic sight.''

"Could have been the black woman," Bolan said. "She's a pro."

"Right. Well, don't forget she's seen you. She knows what you look like, and the mustache isn't going to fool her. She could be in any window, in any car."

"What do you suggest? That I leave town?"

Stein shook his head. "No. You've shaken up this city the way nobody's been able to in my memory. But don't forget something else—you've made as many enemies as friends. A hell of a lot of guys, including guys who think they're honest, were living comfortably with the cozy arrangements they'd made with the Families."

"To make money in business, you need calm and certainty," Coppolo interjected. "To borrow a phrase from politics, 'He may be a crook, but he's *our* crook.' The Families rip them off for millions, but they've learned how to deal with the Families and don't want the uncertainty that goes with change."

"I suppose there's some point in all this?" Bolan asked.

Stein sighed heavily. "It may be too big for you."

"You getting heat?"

Stein nodded. "Even from Albany. The director says hang in there. So do I. But I have to sneak around like this to talk to you. Another thing. There's a fund. I mean, the honest—well, sort of honest—contractors are raising a fund. It's going to be a lot of money. The idea is, if anyone can contact you, it will be offered to you to get out of town. If you don't accept, it becomes a reward for your arrest."

"Pay off a hitter?"

"No," Stein denied emphatically. "Reward for information leading to the arrest and conviction of the man who twice robbed Teddy Brannigan, collector of union dues. If they could get you in custody, they could hold you on the strength of Brannigan's identification. He has a record, but they can make him out as a reformed character with an honest job collecting dues. All of which makes for one more danger to contend with."

"Who's more dangerous?" Bolan asked dryly. "The Families or the citizens?"

"If the city and state authorities had their choice..." Stein began.

"They don't have a choice," Bolan said coldly. "Even before Joan was murdered, they didn't, and they sure don't have one now."

"What are you going to do?" Stein asked.

"You don't want to know."

"ONE LAST THING," Stein had said when he dropped Bolan on a Midtown street. "A couple of old friends of yours are back in town—released from a New Jersey slammer. Sandy Mac and Louey Vig."

He was talking about Luigi Vigaldo, the gunman who had tried to kill Bolan and Coppolo on the Garden State Parkway, and Patrick McMahon, the driver that night. A pair of free-lancers, Stein had said. They worked for any Family that paid them.

The fact was, the Families didn't trust either man and didn't want them as members. Neither was a made man, a member of the Mafia. Vigaldo was thought of as mentally unstable. McMahon, besides being of the wrong ancestry to be accepted, was known as the man who had beaten and scarred a nineteen-year-old girl just for the fun of it. La Cosa Nostra had its standards. Neither would ever be accepted.

Even so, Barbosa had used money and influence to get them out of the New Jersey jail. His lawyer had come back saying they were thinking about telling who hired them to shoot the federal agents. Better to have them back in New York, where, if nothing else, they could be disposed of.

Saul Stein had informers. One of them had told him Sandy Mac and Louey Vig had been offered the same deal as everyone else: a million dollars to the man who knocked off Bolan.

Bolan and Coppolo sat down for lunch in an Italian restaurant on the Upper East Side.

"I don't care what Saul says, the mustache makes you harder to recognize."

"Forget me. It's you I'm worried about. For every guy in town who'd know me, even without the mustache, there have to be twenty who'd know you. I guess there's no point in telling you to lay low."

Coppolo shook his head. "But I got an idea. Something I did for a little while when I was with the force." He paused, tipped his head and smiled. "Being a little fellow, I, uh, was sent out as bait for sex maniacs. You know what I mean? I mean, dressed like a woman. The fact is, I can be pretty damned convincing. Wig, makeup...you know. And I got another idea. Mr. Joe Businessman could have a woman with him. It'd make you harder to spot, too."

By the middle of the afternoon, Joe Coppolo was transformed into a pretty little woman. First he bought a wig—dark brown to match his eyebrows—then a kit of makeup, then clothes. It was only when he wanted the padding to fill out his figure that he ventured into a costume shop. They offered him a dressing room, and the fussy little proprietor helped him with his transformation. When, after half an hour, he emerged from the dressing room, Bolan—who had expected to laugh—stared in amazement.

Coppolo had bought two outfits. This one was a loose, wind-driven red skirt, worn with a white T-shirt and a red linen jacket. He needed long sleeves to cover the muscles in his arms, even though he had shaved off the dark hair. The heels of his red shoes were just high enough to shape the calves of his legs. He had shaved his legs, too, and his stockings covered the darkness that remained. As for makeup, he and the man who helped him had avoided the excess that would have made him look like a man dressed as a woman. Joe had chosen rose-colored lipstick, not red, and an overall foundation that covered the darkness of the whiskers under the skin of his cheeks. He wore a pinkish blush on his cheeks and a slight touch of blue eye shadow.

When they were on the street, Joe opened his shoulder bag, and Bolan surreptitiously slipped in his Browning automatic.

They caught a cab for the Barclay. Bolan found himself not in the least self-conscious walking through the lobby with this figure at his side. Coppolo looked anything but grotesque. A small man, he was able to fit into this role with ease.

JOE ROSSI MAINTAINED a hideaway apartment and two homes—an apartment on East Seventy-second Street and a house in Chappaqua, forty miles out in Westchester County.

His wife and children lived in the house in Chappaqua, where Rossi was known only as a New York businessman with extensive interests in real estate. His neighbors knew that a chauffeur and a houseboy lived in an apartment above the garage. They didn't know that these men carried heavy weapons. They knew that a maid came to the house every morning at eight, just before Mr. Rossi left for the city, and that she drove his children to school each day. They didn't know that this woman, too, carried an automatic in her handbag.

The Chappaqua neighbors didn't guess that the handsome Mrs. Rossi—Roxanne, known as Roxy—had a license to carry a pistol and was almost never without the .25-caliber Baby Browning automatic. Once a Las Vegas showgirl, Roxy was tall, blond, and a fading, though still striking, beauty. She carried off her Ivy League, businessman's-adoring-wife role so well that few of her friends realized she had only a high school education. She was active at St. Joseph's, in the Art League and played a creditable round or two of golf every week when the weather permitted.

In the apartment on Seventy-second Street Joe Rossi kept a twenty-year-old Brazilian girl named Eva Mueller and their two-year-old child, Joey—as Roxy Rossi well knew. Eva was a miniature, twenty-four-years-younger version of Roxy. Though she had almost no formal education, she knew far more about the Rossi Family businesses than Roxy had ever been allowed to know. It was in her blood, as it wasn't in Roxy's, since her father's position in São Paulo wasn't very different from Rossi's in New York. Her father had—to cut the deal to its essence—given her to Rossi when she was sixteen. She had never resented that, never regretted it. He was old enough to be her grandfather and was minimally demanding, and, like a good grandfather, he was generous. She knew enough about business to know that the trust fund he had established for her and her child wasn't dependent on the Rossi Family businesses. She lived in luxury and always would.

Unlike Roxy, Eva never carried a gun. She traveled about the city without a bodyguard. She could. She was anonymous. Also, she understood, as did anyone who might have wanted to kidnap her, that she was expendable. Joe Rossi would surrender nothing important to save his mistress, and all a kidnapper would earn was the undying animosity of the most powerful don in New York.

The apartment that Roxy had never seen was furnished with distinguished works of art by eminent twentieth-century artists. Here Joe Rossi had made no compromises with Roxy's more conventional tastes. Here he displayed what he had collected over the years, which Roxy couldn't appreciate. Maybe Eva couldn't appreciate his art, either, but Eva's tastes made less difference to him; her status in his apartment was different from Roxy's in their house.

The men who came to the apartment for business meetings could not appreciate it, either. Tonight, for example, three men sat at his dining table, in a room dominated by a sort of lopsided bull's-eye done in red-and-blue paint and gold leaf. Their eyes lingered, not on the painting, but on the figure of Eva, proudly displayed in a short, snug-fitting emerald sheath. The tabletop was glass, and they could see her legs almost to her hips.

The youngest of them was ten years older than Joe Rossi. One had been born in Sicily before the First World War. The other two were sons of Sicilian fathers: Lucky DeMaioribus, from Providence, Rhode Island; Peter DiRenzo, from Miami; Vincenti Sestola, from Baltimore—members of the Commission.

The Commission was the governing council of La Cosa Nostra. The members were the dons of the most powerful Families in America. Only four were here tonight—Joe Rossi, too, was a member—but the Commission was an informal body, and only rarely did all the members meet. The four could discuss and decide anything, then secure acquiescence from most of the others, and their decision became the decision of the Commission. The group assembled tonight had come together to discuss the disintegration of the peace in New York.

MACK BOLAN and Joe Coppolo didn't know that the members of the Commission were meeting in Rossi's apartment. They came to look for an opportunity to shake Rossi's cool self-possession. Bolan had insisted that no matter what opportunity they found, they were not going to kill Rossi. Before he attacked Rossi, he wanted more hard evidence of Rossi's complicity in the death of Joan. No, it would be better to shake him, the way he had shaken DePrisco, make him think he was a target, maybe of the killer who had taken out Phil Corone last night, maybe of Angela Corone, maybe of Barbosa or Segesta.

The first problem was how to enter the building. Saul Stein had warned them it was a secure building. Celebrities lived there. The staff was alert to keep away people who might come to annoy them.

Bolan and Coppolo walked east from York Avenue, on Seventy-second Street. The left side of the street was a row of three-and four-story brick apartment buildings. On the right at the end, the target building was a ten-story white stone building. The street ended at a barrier, some fifteen or twenty feet above FDR Drive. At the end you could stand at the barrier and watch the traffic speeding in both directions—and beyond, the traffic on the East River.

"Who you figure is sitting in the black Caddy over there?" Coppolo asked.

"I'd take that for somebody keeping an eye out. I'd guess that since last night, Brother Rossi has gotten a little nervous."

"Which means that you and I get just one approach," Coppolo concluded. "If we walk away and come back, that's suspicious."

"We can stand and look at the river for a couple of minutes."

Coppolo was wearing the second of the two outfits he'd bought that afternoon—a short, tight black skirt, dark stockings, black shoes, a black tank top and a loose white scarf around his shoulders. Once again, his appearance was anything but that of a hard-muscled man dressed as a woman. He didn't look like a hooker, either. To complete the image, he walked arm in arm with Bolan. In his businessman's suit, Bolan looked like a man taking his girlfriend for a walk before he had to leave her, reluctantly, and catch a late train for a home and wife in the suburbs.

"I have a feeling the Caddy isn't the only car with a watchman in it," Bolan said. "There's a BMW across the street with a man in it, too."

"Well, if a don lives in the neighborhood, you can figure he'll be guarded."

"Something odd, though," Bolan stated. "The Caddy's got a Rhode Island license plate."

"Okay. Are we going to try our little gimmick or not?"

"We're going to try it," Bolan replied. "If it works, we're in. If we're in, who cares what hardmen are out here?"

They walked to the apartment building, up the three steps to the wide glass doors and into the lobby.

The uniformed attendant who sat behind a table reading a newspaper looked up. "Yes?"

"Uh, my friend is nauseous," Bolan stammered. "Thinks she might throw up. Do you have a ladies' room available where she could get some cold water and—"

"Buzz out, buddy."

"How long have you been working here?" Bolan asked, feigning indignation. "Is that the way the building management expects you to talk to people? Listen, my friend Joe Rossi lives here, and—"

"Rossi?" the attendant asked skeptically, getting up. "You know Mr. Rossi?"

"Certainly," Bolan said, still playing the businessman outraged by the rudeness of a uniformed lobby man. "And I've never been talked to this way in this building before. You buzz Mr. Rossi. He'll tell you."

"Mr. Rossi isn't here, buddy," said the man who by now had revealed clearly that he was no apartment building lobby attendant.

"I know he is."

"Well, I say he's not," the hardman snarled.

He grabbed at something inside his double-breasted gray jacket. With his attention fastened only on Bolan, without an inkling that the little dark-haired woman might be a threat to him, the hardman was a sucker for the punch Coppolo threw at him. The agent's hard fist caught him on the temple, just forward of the ear and a little above. The hardman crumpled.

In an instant Coppolo was down beside him. He reached inside the double-breasted jacket and pulled out a Smith & Wesson .38.

"We better pull him into the elevator," Coppolo suggested.

Bolan dragged the stunned hardman into the elevator, out of sight from the street. The guy shook his head to clear the fog and began to mumble. Coppolo drove a fist into his nose, bloodying it.

"You're in deep doo-doo, mouthy," he growled into the hardman's face. "So talk. What's goin' on? Where's the real lobby man?"

The hardman cupped his nose in his hands, and blood oozed out between his fingers. "Paid good," he mumbled.

"How many more guys you got in the building?" Bolan asked.

The hardman shook his head. "Nobody. Everybody else is on the street."

"How many?"

"Two. I mean, three. Three. Who the hell are you guys?" He blinked at Coppolo. "My God! You ain' no woman!"

"Why?" Bolan asked. "What's coming down?"

The hardman shook his head. "Nothin'. The guy's scared because of what happened to Corone."

Coppolo slapped him across the nose, which was already beginning to swell and become excruciatingly sensitive.

"So, you guys paid off the regular lobby man—if that's really what you did—and set up inside-and-outside security because Rossi's scared? If he's scared, you lying son of a bitch, he's not just scared tonight. No way. This is something special. So what's special tonight?''

"What's special is that the Commission is meeting upstairs. They'd kill me for telling you...."

Coppolo sneered. "We figured it out for ourselves," he said. "Which floor?"

"Nine."

Bolan was at the controls of the elevator. He ran it up to the top floor, a utility floor above the penthouse. They led the stumbling hardman to the control room for the building's air-conditioning system and bound him securely to a heavy pipe, using the cord from a vacuum cleaner Coppolo found in a nearby service closet. They stuffed the man's mouth full of cleaning rags and tightened more cord around his neck and jaw to hold it in. When they closed the door, even the sound of his grunting was covered by the roar of the air-conditioning equipment.

"Nine, huh?" Coppolo adjusted his wig and checked his makeup. "Ninth floor. The *Commission*, yet!"

EVA HAD SUPERVISED the serving of coffee and brandy by the maid, then she had smiled on the men seated around the dining table and left them to talk business. She looked in on her child and found him sleeping peacefully. From there she went to the master bedroom, where Joe would join her later, and changed into something he would like.

In the dining room, behind closed doors, the four men began to talk earnestly.

"Phil Corone was an expensive man to know," said Miami's Peter DiRenzo. "I sent him two hitters and he lost both of them."

"Barbosa did," Rossi said. "It was Barbosa who sent them to that book."

"Two days later my *consiglière* disappears," DiRenzo continued. "It's got something to do with the same deal. I don't know what."

"The heads of two Families have been killed in a week," DeMaioribus added. "Tell us, Joe—is New York out of control?"

Rossi clasped his hands before his chin. "The death of Philip Corone was no loss," he said. "The death of Carlo Lentini is something else. I have a strong suspicion that Corone arranged the murder of Lentini."

"So, what happens?" Sestola asked. "Who takes over the Corone and the Lentini families?"

"Maybe we should discuss that," Rossi suggested.

WHILE EXPLORING the utility floor, Bolan and Coppolo found a service elevator. A buzzer was sounding in the elevator, so they sent it down. They used the service elevator to descend to the ninth floor.

The elevator doors opened on a service room with access to both the apartments on that floor, whose doors were marked A and B. They had no idea which apartment was Rossi's, but both doors were locked anyway.

They listened at each door and could hear nothing. Coppolo took a serrated tool from his bag and set to work on the lock on the B door.

"So," he grunted after a minute.

He turned the knob and slowly, cautiously opened the door. It opened into the kitchen of the apartment. The room was lighted by a fluorescent fixture under a cabinet and over the sink. The ruby light on the coffee maker showed that the pot of coffee was hot.

Coppolo turned and shrugged. There was no way to tell whether this was the Rossi apartment or somebody else's.

Bolan nodded at the other door, and the Justice agent crossed the service room and went to work on that lock.

The kitchen beyond this door was much like the other. Except the dishwasher was running. The coffee maker was steaming, brewing a pot of coffee. And the air was heavy with cigar smoke.

"The Commission," Bolan whispered to Coppolo. "Probably."

Bolan stepped inside. Three doors opened off the kitchen. A swinging door obviously was the door to the dining room. Beyond another door was a pantry. A third one, closed, probably opened onto a hall so that the kitchen could be entered and exited without passing through the dining room.

Bolan stood close to the swinging door. He could hear conversation, men's voices, one of them gravelly. The Commission.

Coppolo was looking around the kitchen, looking for anything that would prove this apartment was Rossi's. He had found it, an envelope in the trash, when he and Bolan started at the sound of a doorknob turning.

Bolan leaped across the room, grabbing Coppolo, shoving him into the pantry and pushing in behind him. They crouched on the floor.

The door opened. A young woman entered the kitchen, exquisitely beautiful. She was tiny, hardly more than five foot two, blond, and she was dressed in a tight black corselet, high-heeled shiny black shoes and long dark stockings held up with short straps from the corselet. She went to a cabinet, took out a mug and poured herself a mug of coffee. Then she paused for a moment, until, as if on a sudden impulse, she reached for a brandy snifter and the bottle and poured herself a generous drink of brandy.

She moved languidly, in no hurry at all—which was a good thing, for if she had come through the door faster, she would have spotted Bolan and Joe before they could throw themselves into the pantry.

She took a sip of her brandy, then turned up the bottle and replaced that sip. With coffee in one hand and brandy in the other, she left the kitchen.

Coppolo sighed. "I'll never look like that, no matter how hard I try," he whispered.

"Rossi's mistress," Bolan said.

Bolan returned to the dining-room door. Coppolo spotted a wooden wedge apparently used to hold the swinging door open, and he wedged it under the door into the hallway. Both of them stood at the door and listened.

"IF THE LENTINI gambling businesses were fairly divided, it would strengthen the other four Families," Peter DiRenzo said.

"I think Joe might suggest that we shouldn't strengthen all four," Sestola offered, smiling. He sucked smoke from his cigar and blew a heavy gust across the table. Then he reached for wine. "Of course, if there aren't Five Families anymore, then—"

"Then one of the New York Families might become unacceptably strong," DeMaioribus interrupted.

"If you're thinking of my Family," Rossi said, "let me tell you I don't want the Lentini books and loan sharks. I'm interested in very different businesses."

"The Corone Family must have a leader," DeMaioribus growled in his gravelly old voice. "That woman... A woman can't control a Family."

"I'd be willing to see her try," Rossi told him.

"A few months..." Sestola turned down the corners of his mouth and shrugged. "See what happens."

"Then we let the Lentini Family dissolve?" DiRenzo asked. "Their capos—"

"We shouldn't try to tell a man like Carmine Samenza that suddenly he works for another Family," Rossi advised. "Let them bid for him. If he were younger, if he wanted it, I'd say let Samenza take over the Lentini businesses, all of them."

"Ask him again if he wants them, before we give any away," DeMaioribus suggested.

Joe Rossi reached for the brandy bottle. "Actually," he said as he poured, "our biggest problem in New York probably isn't the Corone or Lentini Families. It's Luca Barbosa."

"No." DeMaioribus shook his head firmly. "Your biggest problem in New York is Bolan."

"That name is a rationalization for everything that goes wrong in business," Sestola scoffed.

"Maybe," DeRenzo said, "but what are we doing about it?"

"We have a million-dollar contract out on him," Rossi stated. "We've used our political contacts to get a twenty-man detective force assigned to tracking him down. I've assigned the best hitter I've ever seen to do nothing but find and kill Bolan." He shrugged. "The man is still loose."

"I imagine we have to leave the Bolan problem to you," DiRenzo said. "I don't know what more we could do to help you. He took out the best hitters I had."

"Joe," DeMaioribus said grimly, "who murdered that woman who worked for the Organized Crime Task Force?"

"I have to confess something," Rossi announced. "It was my hitter. She made a mistake. She was trying to take out a woman that Bolan's got some kind of attachment to, to smoke him out and she hit the Warnicke woman when the other woman's boyfriend knocked her down and out of the line of fire."

"A mistake like that!" DeMaioribus protested. "How good can she be?"

"She did the Grieco job. The council of the Five Families agreed that he wasn't the man to take over the Corone Family. Besides, he held Arturo Corone practically a prisoner in his own house and treated him

with total disrespect. Her assignment now is Bolan.
Nothing but Bolan.''

"It was a *big* mistake, Joe," DeMaioribus growled.

"I agree."

"Who is this hitter?" Sestola asked.

"A black woman, from Detroit originally. She's
absolutely cold. I think she'd shoot her own mother if
you paid her enough. She's smart, quiet and she almost never fails. She's done damned good work for
me, for some time. I've trusted her, and she's re-
deemed my trust."

"I would suggest to you that she knows too much,"
DeMaioribus said. "The killing of that lawyer is the
worst thing that's been done in New York for a very
long time. If your involvement becomes known, nobody can save you."

"The Commission will want your ass," DiRenzo
added. "Heat won't be your worst problem."

Rossi blanched. "The, uh, Commission—" he
stuttered.

Lucky DeMaioribus smiled wryly, sucked the smoke
from a cigarette and nodded. "What you have con-
fessed to us, Joe, stays in this room. The other members of the Commission need never know it." He
sighed. "Assuming you take care of it."

"Taking care of it means . . . ?"

"Well, let us hope you succeed in eliminating Mack
Bolan, the legendary Executioner," DeMaioribus said.
"If you achieve that, the world is your oyster, my
friend. In any case, your hitter is dead. However you
do it, Joe—she's dead. She must be dead."

Rossi nodded. "I had meant to get rid of her as soon as she gets Bolan. The million... We can live with that. Salina Beaudreau alive and able to testify... no. I never thought so. Is it your judgment, gentlemen, that she must go, whether she gets Bolan or not?"

"No," Sestola said emphatically. "Nothing is more important than getting Bolan. Anyway, she won't betray you while she's looking at a million for the Bolan job. Let her try. But if you talk to her, tell her it's Bolan, and nothing but Bolan—as you put it yourself. Five minutes after she hits Bolan successfully, this Salina Beaudreau isn't worth a plugged nickel."

"Except to the cops and Feds," DeMaioribus added. "Her testimony would be worth a lot them."

"I'll take care of her, one way or another," Rossi told them glumly.

JOE COPPOLO HAD TAKEN his 9 mm Browning from his shoulder bag. "I guess we know all we need to know," he whispered to Bolan. "Rossi sent the hitter that killed Joan. And in that room are four members of the Commission!"

Bolan shook his head. "What's the point? What did Joan die for? Not to get rid of four big mafiosi, Joe. To break their hold on the construction industry in New York. And more, on the city itself."

"Hey!"

Bolan seized Joe by the arm. "Listen!" he muttered under his breath. "I don't know who those men are, but from the sounds of their voices I'd guess they're old men. Eliminate one and some younger guy jumps in and takes his place. Kill Rossi, somebody picks up where he left off. I didn't come to New York to take out a few big criminals. I came to break their hold on the town.''

"Yeah, but what are you going to do right now?''

"I'm not going to burst into that room and kill everyone. I don't work that way.''

Coppolo let out his breath. "So, what do we do?''

"I want your promise you'll do exactly what I tell you to do.''

He nodded. "You got it.''

"Okay. We've talked about rattling their cage. Suppose the Commission gets the idea that New York is entirely out of control. Like, suppose they find out that Rossi can't even promise them safety in his own apartment. I want to shoot it up in there, but nobody dies.''

Joe Coppolo nodded once more.

"I mean nobody," Bolan emphasized. "This is an apartment building. Slugs will go through the walls. Every shot fired has to be toward the outside wall.'' He gestured to his right.

"I got it.''

"If somebody pulls a gun, that's something else.''

"Okay. Let's do it.''

Bolan kicked the swinging door and jumped to the left, putting himself at an angle to fire toward the outer wall. His first shot, from the unsilenced Beretta, shattered a wine bottle on the dining table and sprayed wine over the four members of the Cosa Nostra governing Commission. Coppolo's first shot, from the barking Browning, plowed into the table, shattering a serving plate, and passed on to explode the plaster under the window behind Lucky DeMaioribus. Bolan fired a 3-shot burst at the chandelier above the table, blowing it to pieces and showering broken glass on the table and the four stunned mafiosi.

DeMaioribus threw himself sideways and to the floor; Sestola sat petrified, just staring at the two men who were firing at the table; Rossi ducked under the table. Only the Miami don, DiRenzo, went for a gun.

Bolan saw that. He took quick but careful aim on DiRenzo's right shoulder and put a 9 mm slug through it.

DiRenzo howled, then groaned and slumped over the table as if mortally wounded.

Coppolo exploded the brandy bottle, then put a slug through the telephone that sat on a credenza behind where Rossi had been sitting.

Women in other rooms—the maid probably, and Rossi's girlfriend—shrieked in shrill terror. A child began to wail.

Bolan and Joe exchanged glances.

The warrior tipped his head toward the door.

Joe Coppolo leveled his Browning on the cowering men under the table and for a moment stood sneering. "Good night, brave gentlemen. We'll see you later, no doubt."

"WE DON'T JUST WALK out of here, you know," Bolan said as they walked toward the service elevator. "In fact I don't think the elevator is a good idea. An elevator can be a trap."

Hiking his tight skirt high to make longer strides possible, Coppolo hurried into the stairwell. They trotted down three or four floors, then stopped.

"Any kind of smarts," Bolan told him, "and they'll have the stairs covered at the bottom."

"Three guns outside, the wise guy said," Joe recalled. "Not enough artillery to cover everything."

"Plus four senior men upstairs. What will they do?"

"I bet Rossi sits tight and does nothing," Coppolo said.

"Probably. But he could have a man or two around somewhere, besides the guys on the street."

Coppolo was taking this moment to push cartridges down into the clip of his Browning. It had a 13-shot clip, but he replaced the cartridges he'd fired just the same. Bolan shoved a new clip into the Beretta.

"Hell of a lot of banging up there," the Justice agent observed. "Somebody in the building has called the cops for sure, which means we've got to get of here pronto."

Bolan screwed the silencer onto the muzzle of the Beretta. He nodded. "Stand back, Joe. I'll go down ahead of you."

Coppolo frowned but said nothing. He took off his high-heeled shoes and stuffed them in his shoulder bag.

Bolan went down quietly.

They saw after a moment that Joe could hang out over the railing on each landing and peer down as Bolan slipped down each flight. They followed that routine—Bolan edging down, staying near the wall,

Coppolo leaning out above, aiming the Browning, watching for anyone who stepped out.

The hardmen from the streets were pros. They-weren't waiting on the ground floor. As Bolan worked his way cautiously down from the fourth to the third, a door suddenly opened at the third-floor level, and a heavyset man stepped out into the stairwell. He spotted Bolan immediately and raised his revolver.

Immediately wasn't soon enough. Bolan was alert and had the Beretta up and ready. It spit silently, and the heavyset man fell back.

Coppolo hurried down, but Bolan raised a hand and stopped him. He wanted to follow the same routine—floor by floor, Joe alert above while he edged down cautiously.

Bolan reached the ground floor. He signaled to his companion to hold back. The door into the foyer was heavy, but the sound of angry voices was clear enough, even if he couldn't understand the words. What was worse, he couldn't be sure who was out there. Police? He wouldn't fire on them. Tenants of the building?

He slipped back up the stairs, halfway to the second floor.

"Lobby's full of people making conversation," he said. "Let's give them reason to go somewhere else."

"By...?"

Bolan nodded at the Browning. He opened the door between the stairwell and the second-floor hall. He pointed down into the stairwell, then at the Browning.

Coppolo got the idea. He loosed three quick shots into the concrete-and-steel stairwell, the bark of the pistol reverberating off the hard walls.

"C'mon!"

Bolan ran down the stairs and out into the foyer. Half a dozen startled men gaped and cowered.

"Police!" he yelled.

Coppolo followed. "Clear the way!" he screamed, in the highest voice he could muster.

"Get an ambulance!" Bolan yelled at the lobby crowd as he and the Justice agent raced out the door. He pointed toward the door to the stairwell. "Wounded man up there!"

They were on the street. The flashing red lights of police cars dominated the scene. One after another, they careered onto Seventy-second Street.

The driver of the Cadillac with the Rhode Island plates stood beside his car, conspicuously terrified by this show of police force. Because they were alert to him, Bolan and Coppolo saw him toss his automatic into a window well.

"Out of here," Joe muttered. He paused to take his high-heeled shoes from his bag and slip them on his feet.

They crossed the street and walked toward York Avenue.

"Hey!"

"Oh, God!" Joe yelled. "Somebody shot somebody in the building! All kinds of shots! Ohh..."

The policeman gaped for a moment at the dark-haired little woman who clung to the tall, hawk-faced man. "Uh, you were where when all this happened?"

"Our friends the Dugans!" Joe feigned weeping. "Fourth floor... Shooting all up and down, above us and below us and all over! Somebody's dead! I *know* somebody's dead!"

"Do me a favor, ma'am—and sir," the officer said. "See the car at the end of the street. Number 434? Stop there and give the lieutenant your names, in case we need to ask you some questions later."

Bolan nodded. "For sure. We'll do that, but I do want to get her out of here."

"Sure," the policeman said sympathetically, frowning at Joe Coppolo and never suspecting he was anything but a frightened woman. "Just take a sec to say hello to the lieutenant."

Bolan nodded again. "Right. And be careful. I think they're still in there, with their guns."

As they rounded the corner and walked south on York Avenue, Bolan pulled his arm out of Joe's grasp. "Want an acting award?" he asked. "I'll nominate you."

CHAPTER FIFTEEN

Bolan ordered breakfast, brought up by room service, and Coppolo waited in the bathroom until the waiter had left the cart. He was wearing pants and a white T-shirt, his own face, and no wig. As he came out of the bathroom and was about to sit down to eat, the telephone rang.

"Hal," he suggested.

"It had better be," Bolan replied, meaning that no one but Hal Brognola was supposed to know where they were.

The call was from Brognola. "I've checked out the name you gave me," he said. "Salina Beaudreau. Absolutely clean. A black female hitter... Negative again. So I ordered a check of murders committed by black women who remain unidentified and presumably at large. There are several of those. Does the name Jésus Domingo mean anything to you?"

"Not to me," Bolan said. "Let me ask Joe." He turned and asked.

"Damn right," Coppolo replied. "Colombian cocaine baron. Reputedly a billionaire. Made a visit to New York in 1987 and... poof! Blown away on the street in front of the Waldorf. A rifle shot from across Park Avenue. Explosive bullet— Hey! Same way Phil Corone got it!"

Bolan spoke to Brognola. "Joe knows the case. He was taken out with an explosive bullet fired from a rifle, the same way Phil Corone was."

"Right. And ask Joe later how many Barbosas and Corones died when the Colombians took their revenge. Those guys play hardball, Striker. Okay. Two witnesses talked about the shot being fired by a tall black woman."

"Interesting."

"I focused the file search on victims tied to organized crime. That brings up the file on the Domingo killing. Two witnesses out of thirty-four. Thirty-two swore to all kinds of things. Two witnesses swore they saw a black woman out on a marquee. One said he saw a rifle. Whoever fired the shot had to be at a window or on a marquee. You couldn't fire across Park Avenue at ground level, through the traffic. Damned fine shooting, in any case."

"A pro."

"Professional enough not to get caught," Brognola said. "Professional enough not to acquire a record."

"And dangerous," Bolan added. "Only she's gotten careless, Hal. I mean, lately. She hit Michael Grieco in view of witnesses. She killed Joan Warnicke in view of witnesses."

"She's getting ready to retire—after she takes out Mack Bolan," Brognola told him. "And she gets around. Now she's working for Rossi."

"She's been working for Rossi all along," Bolan countered. "It fits. The Colombians knew the Rossi Family wasn't into the cocaine trade. They knew the

Corones and Barbosas were—or wanted to be. When Domingo was killed, they went after the Corones and Barbosas. Their revenge weakened those two families. To whose benefit? Rossi's. Rossi killed Domingo, which was smart. And Rossi had Phil Corone killed. Last night they talked about splitting up the Lentini businesses. The Corone Family is in the hands of a woman. Rossi figures he'll take care of her, sooner or later. Luca Barbosa is old. Segesta is a Mustache Pete. Rossi sees himself godfather of New York. Five Families? No more. *One* Family.''

''Do I hear you changing your focus, Striker?''

''No. Rossi makes his chief money by corrupting the construction industry. Some of the others make a lot by corrupting the unions. Either way, it's a multibillion-dollar jackpot for the Five Families. Or the One Family.''

''Your targets?'' Brognola asked crisply.

''Rossi, for sure. He killed Joan.''

''Striker,'' Brognola said quietly. ''Something else is coming down. The Man wants to know when you'll be available to look into something ten times more dangerous than what you're looking at in New York. We've got reports that Colonel Khaddafi and some other crazies are building plants to manufacture chemical-warfare agents for export. Poison gases may become the poor man's A-bombs, and suddenly the world's a lot more dangerous. The Man wants to know when you'll be available to tackle this one.''

Bolan glanced at Joe, who had poured himself a cup of coffee but was otherwise waiting before touching the food.

"Striker?"

"Give me a few more days," he said.

"I don't *give* you anything, big guy. I'm just telling you there are other jobs waiting."

"Less than a week," Bolan said grimly. "Count on it."

JUST AS Bolan was finishing his conversation with Hal Brognola, Luca Barbosa was leaving St. Bonaventure's Church in Riverdale. Don Barbosa was a widower whose children lived in Florida and Texas, and he had attended Mass alone.

He had sat in church without even a bodyguard, secure in a strange, fatalistic sense that no enemy would attack him in God's house, or if he died there he would be translated to heaven, after only a short stay in purgatory, as a reward for his confidence in divine protection. Sins lay heavy on his soul, he knew. Some things a man couldn't confess. But he had considered what he had to pay for, and what he had counterbalanced by good works, and he remained confident that he wouldn't remain forever excluded from heaven.

This morning he had put a hundred dollars in the collection. He put in a hundred from time to time. Not more. Putting in too much aroused suspicions among the priests that a man had much on his conscience. The hundred now and then was a nice balance.

Two good men were alert outside, his driver and a guy recently made, who had proved reliable. As he emerged into the summer sunlight, the new guy stood halfway down the walk. The driver remained in the car.

"Thank you, Father," Barbosa said to the priest who stood by the door.

"Thank *you*, Mr. Barbosa. Your generosity is appreciated."

People nodded at him as he strolled along the walk toward the steps that led down over the terrace to the street. His eyes met those of his bodyguard, who winked. Wink . . . Why did he wink?

The bodyguard's knees buckled and he slipped quietly to the stones of the walk. Luca Barbosa froze with knowledge and fear. Then he felt the first slug drilling into his chest. He opened his mouth to scream, but his throat was full of blood. A second slug hit home, quietly.

A tall woman in a black dress shrieked. She continued to shriek as people ran to Barbosa and knelt over him. The priest ran down the steps of the church. After a minute they realized that Mr. Barbosa hadn't suffered a heart attack but was bleeding from bullet wounds. Then others screamed. They realized another man had fallen. And finally they realized that the woman who had shrieked was gone. Where? No one knew. Just gone.

MARCO NAPOLITANI LIKED to spend his Sunday afternoons at Luciano's, where he would sit at one of the back tables, drink wine and play cards with his friends. He was a Barbosa capo, but he was all but retired. His business had been drugs, all kinds, which he had sold through pushers who worked the streets and reaped a weekly take big enough to make Marco a very rich man. He was out of that business now. Others had muscled in on it. What he did mostly now was lend money. He had a couple of legbreakers to collect for him, and he did all right, without much hassle.

Don Barbosa had called him for a sitdown yesterday afternoon to talk about what had happened to Lentini and Corone. The don thought Bolan was responsible. Bolan—just a name for everything that went wrong. A myth. Like Santa Claus. What was really wrong was that somebody was making war. It was the old story. It happened from time to time.

"Marco."

He looked up from his game of cards. Jackie, one of his breakers, had come in—a reliable young man, invariably well dressed, like a Wall Street broker. He was tossing his head significantly, meaning he had something to say. Napolitani sighed and got up.

Jackie spoke under his breath. "Don Barbosa's been whacked. I got it off the radio."

Marco Napolitani was sixty years old, still a powerful man, but the news of the death of Luca Barbosa staggered him—he gasped. He walked out of Luciano's into the sunshine of a summer afternoon. He stood there, blinking, full of thoughts. He hardly noticed the cab that pulled away from the curb down the street and approached him. He didn't see the shotgun protruding from the rear window, and he didn't hear the blast.

Augie Karas tossed the sawed-off shotgun on the floor of the car and shoved it under the back seat.

"Nice work, man," said the driver, "Sandy Mac" McMahon. "Like you did it every day of your life."

"With the new boss-woman calling the shots, we *may* be doing it every day," Augie said quietly.

NONE OF THE MEMBERS of the Commission had left New York. By noon on Sunday they were again in Joe Rossi's apartment on East Seventy-second Street, ringed around the bullet-shattered table where they'd been sitting last night. DiRenzo's right arm rested in a sling.

Rossi had hurried the three dons to the roof the previous night. They had scrambled down a fire escape on the rear of the building, to a service alley at the rear. They'd been away from Seventy-second Street long before Bolan and Coppolo.

Rossi and Eva had insisted to the police that they'd been dining alone when two men burst into the dining room and started shooting. The maid who had served their dinner confirmed it—there had been no one else in the apartment. The detectives had been skeptical, but half an hour after the first of them arrived, a captain from downtown joined them. After he arrived, the detectives dropped the question of how many people had been at the table. If Mr. Rossi said only two, that was how it was.

Eva knocked on the door, then entered. She told Rossi there was a telephone call for him. The instrument in the dining room had been shattered by a bullet, so he went to the living room to take the call. Then he rejoined the others.

"Gentlemen, I have bad news. Very bad news. Luca Barbosa has been killed."

Peter DiRenzo slammed his fist down on the table, spilling coffee. "New York is out of control!" he yelled.

Lucky DeMaioribus spoke quietly, in the voice ravaged by decades of heavy smoking. "It seems to be true. Lentini, Corone and now Barbosa. Even we, even in your house, aren't safe."

"That was Bolan last night," Rossi said.

"Was it Bolan who killed Barbosa?" Vincenti Sestola asked.

"They say it was a woman."

DeMaioribus frowned. "Your hitter, Joe?"

Rossi shook his head.

The three older men exchanged glances. Then their eyes, hard with accusation, settled on Rossi.

"Lentini, Corone, Barbosa," DeMaioribus said. "I think I would be very cautious if I were Alfredo Segesta."

THE SAME THOUGHT had occurred to Segesta. If it hadn't, it would have been impressed on him by a visitor who arrived at his Staten Island home late in the afternoon.

"Rossi!" Angela Corone spit. "Not Bolan!"

Johnny DePrisco was there, too. He nodded emphatically, agreeing with Angela.

"War," Segesta muttered. "Johnny, call Samenza. He'll have to speak for the Lentinis. And who now speaks for the Barbosa Family? Napolitani?"

"No, not Napolitani," Angela Corone said. "I'm taking over the Barbosa Family."

"Oh? Just like that?"

"With your kind consent, Don Segesta," she murmured with a wry little smile. "And you will take over the Lentini businesses. Samenza will agree to it."

Segesta shrugged. "Who is there to deny us?" he asked.

"Only Rossi."

DePrisco raised his chin high. "And Bolan."

MACK BOLAN and Joe Coppolo sat at a window table in a small, quiet Hungarian restaurant on East Seventy-second Street. Though it was on the corner of York Avenue a block away from the Rossi apartment at the far end of the street, the restaurant afforded them a good view of the traffic that entered the cul-de-sac and had to slow and turn around.

They were unsure of what they could accomplish sitting there. At best, if they had the kind of luck that almost never happened, they might spot Salina Beaudreau. At worst they would snack on savory Hungarian food and sip at a glass of Hungarian wine.

"I know the guy in the light blue Ford," Joe said, nodding toward a man sitting in a car on the opposite side of the street and halfway to the end. "His name's Rocco. Ex-cop. He's on the staff of the Organized Crime Task Force."

"Would he know you if he got a close look at you?"

Joe shook his head. "What do you think? I doubt my mother would know me—God forbid she should see me in this dress. As far as I can tell, the guy's the only stakeout on the street. He'll be taking pictures of everyone who goes in or out of that building."

"There's the Caddy with the Rhode Island plates," Bolan said. "Nobody in it."

"You don't suppose—"

"That the three old men are in the Rossi apartment again? If they are, they've got plenty to talk about."

Radio and television newscasts were full of talk about two more "gangland executions." Luca Barbosa was described in such terms as "reputed mobster" and "Mafia kingpin," while Marco Napolitani was called a "high-ranking mafioso." The broadcasters talked about a gang war erupting in the city.

As they watched, a taxi pulled up in front of the apartment building. The man in the blue Ford stirred himself. He leveled a fat telephoto lens and began shooting film. Two men got out of the cab. One was elaborately deferential to the other, and both of them hurried into the building.

THE NEW ARRIVAL was Gaspare Nicolosi, from Los Angeles, a fifth member of the Commission.

Eva knew who he was. He had visited her father in Brazil. She offered her hand, murmuring, "You do our household great honor, Don Nicolosi."

The white-haired don turned over Eva's hand and kissed her palm—a far more intimate greeting than simply kissing the back of a hand. It was a gesture pregnant with meaning.

The dining-room door swung open, and Joe Rossi came out, arms wide, to embrace the Los Angeles godfather. "Thank God you're here," he whispered. "The others are—" He shook his head grimly. Don Nicolosi would take his meaning from the omitted words. "And thank you for coming so far."

Nicolosi hadn't flown in from Los Angeles. He'd been enjoying the clean, cool air of the Maine coast. Rossi's call had reached him not long after noon, and he had taken a private plane to Boston, then an airline flight to New York.

Don Gaspare Nicolosi was a tall, muscular man. He moved with the self-confidence of an athlete, obviously aware that his was a commanding presence. His hair was thick but white, and his tanned face was deeply lined. At sixty-two he remained the handsome man he had always been. If there was a flaw in his appearance, it was in his hazel eyes, which exuded a threat of ruthless cruelty.

Rossi admired Nicolosi. There weren't five different Families in Los Angeles, only the Nicolosi Family, and Don Gaspare Nicolosi answered to no one.

He walked into the dining room, where his appearance was a surprise to DeMaioribus, Sestola and DiRenzo.

They understood why he had come. Since they had received word of the death of Barbosa and Napolitani, they had been putting severe pressure on Rossi. DeMaioribus had in fact accused him of breaking the peace in New York, of an ambition to take command of the city, and it had been distressing to Rossi to hear his own secret thoughts issue from the mouths of three angry old men. Rossi had somehow thrown a rock on his side of the scales. The Commission had twelve members. By no means were they equal. The Los Angeles don commanded ten times what the Providence don could command. Ten times? Fifty times.

Don Nicolosi sat down at the table. With a quick sweep of his eyes he took notice of the bullet scars. His eyes stopped no longer on DiRenzo's wound.

"New York is in chaos," DeMaioribus stated.

Nicolosi shrugged. "Sometimes we have to shake out a town."

"Never," Peter DiRenzo said firmly, "has all of New York been controlled by one family."

"Los Angeles is controlled by one family," Nicolosi replied. "Chicago, Miami, Boston, Philadelphia. But, anyway, who says New York is to be controlled by one family?"

"The heads of three families are dead," Sestola said soberly.

"Lentini," Nicolosi said. "That's too bad. He was a good man. Phil Corone..." He shrugged. "Which of you will deny it was good riddance? And as for Luca Barbosa, he has for a long time refused to enter the twentieth century. Or its final decades, anyway." Nicolosi paused and frowned. "This woman, Angela Corone. She must be disposed of."

"Don Rossi has the hitter who can do it, I think," DiRenzo sneered.

"The hitter who took out Luca Barbosa and Phil Corone," DeMaioribus muttered.

"But not Don Lentini," Rossi said. "I swear it. And not Marco Napolitani. Somebody else... Bolan."

"If one man," Nicolosi pronounced, "is strong enough to restore the peace, then let him restore it."

"And what of Bolan?" Sestola asked.

Nicolosi settled his cold eyes on Rossi. "Let him solve that problem, too."

A BLUE-AND-WHITE POLICE CAR turned off York Avenue and onto Seventy-second. It cruised slowly down the block, turned at the end and cruised back again.

"The precinct isn't too interested," Joe said. "One car. No stakeout."

"It's a big city to cover," Bolan replied.

Joe shook his head. "That's the Commission meeting in there. They know it, too. They have to know it."

Bolan took the check from the waiter in the little restaurant and counted out the amount, adding a tip. They had sat as long as they could at the window table, and now they stepped out on the street. They walked along slowly, still playing the roles of a businessman and his woman. The scene hadn't changed. At the end of the street they stood for a minute or two and looked down on FDR Drive and the East River.

"Look at the Caddy." Coppolo pointed at the vehicle.

Bolan glanced at the car with the Rhode Island plates. No one had been in it before. Now a man sat behind the wheel, smoking a cigarette and scanning a tabloid newspaper.

A cab turned into the street.

Bolan and the Justice agent walked back along the north side of the street. Another cab turned in.

A man appeared in the door of the apartment building—an old man, shrunken and gray. He stood alone for a moment looking around, and then the man in the Rhode Island Cadillac hurried toward him.

"That figures," said Bolan. "Lucky DeMaioribus, Providence."

Three more men appeared in the doorway. One of them trotted down the steps and spoke to the driver of the first cab. One of the two men at the door was tall, white haired, ominous. "Nicolosi," Bolan tagged him. "Los Angeles."

"The big guns."

"Very big."

Nicolosi snapped his fingers. The man standing by the cab heard the sound—apparently he was alert to it—and trotted back toward the doorway. Nicolosi pointed at the blue Ford halfway up the street, where Rocco held the small camera with the big lens to his face, aiming it at the door of the apartment building. Nicolosi's man strode toward the Ford.

"Uh-oh," Joe grunted.

He grabbed the Browning out of his shoulder bag and shoved it under his jacket. Before Bolan could stop him, he walked across the street toward the Ford.

Nicolosi's man was direct. He opened the door of the Ford and grabbed the camera out of Rocco's hands. Rocco, who was a big enough man to defend himself and his camera, had been so intent on what he saw through his viewfinder that he hadn't noticed the hood approaching. Before he really knew what was happening, his camera was gone, and the man outside the car was smashing it on the sidewalk.

Rocco scrambled out of the car. Nicolosi's man was busy smashing the camera and didn't see the heavy fist driving toward his ear. It hit him, and he staggered back and slumped against the wall of a building. He blinked and shook his head, and then his hand went inside his coat and came out with a stubby revolver in his grip.

Nicolosi's man aimed at Rocco, but a 9 mm slug from Joe Coppolo's Browning flopped him on his back before he could pull the trigger.

On the steps of the apartment building, DeMaioribus's man shoved him roughly inside the lobby, out of danger. Then he ran back out, pistol in hand, and spread his legs to take aim on the little woman who had just blown away Nicolosi's bodyguard. Bolan's shot took him in the upper chest, and he fell to his knees, then toppled down the steps.

Don Gaspare Nicolosi stood almost calmly, analyzing the situation. He identified his adversaries—a tall, dark-haired man, a slight woman, possibly also the cameraman, who maybe wasn't a newspaper photographer after all.

They all talked of Bolan. Maybe this was Bolan— the man across the street, the tall, well-built fellow, a handsome man. For a moment Nicolosi let his eyes meet that man's, and he knew it was Mack Bolan. There he was, The Executioner, the man so widely feared. Nicolosi extended his arms to both sides. He had no weapon. He never carried iron. He let Bolan see that he wasn't going for a pistol, then he nodded and smiled. Faintly.

He wasn't surprised that Bolan didn't return the smile. But he returned the nod.

It was a fine line. Bolan could have leveled the Beretta on Don Gaspare Nicolosi and probably done a major service for humanity. But he had never heard anything of Nicolosi that definitely made him deserving of the death penalty.

For the moment, Bolan and Nicolosi shared an interest—in getting out of there as quickly as possible.

The Los Angeles don wouldn't take one of the taxis. That could identify him as having been at the scene of the shooting. He walked up the middle of the street, between Bolan and Coppolo, keeping his eyes fixed ahead as if he didn't see them.

Coppolo crossed to where Bolan waited for him. He nodded at Nicolosi, and Bolan shook his head. They followed the don up the street. He continued on Seventy-second Street, across York Avenue. They turned north on York.

Ned McGrory, Assistant Police Commissioner, sat over dinner with Councilman James Benoit. Benoit favored Italian food, and the restaurant was in Little Italy.

"Heat! Man, you don't know what heat is!" McGrory complained. "We've got two cars stationed permanently on Seventy-second east of York—I mean, *permanently*. You got any idea who lives in that building, besides Rossi? Prominent people, and they want Rossi arrested, indicted, sent to Attica, something.... Anything to get him out of their building.

The major can't take a nap but they call! The Commissioner... Me. Heat, man. Heat."

The fat, florid politician pushed pasta into his mouth. "There will be no more envelopes from Chickie Asman," he said. "He's out of business. We couldn't save him once that Seventh Avenue job hit the newspapers. There's just so much you can do, you know. Asman Construction couldn't build a chicken coop in the City of New York right now."

"That was Bolan on Seventy-second Street last night and this afternoon."

"Well? What are you guys doing about him?"

McGrory sipped wine. "Everything we *can* do. Every cop in the city is looking for him. But—"

"But? But what?"

"The guy just disappears."

"What about Coppolo?"

"Gone. Disappeared. He's a Fed, and I have a feeling he's been called out of town."

"Well, Bolan's not out of town," Benoit complained through a mouthful of pasta. "He's here, and you guys aren't—"

"There's a limit," McGrory interrupted. "NYPD can't declare war on Bolan and literally put every man on him and nothing else."

"He's destroying us," Benoit said. "There's a war among the Five Families, which I bet you he started."

"I'd shoot the SOB myself," McGrory said, "but I don't even know what he looks like."

Benoit put down his fork and focused his eyes soberly on the assistant commissioner. "Asman Construction is ruined. What happened there can happen to half a dozen others. Lentini is dead, Corone is dead, Barbosa is dead. Every damned thing can dry up, my friend. Every damned thing. I mean, Ned, do you want to live on the salary of an assistant commissioner of police? Do I want to live on the salary of a councilman? The idiot mayor lives on his city salary and pronounces himself happy."

"The damned building inspectors—"

Benoit interrupted. "You see the mayor's speech? He called the inspectors in for a meeting and read the riot act. Talk about living on your salary! They booed him, but he slammed his fist on the podium and ordered them to enforce the damned laws. He promised those guys indictments if they don't enforce every line of the regulations. Guys that've been on the take for thirty years won't accept an envelope."

"They're scared," McGrory said. "Everybody's scared."

ONLY ONE of the Five Families remained untouched—Segesta's.

The Segesta house on Staten Island was modest by comparison, for example, with Rossi's house in Chappaqua. It was old, a red-brick, three-story building surrounded by a brick wall. At the front the house faced a quiet, tree-lined street. Behind, the wall enclosed a half-acre vineyard, and there was land there also for Mama Segesta to grow her small garden of tomatoes and cooking spices. From the terrace at the rear of the house, Segesta and his family had a view of Upper New York Bay, though streets and docks intervened between the house and the salt water.

It was a comfortable house. The neighbors knew that Alfredo Segesta was godfather of one of the Five Families, so they understood why there was almost always a car or two parked on the street, with men inside, watching. Because they had read the newspapers and watched television news, they also understood why more hardmen than usual were evident on the premises.

Segesta was worried. He and Joe Rossi were the only two Family heads left alive. The others . . . ? He had supposed Bolan had hit them. Angela Corone argued it was Rossi. Either way, the situation was dangerous.

He had asked Carmine Samenza to meet with him this evening, and the big man was with him for dinner, speaking painfully slowly because of his stroke but speaking wisely, Segesta thought, with humor to back his points. As Angela had said he would, Samenza raised no objection to transferring his allegiance to the Segesta Family.

John DePrisco had also stayed. Johnny, he supposed, would sleep with Claire tonight. Okay. That was what Claire wanted. So why not? Why not his best young capo for a son-in-law?

Except for the threats of Bolan and Rossi, this would have been a wonderful day. He had a new ally in the powerful Samenza, and maybe his daughter had a man at last. Segesta could have been happy but for Rossi and Bolan. He wondered where they were, when they might make a move.

BOLAN WAS fifty yards away. The street was lighted by lamps hung above the intersections, and he had kept in the shadows of the trunks of big trees as he approached the Segesta house. He'd had to search for the address, but now that he was on the street and on the right block, it was evident which house was Segesta's—the one with two cars parked in front, two cars with hardmen inside.

The wall surrounding the property wasn't very high and wasn't difficult to get over. He wondered whether Segesta employed a security service and whether anyone climbing the wall would set off an alarm.

There was only one way to find out.

The neighbors' shrubs and hedges were an advantage to him. So was their anxious knowledge that something ominous was going on at Don Segesta's house. They kept away from the windows. The neighborhood was, in fact, unnaturally quiet.

Bolan slipped forward in a low crouch. He covered a few yards, stopped to look and listen, then moved forward again.

The Segesta house was lighted, upstairs and down. The don and his men were alert, as they should have been.

On the last lawn before the wall he knelt in the grass, in the shadow of a tall blue spruce, and watched the house for several minutes. Very slowly he approached the brick wall.

He judged that Segesta lived without elaborate security—or had until now, anyway. His neighbors' trees rose above his wall. A man could climb up and look down on the grounds on the other side. A man with a rifle—a woman with a rifle—could climb up and take aim on anyone inside those lighted windows.

Bolan reached the foot of the wall. To the right was the rear of the house, to the left the front. He decided to check the front first to see what the men in the cars were doing. Clinging to the base of the brick wall, he worked his way forward.

The neighbor had planted the foot of the wall with innocent yet sticky shrubs—bayberry and holly. As Bolan worked his way forward, the first drops of a light rain hit him.

Three bulky shapes lay in the grass just ahead of him. The warrior drew the Desert Eagle, released the safety and crawled toward the indistinct shapes.

They were corpses. Bolan knelt over the first body and examined it as best he could in the darkness. He smelled bitter almond. The man had inhaled cyanide gas.

And so had the other ones.

Cyanide gas was a deadly killer. Silent. A single whiff of it killed a man. It left a corpse with a characteristic odor, once smelled, never forgotten—and a characteristic smear of white foam around the mouth.

Three men had died of cyanide poisoning, and their bodies had been dragged along the wall and abandoned.

Don Segesta was under siege and didn't even know it.

MAMA SEGESTA POURED black coffee into two vacuum carafes, then tucked handfuls of anise-flavored cookies into two brown bags.

"Claire," she said to her daughter. "Some coffee and cookies for the boys on the street. Hmm? You take them out. One carafe and one bag for each car. Okay?''

Claire was in a cheerful mood. Johnny was staying, and she expected a repeat of her experience of Friday night, when they had gotten away from the pier and to their private place before Phil Corone was shot. They had spent a glorious night together. They hadn't heard the news about Phil until Johnny had brought her home in the morning.

"Sure, Mama. A snack for the boys outside."

BOLAN HAD REACHED the corner of the wall. He pressed himself into the prickly shrubs and peered at the two cars.

Three men had died here within the past half hour or so. He was cautious.

The hinges of the wrought-iron gate squeaked. A plump young woman had come out of the house. In one hand she carried what looked like a big shopping bag, in the other an open umbrella.

"Hey, Fredo!" she called. "Coffee! Eh?"

The door of the vehicle in front of the gate opened and the woman hurried up to it.

Then she shrieked.

The man who had opened the door leaped out of the car and grabbed her around the throat. Her shopping bag and umbrella fell, and he wrestled her toward the car. The other man had jumped out of the vehicle and had hurried around to open the back door. He threw her roughly into the rear seat and shoved himself in on top of her while she continued to scream.

Bolan was on his feet in an instant. What was happening was pretty obvious.

He heard the starter grind, and the Chevrolet roared. Bolan leveled the Desert Eagle. As the vehicle careered into line to speed west, he fired once at the hood.

The engine grunted and howled, and a plume of water and oil spewed from under it. The huge bullet had cracked the casting, and the pistons were driving out fluids, leaving the engine dry and hot. The Chevrolet traveled no more than twenty yards before the engine locked.

A man bolted from the Toyota parked across the street, pistol in front of him, looking for a target. He tracked the shadows in front of him, but he didn't spot Bolan.

The two men in the Chevrolet scrambled out, leaving the young woman in the back seat.

Bolan took aim on a front wheel of the Toyota. The shot crippled the car, and the mangled wheel collapsed.

Another man got out of the Toyota. Now there were four of them. They knelt and concentrated a wide, destructive fire on the gate in the brick wall, thinking, apparently, that the shots that had immobilized their vehicles had come from there. They walked toward the gate, firing through it and into the house.

The warrior raced across the neighbor's front lawn toward the crippled Chevrolet. He reached it, circled it then opened the back door.

The young woman cowered on the floor, whimpering.

"Come on," he grunted.

She turned her head and looked up into his face, her eyes wide with fear.

"Let's go!"

"You work for my father?" she whispered hoarsely.

"It looks that way," he replied.

Bolan grabbed Claire Segesta by her right arm and pulled her out of the Chevrolet. He knelt with her on the street, on the west side of the car, out of sight of the hardmen who were firing at the gate and at the door of the Segesta house. She was trembling.

"What happened to Fredo?" she muttered.

Fredo, he guessed, was one of the dead men lying along the wall. The four hardmen had sneaked up on the Chevrolet and Toyota and tossed in cyanide bombs. The three Segesta hardmen had died in seconds, and the others had dragged their bodies away, aired out the two cars and taken their places.

Now the firing stopped. The four gunmen had to reload. No gunfire was returned. The house was silent. Lights went out in houses up and down the street. The four hardmen held the street and reloaded without interference.

"*Hey!* Come back here, bitch!"

One of them had seen that Claire was no longer in the Chevrolet. He loosed a shot at the car, shattering the glass in a rear window. He began to double-time it toward the car, his revolver out in front of him.

"It's come with us or go to hell," he growled as he neared the vehicle.

He fired another bullet into the Chevrolet, careless of where the slug might go after it punched through the glass.

Bolan's .44 Magnum round hit the hardman squarely in the chest with enormous force that shattered ribs, lungs, heart and spine and threw the man on his back on the pavement, a shattered, lifeless body.

The other three had watched. For an instant they stood where they were, too terrified to move. Then they ran.

Claire Segesta was on her hands and knees on the street, still trembling. She tried to speak, swallowed, then tried again.

"Who are you?"

Bolan glanced toward the house. Segesta hardmen were venturing out. He decided to move out. He looked down at the woman he had guessed was Segesta's daughter.

"The name's Mack Bolan. Tell your father there's a war on and not to send defenseless women out on the street in the middle of it."

NATALE PLUMERI SAT in Rossi's living room in Westchester. He was one of the very few business associates who had ever seen the inside of the Rossi country home. Roxy Rossi knew who he was and had seen to it that a good dinner was put on the table. She had no idea who the exotic black woman was and still didn't know even after Salina Beaudreau was introduced. She could only guess, and she disliked both of the ideas the woman brought to her mind.

When they had eaten, she went to their master bedroom suite, as Eva did in the apartment in the city.

Eva and her child weren't in the apartment. The neighbors were so hostile that Rossi was considering selling the place and setting Eva up with a suburban home. Right now, Eva and the child were at the Hyatt Regency Hotel in Greenwich, Connecticut. They were under the protection of the Murese Family, and Italo Murese alone knew they were in Connecticut. Murese had consented that Eva should be guarded by two Rossi hardmen, so she was doubly safe.

The house in Chappaqua was surrounded by an invisible army. It was protected, too, by an elaborate system of electronic surveillance. Rossi had retreated to the country after Bolan's two appearances on Seventy-second Street, and he had called on his capos to send him twenty men. They were out there in the dark, under strict orders not to become obvious to the neighbors.

"We understand one another," Rossi said to his visitors. "We are on the verge of undreamed-of success...or a nightmare catastrophe. I promise both of you a full share. Of either." He paused, smiled. Then he spoke directly to Salina. "With success... We have spoken of a million. Five million. Maybe ten."

She was calm in the face of what she very obviously took as a grandiose promise. "First we gotta get Bolan," she said quietly.

"First Angela Corone," Rossi countered.

"No. First Bolan. We've had too many distractions. Bolan, man. We've got to get Bolan."

"I've seen him," Rossi said. "I looked at him face-to-face. I—"

"So have I," she interrupted. "You didn't see a killer in his eyes, did you? Neither did I. But let's not forget his record."

"All of this," Plumeri interjected, "is pointless talk. Bolan isn't going to step out in front of you with a target pinned to his chest. If you want to hit Bolan, you have to draw him to you, set him up in front of your sights."

"Okay," Rossi said crisply. "How?"

"Think," Plumeri urged quietly. "How did you describe him? How did Don Nicolosi describe him? A man with a woman. Hmm? A man accompanied by a dark-haired woman."

"The Mohawk Indian!"

Plumeri nodded. "Find that woman. Take her. Make Bolan come and get her. That brings him into your sights. Hmm? That brings you Bolan."

CHAPTER SIXTEEN

Joe Rossi had never met James Benoit. He thought that politicians were chronically stupid. They were never to be trusted. They could be made to talk.

Usually he didn't want his capos to talk to politicians, either. He liked to have three or four layers between him and the politicos. In this instance he had consented to a sitdown between James Benoit and Natale Plumeri. No matter what, Plumeri would never talk. Plumeri adhered absolutely to the tradition of *omertà*. Unconditionally.

"It is very simple," Plumeri said to Benoit. "The necessity is to effect a hit on Bolan. How can that be done, when none of us know where he is or where he may be going?"

"NYPD—" Benoit began.

Plumeri snorted. "NYPD doesn't know its right shoe from its left. But I have a job for it. I want the Mohawk woman—Gina Claw."

Benoit shrugged.

"Even the famous New York Police Department ought to be able to find a Mohawk Indian woman from out of town. Half the work's done. Who were the Claw family's friends? Didn't they find out all about that when they looked into the murder of her father and grandfather? Who's providing her a place to sleep? Or is she staying in a hotel? If so, which one? A simple job. To be done today."

"Today? Hey—"

"Today," Plumeri repeated. "By five o'clock. It's our best chance to find Bolan, and we want it done now. Now, you understand?"

"I— Hell, man. I don't know."

Natale Plumeri put his hand on Benoit's. It was like the touch of a snake, cold and threatening. "By five o'clock, Benoit." His eyes were like the eyes of a snake, too. "Cash your chits. Get results. *For sure.*"

ROBERTO ORTEGA WAS an honest young cop. He planned to make the NYPD his lifetime career, and he looked forward to the day when he would have enough years in service to qualify for the detective sergeant's examination.

He was entitled to a midshift break. He unclipped the handie-talkie from his belt and advised the dispatcher that he would be off the street for fifteen minutes. Then he walked into Howard Johnson's Motor Hotel and into the coffee shop, where he sat down and ordered coffee and a Danish.

The girl behind the counter called him by name and smiled warmly at him. She was the reason he came to this particular coffee shop. Her name was Maria.

While Maria went to the glass cabinet to select the best cinnamon Danish, Roberto looked around to see who was sitting in the coffee shop.

It was Ortega who spotted Gina Claw. The shift briefing had been to look for a Mohawk Indian woman, good-looking, in her twenties, long black hair, possibly in the company of a blond man. He was not to approach her, but should notify the dispatcher. Surveillance was to be maintained until he was relieved.

Roberto followed orders. He went outside and reported on his handie-talkie. Then he returned to the counter and kept an eye on the woman and the man until, five minutes later, two detectives came in and took over.

The detectives were honest cops. They had looked at photos of Gina Claw and satisfied themselves that the woman in the coffee shop was the same. They reported to their precinct captain that they had the Claw woman under observation.

The captain was an honest cop, but he reported to Assistant Commissioner Ned McGrory.

AT THE SAME TIME that Natale Plumeri was meeting with Councilman James Benoit, Joe Rossi was meeting with Alfredo Segesta. The sitdown, on neutral turf, had been arranged by telephone during the night. It took place in a Holiday Inn in Ridgefield, New Jersey, in the breakfast room, where the two dons sat down alone, intently observed by two Rossi hardmen and two Segesta hardmen at other tables.

Segesta told Rossi about the attempt to kidnap his daughter. He said he didn't think a kidnap had been planned, that it had been a spur-of-the-moment thing by men who had come to hit him if they could and had used Claire as a possible way to get him out of his house. Rossi swore he had nothing to do with it. Segesta said he never suspected Rossi had.

They agreed that they had two problems—Bolan and Angela. They also agreed Bolan was the critical problem; Angela Corone could be taken care of later.

Over that table, over ham and eggs, they formed an alliance—the two remaining godfathers against the gravest threat they had ever faced. At Segesta's suggestion, they also agreed to call on Samenza, to treat him as if he were head of a Family.

Then they began to plan.

GINA AND ERIC HAD LIVED for days at Howard Johnson's. Eric complained every day that their staying in New York was eating up his life's savings and that all they had managed to do was get shot at. Gina watched the news and read the newspapers. She read every detail of the death of Don Luca Barbosa with satisfaction. He was the man who had killed her father.

"Don't you see?" she said to Eric. "It's all falling apart! The whole deal. The Five Families, their domination of the construction business, everything . . ."

"It doesn't have anything to do with us anymore. I mean—"

"Nothing to do with us? Eric! It's Bolan who's doing it all, and he's in New York because I went out into Connecticut and found him. Not to mention that I shot the hitters who came to New Jersey to kill him."

"Yeah. Well, he hasn't even called you."

"He's trying to protect me."

"So'm I. And the way to do that is go back to California."

They'd had this argument twenty times. Gina wouldn't leave New York. She was going to be there for the kill, as she put it. And Mack Bolan would contact her when he thought it was safe.

They had rarely left the hotel during their stay. At first they had eaten only what they ordered from room service. Then they had ventured down to the coffee shop and dining room. And last night they had gone out for dinner.

It had been a celebration party, at least after they heard of the death of Don Barbosa. Also, that death seemed to make New York a little safer for Gina Claw. Surely now the Barbosa Family was fearful and confused, certainly for a little while. With that idea in mind, they decided to go out again tonight.

JOHNNY DEPRISCO WASN'T happy. Taking a direct, personal part in a snatch wasn't his idea of the best way to live a long, comfortable life. Guys who got involved in stuff like this had a way of getting hurt or of getting long sentences to uncomfortable places.

It had been a long time since Alfredo Segesta had reminded him who was don and who was capo, but he'd reminded him this afternoon, in forceful terms.

Johnny was carrying hardware—a Smith & Wesson 9 mm automatic, a little fellow, easily concealed inside a well-tailored jacket, but packing enough power to do just about any job a man had to do. He had no permit for the weapon, and he didn't like carrying it. But Alfredo had issued the order, so he had no choice. The pistol was tucked into the waistband of his slacks, under his left arm, where it wasn't very comfortable, and every few minutes he checked to be sure it wasn't falling out.

Plumeri sat in the lobby of the hotel, reading a newspaper, looking old and feeble. He was old but hardly feeble, as Johnny well understood. The Rossi Family had no *consiglière*, but if Joe had had one, it would have been Plumeri. He, too, was carrying iron, an old-fashioned, snub-nosed, round-grip .38 revolver.

And sitting beside Johnny in his double-parked Maserati was Carmine Samenza.

Two old men, Johnny reflected. Two old men, plus him. The two surviving godfathers had handed this job to their top men, not to bonecrushers. The orders were specific. If the woman and her boyfriend didn't come down from their room, then go in and get them.

ERIC WAS ANNOYED by the amount of time Gina spent in the bathroom. When she came out, he was glad she had taken that time. During the weeks in New York she hadn't been quite the Gina he had fallen in love with. The death of her father and grandfather, the breaking-up of her home and relocating her mother, the experience she'd had with Bolan . . . all that had marked her. She'd become a haggard, harassed young woman. Now, as she came from the bathroom, she was the girl he loved.

Gina wore pink lipstick that had a distinctive suggestion of violet, matched by eye shadow of the same shade. Her shiny black hair was brushed down behind her. Her dress was a black mini, with the skirt six inches or more above her knees.

Fric pulled out a checked jacket. Then they went down in the elevator and out onto the bustling, brightly lighted streets.

They hadn't noticed the austere old man in the black suit, sittin_ behind his newspaper in the lobby. They might have been alarmed if they had seen with what alacrity he had left his chair and rushed toward the door after them.

They didn't recognize the old man as anyone they had ever seen before when he passed them on the sidewalk, walked out fifty feet or so ahead of them, and then began to cough and stagger.

Natale Plumeri stumbled over the curb and collapsed against a car—a red Maserati.

"Hey, can we help you?" Eric asked the old man.

Eric stood agape. The old man he had rushed to help was pointing a revolver at his belly.

Gina looked first at the face, then at the pistol of the handsome man who had gotten out of the beautiful red sports car. It was odd how much he looked like Mack Bolan.

"In the car, kid," Bolan's look-alike ordered.

In the back seat of the car, a third man spoke with pronounced hesitation, as if he had suffered a stroke. "Hands behind your back, Miss Claw," he directed. When she did as ordered, he fastened on a pair of handcuffs.

Eric sat down on the front seat of the Maserati, driven by the threat of the revolver pointed squarely at him. The old man in the black suit bent over him and handcuffed his hands behind his back.

The young man came around and took his place behind the wheel. "See ya later, ol' buddy," he said to the old man.

Natale Plumeri saluted, and Johnny DePrisco pulled away from the curb.

AT ELEVEN O'CLOCK the telephone rang in Bolan's room at the Barclay.

"Belasko."

"Hal."

"What's up?"

"I had a call from a friend of yours this evening," Brognola said grimly. "Gina Claw. She's been kidnapped. And Mack—*Dammit*. She's so scared that she told them she could get a message to you through a friend—me. And she did. I don't know who's got her, and she doesn't know who's got her."

Bolan tipped his head back and blew a deep, loud sigh. "Damn. Do you have any idea where?"

"Hell, no. But I can tell you this—they didn't kidnap Gina because they want Gina. They want you dead, or you lay off. That's what she told me."

"Lay off.... That's what they really want?"

"Not really," Brognola said. "You know better, big guy."

Brognola was silent for a moment. "My guess is that sooner or later you're going to find out where she is, one way or another. And that's the trap. They want you to walk into the trap."

"You put rules on this, Hal?" Bolan asked quietly.

"No rules. Whatever you need. Do it."

Eric Kruger, no New Yorker, had no idea where he was when they pushed him out of the car. He had recognized the big bridge, thought it was the George Washington Bridge, and after that had been wholly lost.

In fact DePrisco had driven up the Palisades Parkway to the Rockleigh exit, then north on Rockland Road and Broadway Avenue to a deserted stretch of road, and there they had let him out. By the time Kruger hiked to a house where they would let him use the telephone, the Maserati had sped on for twenty miles.

DePrisco had driven north a few more miles, crossed the Tappan Zee Bridge into New York and Westchester County, and from there had driven northeast to an airport at Waterford, Connecticut.

The airport at Waterford was unusual. It had an instrument landing system, but there was no control tower. No one monitored approaching and departing flights. After midnight the field was all but deserted. The runway lights could be switched on from the air by setting the radio to the correct frequency and repeatedly pressing the transmit key on the microphone in the cockpit. A small plane could come in almost unnoticed. It could depart unnoticed—particularly if it didn't approach the ramp and the twenty to fifty planes parked there. A score of planes did, every night.

The pilot of the high-winged Cessna that had come in an hour earlier and parked a hundred yards from the ramp saw the lights of the Maserati. He checked the heavy automatic under his jacket, then walked toward the ramp and the parked airplanes. If it was cops . . .

It wasn't. The single security officer on the field sat in his little office and watched a late show on television, as he did every night. Johnny DePrisco walked out on the ramp and identified himself to the pilot. Then he returned to the Maserati and dragged Gina Claw out of the vehicle.

Her hands remained cuffed behind her. They led her across the dimly lighted airport ramp to a telephone booth. There they took off the handcuffs and she made the call she had told them she could make. Brognola.

Then they led her to the Cessna. Under the wing of the plane the pilot strapped her into a straitjacket, which rendered her helpless. He had to have DePrisco's help to boost her into the airplane. When she was seated in the right seat, he bound her legs together with a heavy leather belt. Finally he secured her to the seat with the airplane's seat belt and shoulder strap.

Gina wept.

"Don't need a gag, do you, honey?" the pilot asked. "Aren't gonna yell and make me nervous?"

She shook her head and subdued her sobs.

Five minutes later the runway lights were on for another few minutes—switched by the radio in the Cessna—and the common, forgettable little airplane rushed down the runway and rose into the air.

DePrisco and Samenza watched the blinking lights until the airplane was all but out of sight. Then they returned to the Maserati, and DePrisco headed for New York.

"THE WORD WAS OUT TODAY," Joe Coppolo told Bolan. "I mean, every watch was given the word—find Gina Claw. The official word now is that they had discovered a plot to kidnap her and were trying to set up protection for her."

"You believe that?"

"I would if it came from anywhere but McGrory's office. She's in big trouble, and I think we're going to have a tough decision to make. I have a suggestion."

"Spit it out."

"She's a hostage. So, we take one of our own, then we trade."

Bolan shook his head. "I don't want to work that way. Who you have in mind?"

"I can think of two possibilities. Rossi has a girl-friend and a wife."

"No way," Bolan stated firmly.

"Okay. He has a favorite capo, an old-time mafioso named Plumeri."

"That's more to my liking. Give Alex Campbell a call. Maybe he can give us an address."

PLUMERI LIVED on Woodbine Street, in Brooklyn. Bolan stood across the street, staring at the building he had walked past only a few minutes earlier. The street was quiet. It was odd that an important capo would live without protection, but he hadn't yet detected any.

Coppolo had done the preliminary recon, strolling down the street at a leisurely pace, checking every car.

"Nothing," he pronounced after rejoining the Executioner.

"Okay. I'll move in. Cover me."

Bolan crossed the street, careful not to attract attention by looking too purposeful. He walked up the three stone steps to the door of the modest redbrick apartment building.

It was a typical New York apartment building, with buzz-in doors. The lock could be buzzed open from the third floor—which the bell labels indicated was where "Mr. Plumb" lived—but could not be opened at ground level without a key.

It was exactly what Bolan and Coppolo had expected.

They had come prepared. As an agent of Brognola's Sensitive Operations Group, Joe Coppolo's credentials entitled him to access to federal facilities and matériel. The FBI agent who had ultimately issued to him the equipment he'd demanded in the middle of the night had made a telephone call to Washington before he'd accepted either credentials or authority. That done, he was generous with the Bureau's equipment.

At the rear of the building a fire escape rose to platforms at each of the three floors. It was one of those fire escapes with a bottom ladder that people coming down could lower from ten feet above ground level. Also, obviously, lowering the ladder set off an alarm. Both Joe and Bolan knew how to cope with that.

They stood below the fire escape for a minute or two to see whether anyone had noticed their intrusion into the service area behind the building. No one had. Any sounds back there would more than likely be taken as the prowling of dogs investigating the overflowing garbage cans. The apartments were dark except for the dim glow of night-lights in two of them. No one expected burglars in this modest neighborhood. The only likely burglars would be kids looking for a few bucks to sustain the habit, and they would look for easier pickings than a buzz-in front entrance and alarm-equipped fire escape.

Bolan swung the nylon rope and tossed it. The little hook at the end made a secure purchase on the fire escape. He tested it, then climbed briskly, followed by Coppolo. They reached the first platform easily, without pulling down the ladder or tripping the alarm.

The climb up was easy. They went slowly, pausing every few steps on the grimy, long-disused steps to be sure the faint sounds of their ascent had not wakened anyone.

There were six apartments in the building. From the location of the buttons at the front door, Bolan had judged that 3B was the right-hand apartment on the third floor. He and Joe crawled on the third-floor fire-escape platform, peering in, trying to gain a clue from anything they could see through the window.

"Hsst..."

Bolan responded to Coppolo's signal. The agent pointed through the window of the left-hand apartment, where a night-light burned in the kitchen.

On the countertops, visible in the glow of the night-light, they could see bright-colored cartoon characters imprinted on boxes of sugar-coated cereals, plus little mugs with similar characters. Kids' stuff. Not likely the belongings of a seventy-year-old Mafia capo.

The kitchen in the right-hand apartment was dark. More likely.

The windows on both apartments were protected by steel grilles. Bolan reached through and tapped the glass gently with a fingertip. No alarm went off. He wrapped the muzzle of the Beretta in a knit stocking, thrust it through the grille and tapped harder. No sound. No alarm.

Coppolo was already at work. He opened a paper-wrapped package of sticky, puttylike material and began to shape it around one of the bars. Thermagron. He packed all that the package had contained around that one bar, then began to wrap the sticky stuff and the bar in rounds of tape. Around he went until the Thermagron was sealed in half a dozen layers of tape. Last he pushed the tip of a penknife through the tape and inserted a thin nail in the hole.

He looked at Bolan, who nodded.

Cupping his hands around the flame, the agent touched the fire from a cigarette lighter to the nail he had pushed through the hole in the tape. It was a magnesium needle. In a moment it flared in a hot, white light, then the fire burned in the hole in the tape and ignited the Thermagron. The tape contained the glare, not perfectly, but well enough. The Thermagron—powdered aluminum and chromium oxide principally—burned for half a minute, and when the hot fire puffed out, the steel bar had been melted through and now hung loose.

They repeated the process on two more bars.

Now the glass, which was easy enough. Bolan first attached a large suction cup to the windowpane, then ripped the glass with a cutter. He tapped the cut line until the cut opened, then lifted the glass out. He reached in and unlatched the window.

Still no alarm.

They had been working in near-darkness, so their eyes needed no time to adjust to the darkness once they were inside the kitchen. The apartment was utterly quiet. Not the smallest night-light burned anywhere. The kitchen opened onto a spacious room, apparently a combined living and dining room. On the west wall of the big room, doors opened onto what would probably prove to be a bedroom and bathroom.

They walked through the living-dining room. Light from the street was enough to let them see it was comfortably furnished. A spinet piano rested along the east wall, making Bolan wonder whether they had entered the wrong premises or whether the old mafioso really played. There was a huge television set and an oversized couch. A big glass ashtray on a coffee table overflowed with cigarette and cigar ash.

While Coppolo stood with his Browning at the ready, Bolan quietly opened the door to the bedroom.

"Not home," Coppolo whispered.

Bolan was less cautious with the bathroom door. "Yeah. He's home," he said aloud.

Natale Plumeri lay in his bathtub. Bolan switched on the lights; it made no difference now. The old man had been soaking in his bath. He was naked, and a cigar lay at hand in an ashtray on the lid of the toilet. He'd been shot three or four times. But before that, he'd been worked over viciously. His face was a mangled mess of broken flesh.

"How the hell'd somebody get in?" Coppolo asked.

A horrible thought occurred to Bolan. He rushed into the living room and to the door that opened into the hallway outside the apartment and to the stairs. The door to Apartment 3A stood open.

The family was dead—parents and a child. What had happened was obvious. Plumeri's killers had entered the building by somehow tricking the family in 3A to buzz them in.

THEY RETURNED to the Barclay, convinced that Rossi couldn't have ordered the hit. That left Angela Corone.

"Good morning, sir and madam."

Alex Campbell had gotten into the elevator behind them. They kept quiet until they reached Bolan's room.

"I've got news for you," Campbell said. "The New York State Police picked up a guy last night. I think you're going to want to talk to him, and I'm trying to figure out a way to arrange that, since he's gonna have a twenty-four-hour tail on him."

"Who?" Bolan asked. Tired, he had dropped into a chair and now sat with his legs stretched out before him.

"Eric Kruger. They drove him up the west side of the Hudson and dropped him off. The State Police brought him into Manhattan about two this morning, and a bunch of our guys interrogated him for an hour and a half. He's back where he started from, the Howard Johnson's, with two guys assigned to watch him."

"Watch him?"

"Partly protection. Partly because some people think he may be contacted by a guy named Bolan. We've got a few guys on the job more interested in getting Bolan than in rescuing Gina Claw."

"No idea where she is?"

Campbell shook his head. "No idea. No contact. No nothin'."

"What did they find out?" Coppolo asked. "I mean by interrogating Kruger."

"She was snatched off the street. An old guy collapsed against the fender of a car, and when Kruger and Gina went to help him, he pulled a gun on them. Then the driver of the car shoved another gun in their faces. They got in the car, where there was still another guy. The old man walked away. The other two handcuffed them and drove off."

"Descriptions?"

"The old man was probably Natale Plumeri. The other two descriptions could fit anybody."

"Plumeri's dead," Bolan told him.

"You guys?"

Bolan shook his head. "Dead when we got there. Together with a young family who lived in the next apartment."

"Not reported yet, I don't think," Campbell said. "I— Hell, I can't call it in. Somebody'd have to know how I found out."

"I want to talk to Kruger," Bolan said.

KRUGER PACED HIS ROOM. He couldn't sleep; he hadn't even tried. A dozen times he'd called the number the detective gave him to ask whether there was any word. They'd lost patience with him and asked him not to call, repeating firmly their promise that they'd call as soon as they had even a scrap of information. And no, right now they didn't have a thing. There'd been no word. Not a ransom demand. Nothing.

He guessed they suspected him, some way. He didn't think they believed everything he'd told them. He was angry as well as frantic. Bolan— Damn Bolan! Why didn't he call? Or come? Or did he even know Gina had been kidnapped?

A knock on the door. What the hell? He opened it.

"Hey, I didn't order—"

The woman with the breakfast tray pushed her way past him and into the room. "Shut the door," she said curtly. "I've only got a minute."

"Who the hell . . . ?"

He pulled off his blond wig for a moment, then he put it back on. "Joe Coppolo," he said. He was wearing a waitress uniform. The disguise was perfect.

"Mack wants to see you. So you do like I tell you. Now, listen."

Ten minutes later Eric Kruger walked out on the street. He followed instructions; he didn't look around to see the two detectives who would be following him. A cab was waiting at the curb, the Off Duty sign lit. He opened the door and got in. The cab sped off.

"Jack of all trades," Coppolo announced, looking over his shoulder. He had rid himself of the waitress uniform but was still a woman, now a cabdriver wearing a baseball cap over the blond wig. "Don't look back. They aren't following yet, but they'll try. If I get stuck in traffic, they might catch up."

Coppolo whipped the taxi through traffic as if he'd been driving a New York cab all his life. He drove a circuitous route until he was satisfied that they had shaken the two detectives. Then he headed east, for Third Avenue, where he soon turned the cab over to another driver—Saul Stein.

Bolan was waiting in a rented black Ford. "Talk," he demanded as soon as Kruger was seated beside him. "Every detail."

Kruger repeated his story, everything he had told the NYPD detectives three times over.

"Again."

"Man, I—"

"Again. Every little detail you can possibly remember. What'd they look like? What kind of car did they take you in?"

"The car was a red sports job. A real bomb. Cost fifty thousand bucks if it cost a nickel."

Bolan pulled to the curb half a block farther on. "Joe, go in there and buy a couple of car magazines. We're going to see if we can find a picture of this vehicle."

When Coppolo came out with half a dozen magazines, Bolan dropped them on Kruger's lap and told him to start thumbing through. They drove nowhere in particular, just kept moving, while Kruger searched.

"Okay," he said finally. "Like that. The car looked a lot like that."

Bolan stared for a moment at the picture Kruger was showing him. "Yeah," he said grimly. He turned and spoke to Coppolo in the back seat. "A red Maserati."

THE DOORMAN ON DUTY in the lobby of DePrisco's apartment building presented a small problem. Bolan solved it by having Kruger go in first and offer the man twenty dollars to come outside and help him change a tire. The man accepted eagerly, and while he and Kruger jacked up the rented car and replaced the tire Coppolo had just deflated, Bolan and the Justice agent slipped into the building and took the elevator to the third floor.

Coppolo was dressed as a man now, in a dark brown suit and a straw hat. The Browning rode in the harness under his jacket. Bolan was in a suit, as well, and carried the Beretta in harness, the Desert Eagle in his briefcase.

The next problem was DePrisco's two bodyguards. The first man dropped under a quick, hard shot from Bolan's fist. The second one jerked a gun out of its holster and fell from a shot to the throat from Bolan's silenced Beretta.

Johnny DePrisco was asleep, sprawled across his bed in a pair of red slingshot underpants. Bolan grabbed him by the shoulders and threw him against the wall. As he rose to his knees, shaking his head, wondering what had happened, the warrior wrapped a hard arm around the guy's neck and began to apply pressure.

"Starting to get the idea?" Bolan growled.

DePrisco gasped and moaned, and tried to focus his eyes. "Hey, don't . . ." he muttered. "Wha' th' hell?"

Bolan jammed the muzzle of the Beretta against DePrisco's temple. "Where is she, Johnny?" he asked.

"Who? Where's who?"

"Who do you think, Johnny?" Bolan snarled. "Let's suppose you just tell us where somebody is. Somebody you think we might be interested in."

"You've got just one little chance, DePrisco," Coppolo added. "If we get the girl back alive, you might—you just might—make it. Otherwise . . . Well, you can figure. And we won't let it be easy. I hate animals like you. It won't bother me at all to work on you for a long time."

DePrisco's eyes were wide with fear. He sucked breath and swallowed in a dry mouth. "Cape Cod . . ." he whispered. "Provincetown."

CHAPTER SEVENTEEN

Carmine Samenza telephoned Joe Rossi in Chappaqua a little after noon.

"What word have you got?" he asked gruffly.

"What word? No word. I'm waiting for word."

"I got word. It ain't the word you're waiting for. Somebody blew Plumeri last night. And that ain't all. They came for me, too. It was a mistake. Not only did we get one of the guys, but who he was tells us for sure who sent him."

"Natale...?" Rossi mumbled. He felt genuine shock at the loss of the old capo. "Who? How?"

"Listen to me, Joe," Samenza growled. "We dropped a guy last night. Early this morning, actually. Guess who? Augie Karas. He worked for Arturo Corone, then Phil, now for Angela. No question about it, Angela Corone tried to hit me last night."

"Then who hit Natale? Angela or Bolan?"

"I don't know. But I'll give you a hint. McGrory tells me they worked the old boy over before they killed him."

"To find out where we were sending the Indian girl!"

"Yeah. Why else? So that means one thing," Samenza said. "Plumeri told somebody about his summer house on Cape Cod, and that somebody knows where your Mohawk woman is. Either Angela or Bolan. And either way, you got trouble."

"Segesta—"

"Segesta is holed up out on Staten Island. He's turned that place of his into a fort, called in half his guys to protect him."

"How many men can you send me?" Rossi asked.

"Send where?"

"To Cape Cod."

"Joe, I ain't sendin' nobody to Cape Cod. What I'm gonna do is send some guys to get rid of Angela. This is the end of the Corone Family, Joe. I didn't want war, but if that's what Angela wants, she's got it."

"Carmine, what about Bolan? What about the plan to take Bolan?"

Rossi understood that the brief moment of silence on the line was the time Samenza was taking to shrug.

"Carmine?"

Samenza spoke with cool precision. "Bolan's not my problem, Joe. The way I run my territory, the way Segesta runs his, Bolan would never have come to New York. *You* got Bolan for us—you and Luca Barbosa. So you take care of him. Barbosa might have helped you. But you had him killed. In a way, I don't blame you. Even Phil Corone might have helped you—temporarily, though what he really wanted was your ass. But you whacked him, too. Hey. Bolan's not after me. He's on your case, not mine."

"But, Carmine—"

"I wish you good luck, Joe. And if you want to have any, you better get out to where you got that woman boxed up. It's gonna come down hard out there, Bolan or Angela, and you got no capo on the scene. For once, my boy, you can't be 'Clean' Joe. You're going to have to get your hands dirty on this one."

"You're right, Carmine," Rossi said somberly. "And no hard feelings. I see your point."

"You can't afford to lose, Joe. You're playing for the big pot."

JOE ROSSI and Salina Beaudreau arrived at Westchester County Airport less than half an hour after Samenza's telephone call.

For almost the first time in his life, Rossi was carrying a gun. He didn't know much about guns, and this one had been given to him years ago and had remained hidden in a closet in his home in Chappaqua, wrapped in the shoulder holster in which he now carried it. It was a Government Model .45 Colt and it felt heavy under his left arm. He didn't know how he would handle it if, God forbid, he had to.

Salina was comfortable with her weapons. She knew a great deal more about them, and she had selected for this job the iron she thought would most likely be helpful. The breakdown rifle with scope and explosive ammunition rode snugly in a leather briefcase. For her chief pistol she had chosen a Glock 17, an ugly 9 mm automatic. Ungainly as it was in appearance, it carried sixteen rounds in the clip and one in the chamber, and it was determinedly reliable. She was wearing a black paratrooper's suit that had plenty of pockets for extra ammo, a knife and some other things she might need.

In a holster strapped to her leg, she carried a Baby Browning—just in case. In one of her pockets she had two watertight packages, one containing a hundred thousand dollars in cash, the other containing a forged British passport and twenty-five pounds sterling— also, just in case.

Two Rossi soldiers had gone to the airport ahead of them. They were loading suitcases into the Lear jet as the Rossi Cadillac drove up to the gate at CEO Aviation. The pilots didn't know what was in the suitcases, but Salina did—she had packed them. They contained four Uzis and plenty of extra magazines.

The chartered jet lifted off, climbed, and turned northeast. It was small enough to land on the short, rough runway at Provincetown, and fast enough to be there in half an hour.

BOLAN WATCHED the waters of Great Peconic Bay slipping smoothly under them at what seemed like high speed, but he knew it wasn't. The helicopter was making a hundred ten knots maybe—not much more. Low altitude gave the illusion of high speed. He glanced at Kruger. The young man obviously knew what he was doing. He was a pro helicopter pilot, but he couldn't coax another ten knots out of this little chopper.

Getting their hands on the little ship had taken some doing—a call to Brognola, some calls around Washington *by* Brognola and finally a call from the White

House. With that—half an hour after the process began—the Federal Bureau of Narcotics had reluctantly handed over to Sensitive Operations Group, in the person of Joe Coppolo, one equipped and fueled Bell helicopter without agency markings.

Bolan sat in the right seat, beside Kruger. He had a little helicopter time and could have taken over if an emergency required it. In the two seats behind were Joe Coppolo and Johnny DePrisco.

DePrisco remained terrified. He knew something even Bolan didn't know—that after they had bound up the second bodyguard in DePrisco's apartment and dumped him in a closet, Joe Coppolo had made sure of his keeping quiet by slugging him hard over the head with the barrel of his Browning. Bolan hadn't seen, nor had he heard the sickening crunch, but DePrisco had seen and heard; Coppolo had made sure of that.

Johnny DePrisco, hands cuffed behind his back, squirmed occasionally to relieve the tension on his cramped shoulders but otherwise kept quiet.

SITTING IN THE CABIN of the jet, Joe Rossi had no sense of the feat of airmanship the two charter pilots performed in putting the Lear down on the short, narrow, windswept runway at Provincetown. He and Salina stayed in the jet on the ramp while one of the hardmen went in and called the house. All four passengers sat and waited until the car pulled up beside the airplane. Then they got out with their equipment, and were driven to the house.

Rossi spoke to the two Plumeri soldiers. He told them that Plumeri had been murdered and who had murdered him. "We think she'll probably show up here with some guys. That's why I brought my people with me."

One of the two soldiers was named Malatesta. He was a beefy but hard-muscled man. His eyes kept shifting past Rossi, to Salina Beaudreau. "Who's the broad?" he asked.

Rossi glanced at Salina to be sure she hadn't heard Malatesta and wouldn't hear his reply. "Don't let her hear you be so disrespectful. She'll put your lights out."

Malatesta stared at her for a moment. "Hey, is she the hitter who took care of Grieco? And the lawyer at Kennedy Airport?"

Rossi nodded.

"I'll explain that to O'Brien," Malatesta said, nodding toward the other Plumeri soldier, a young redhead with a pale, freckled face.

Rossi knew he could trust Malatesta. Plumeri had recommended the big, bearish man. But he had warned him about O'Brien, cautioning that he wasn't one hundred percent stable and had a streak of sadism in him.

He knew he could trust Salina, too. He hadn't made up his mind as to what he would have to do about her. The Commission wanted her dead, and probably there was no way to avoid having to dispose of her. For now she was an important gun.

His own two men, the dark, short, saturnine Appiano and the tall, bald cynical Uccello, were completely trustworthy. They expected big rewards from this day's work, and they were ready to take risks to get them.

Rossi looked in on Gina Claw. She sat unhappily on a bed and had been staring out the window when Rossi opened the door. Her appearance was incongruous—stylish black minidress with dark stockings and shiny black shoes, and the chain around her ankle. She looked haggard.

Salina stepped into the doorway beside Rossi.

"You!" Gina shrieked.

"I think she knows me," Salina remarked dryly as she walked away from the door.

Rossi closed the bedroom door and walked out onto the front porch that faced the breakers fifty yards away. The house was half a mile off the highway, reached by driving a sandy track through dunes and thin salt grass. Anyone approaching from any direction would be seen a hundred yards away. The six of them, heavily armed, should be able to fend off whatever Angela Corone might bring.

Bolan... Well, he didn't know. The stories were that when the Executioner attacked, you were in big trouble no matter what you had to use against him.

But it wasn't likely Bolan would show up. He didn't know about this place.

Salina came out and stood beside him. She lit a cigarette. "Beautiful place."

Rossi nodded. "I expect she'll try some trick," he said. "I mean, Angela will say she wants to talk or something like that. Then she'll—"

"Relax. I'll have her in my sights."

KRUGER TOOK OFF AGAIN after refueling on Nantucket Island. He didn't climb above two thousand feet. The little helicopter swept across Nantucket Sound, over a fleet of fishing boats working the fertile fishing grounds south of Monomoy Point. It crossed the Cape beach at South Yarmouth, crossed the Cape in less than five minutes, and flew north over Cape Cod Bay.

"I swear I don't know, guys!" DePrisco whimpered. "I've never been to the place. All I know is what I heard them say, that they'd land her at Provincetown and the place wasn't ten minutes from the airport. And they talked about it being isolated, so nobody'd notice she was there. That's all I know."

Most of the land on the northern hook of Cape Cod was within the Cape Cod National Seashore, so the number of private homes on the beachfront was severely limited. Even so, as the chopper approached Provincetown, Bolan could see a dozen or more possibles.

Isolated, DePrisco had said. Yeah. Some of the houses were isolated, with the breakers crashing in front and low sand dunes rising behind. People walked along the shore, but the houses sat some distance back. They had their privacy all right. Also, they had good views and fields of fire. You couldn't just walk up to one of them.

ANGELA POINTED, and Sandy Mac pulled the Cadillac into a small gasoline station at Truro. She got out of the car and walked into the little office, where an elderly man sat on a stool behind a dusty glass showcase stocked with cigarettes and candy.

"Hi," she said brightly. "Nice day."

The old man appraised the coarse, brassy woman who had come into his station. He noticed the sneering twist of her lips and noticed, too, that her blue jeans were much too tight for her ample hips. He nodded.

"I'm looking for the house of a friend of mine," she said. "Thought you might be able to help me."

"Who?" he asked.

"His name is Natale Plumeri. Man of about seventy. Know him?"

"Guess so. Yeah. Mr. Plumeri."

"Right," Angela said, trying to hide her impatience. "Can you tell me where he lives?"

"Yeah. Prob'ly can. Mr. Plumeri. Umm-hmm. He's not home."

"Yes, he is," she contradicted. "He flew up this time. Landed at Provincetown early this morning."

"Flew, huh? Well... He plannin' on goin' fishin'?"

Angela's eyes narrowed. She suspected a verbal trap. "Maybe. I never knew him to go fishing, though. He fish a lot when he's up here?"

"No. No, can't say he does."

"Anyway, can you tell me where his house is?"

"You go on about a mile," the old man said, pointing north. "There's a sand lane goes off to your left. Can't see the house from the road. No sign. You just have to know which lane it is."

"Well, how can I tell? Is there some kind of landmark?"

The old man pondered for a moment. "Tell you what," he said. "Day before yesterday some tourists tossed a sack of cans and stuff off the side of the road. When I came by this mornin', it was still there. Prob'ly there yet. If not, you'll just have to try a lane or so till you get the right one.''

"ANY OF THOSE HOUSES!" DePrisco complained. "Or maybe none of them. God, how could I know?''

Joe Coppolo held the muzzle of the Browning against DePrisco's crotch.

"Hey, I really don't know!''

Bolan spoke quietly to Kruger. "I don't see any choice but to land and ask.''

"I'll put 'er down on the airport. Less conspicuous.''

Five minutes later the helicopter sat on the edge of the ramp at the Provincetown Airport. A black-and-white police car approached.

"I'll talk to them," Coppolo said, scrambling out of the back seat. "I've got credentials.''

He walked toward the police car, where a man in sunglasses, a straw hat and a tan shirt looked at him suspiciously and spoke into his radio microphone. As the Justice agent walked up to the car he noticed that the badge on the shirt read Chief.

"Hi, Chief," he said. "Joe Coppolo, United States Department of Justice." He pulled out the little leather case containing his badge and the laminated identification card that bore his picture.

The chief of police pulled off the sunglasses and squinted at the ID. "Jack Schriver," he said as he handed the case back. "What can I do for you?''

"I'm looking for a man named Natale Plumeri. Understand he has a house here."

"You aren't going to find him," Chief Schriver said. "He was murdered last night in New York."

"I know. But there's somebody at his house."

"Lots of 'somebodys.' A Lear jet came in here about an hour ago and brought four more."

"Four *more*?"

"Well, there's been a couple of guys in the house since yesterday evening. I've been trying to find out who they are."

Coppolo turned and signaled to Bolan to come over and talk to the policeman.

"Let me introduce Mike Belasko, Chief. He's my boss. He ought to hear what we're saying. So, you figure there's six men out there?"

"Five men and a woman," the chief replied. "A tall black woman."

Bolan nodded, his lips grimly tight. "Figures," he said. "Actually there's almost certainly another woman in the house. A kidnap victim."

"You sure of that?" the chief asked. "What's comin' down?"

"A gang war," Bolan told him. "Natale Plumeri was a very big man in the Rossi crime family in New York. The black woman is an assassin with at least half a dozen murders on her record. The other woman is a hostage. Also, she's pregnant."

"I've got me and one man here," the chief said dubiously. "I'll notify the Massachusetts State Police."

"Do us a favor and don't," Bolan continued. "It's a federal operation. It's going to be damned delicate, getting the hostage out alive. Also, it's important that some degree of confidentiality be maintained."

"Besides which, we don't have time to wait for reinforcements," Coppolo added.

"But there are only two, three, four—"

"Three," Bolan said. "The one in back's a prisoner."

"Want me to take him off your hands?"

"What we'd really like for you to do, Chief Schriver, is to keep people away. Can you get the people out of adjoining houses?"

The chief nodded. "I'll block the highway. I'll send my man down the beach to clear it. Then he can clear two houses that might be in range if there's shooting."

"There's going to be shooting," Bolan promised. "Now. How do we identify the house?"

THE PAPER BAG of roadside litter remained where the old man in the gas station had said it was. Sandy Mac turned the Cadillac into the lane, and the two hardmen in the white Buick followed.

Angela hefted the Uzi submachine gun, trying its weight. She had never fired one, and she regretted their plan, which put the Uzi in the hands of Sandy Mac.

"If the old boy lied to us—" the Irishman began to say. His thought was that Plumeri might have lied to them about how many men he had at this house. His revenge.

"Do you think he was lying?" she asked scornfully. "Are you starting to feel chicken?"

Sandy Mac shook his head.

"We take out two wise guys and the girl belongs to us. It won't take Bolan long to figure out who snatched her, and when he finds out she's dead—"

"He'll take out Rossi for us," Sandy Mac concluded.

He was skeptical of the whole idea, but Angela had made up her mind, and he was in no position to dispute Angela Corone. He wasn't sure she hadn't killed her own brother. He had watched her kill a kid last night, and then Plumeri. She'd sent Augie Karas after Samenza; and, knowing Augie, Samenza was likely dead. Her only failure had been the try on Staten Island, when they'd fouled up the hit on Segesta. It wasn't out of the question that she was going to wind up boss of a hell of a lot of business. Anyway, she had him by the short hairs. A word from her would put him back in the slammer.

As the car rolled and heaved through the soft sand of the lane, the sea was occasionally in view through gaps in the low dunes. Then the roof of the house was visible.

"Step on it a little," Angela demanded.

Sandy Mac pressed the accelerator, and the wheels churned in the sand and whipped up plumes behind the car. Angela put the Uzi down between them, opened her purse and checked her Beretta. As the Cadillac emerged from among the dunes and was in full view of the house, Sandy Mac leaned on the horn.

The door opened, and a bearish man in a golf shirt and slacks stepped out on the porch. It was the back porch, really; the house faced the sea. He hesitated for a moment, frowning, then came down the two wooden steps and walked across the sand toward the Cadillac.

Angela opened the door and got out. "Hi," she said. "You're, uh, Malatesta?"

The big man nodded.

"I'm Angela Corone. Natale sent me. Plan's changed a little. He wanted you to get the new word in person."

Malatesta nodded. "Okay," he said. "You wanna come in?"

"Sure. I guess. Where's O'Brien?"

Malatesta glanced back over his shoulder just as O'Brien came through the screen door and stepped out on the porch.

Angela grinned. Then, as quick as a cat, she threw herself to the side and down on the sand as Sandy Mac thrust the Uzi through the open window of the Cadillac.

The muzzle of the machine pistol was still pointed at the roof of the house, where the short burst he managed to fire ripped away some gingerbread. The bullet that had exploded in his upper chest, just below his throat, dealt him instant death. The Uzi fell to the ground, and "Sandy Mac" McMahon fell back across the seat of the car.

Angela screamed in terror as she snatched open her shoulder bag and clutched at her Beretta. Malatesta had done exactly what she had done—thrown himself to the sand—and was rolling out of the way.

O'Brien reached through an open window and grabbed an Uzi from a table just inside. He stepped to the edge of the porch, spread his legs to steady his aim and loosed a burst that caught Angela in the belly and threw her on her back. He fired another burst that shook her inert body. Then he stepped down from the porch, leveled the Uzi at her head and pumped 9 mm slugs into it until she was unrecognizable.

The two Corone hardmen in the Buick witnessed all this with shock and horror. The one in the passenger seat grabbed another Uzi, but the man behind the wheel had already thrown the Buick in reverse and had it churning backward.

O'Brien shoved another clip into the Uzi. He fired from the hip at the retreating Buick. Slugs ripped through the grille and tore up the radiator. The driver floored the accelerator, and the Buick kept lurching and rolling backward. When the engine locked, the car was out of sight to O'Brien. The two Corone men abandoned it and ran.

NO ONE IN THE HOUSE—and certainly no one in the Corone group—had noticed the helicopter overhead hovering at a thousand feet. But Bolan had watched the firefight through binoculars and knew that Angela Corone was dead. He watched the two men from the Buick scrambling in panic toward the road.

Just before leaving Chief Jack Schriver, they had given him one of the handie-talkies they would use. It operated on a restricted frequency, and the talk was scrambled and unscrambled in circuits. Now Bolan spoke to the chief of the Provincetown police.

"You've got two Mafia types on foot running away from the gunfire you heard. Be careful. They're armed with automatic weapons. If you get them, you can hold them on weapons possession charges. But be careful, Chief."

Chief Schriver was careful. He left his car blocking the road, emergency lights blinking, and climbed a dune, carrying a short automatic shotgun. When the two Corone hardmen came close enough, he let fly two blasts, one near the feet of each man.

Each was hit by pellets that ricocheted up and shredded their shoes and pants, giving them painful, bloody pellet wounds on their feet and legs. They threw their weapons as far as they could and stood with their hands above their heads until the chief handcuffed them together.

"WHAT THE HELL was that?" Rossi asked tensely. He had heard the two shotgun blasts. "Explosions?"

Salina shrugged. "Those wise guys telling us goodbye. A couple of parting shots, as they say."

"Hell of a piece of shooting," Malatesta said to Salina. "Thanks."

Salina nodded. She was disassembling the rifle, replacing it in its case. "I figure we have three to five minutes before the cops come," she said. "Half of Cape Cod must have heard that Uzi. O'Brien is a total idiot."

"Why's the chopper up there?" Appiano asked nervously.

"Tourists," Malatesta replied. "They sell helicopter rides at the airport. The cops out here don't have a chopper."

Rossi glanced at the redheaded hardman, still on the porch, threatening the landscape with his submachine gun. "Granted," he said.

"We've got a corpse lying in the sand, a corpse lying in that Caddy. I don't see how we're going to explain how those parties got dead," Salina said.

"O'Brien!" Rossi yelled. "Pull the body out of the Cadillac. See if that car's drivable. We're going to use it if we can."

"Pull the bodies inside and torch the house," Malatesta directed. "That'll distract the locals for a little while."

"What do we do with the Indian?" Uccello asked.

"We bring her," Rossi said. "She's money in the bank."

KRUGER CIRCLED the Plumeri house, letting Bolan and Coppolo get a good look at it from every angle. Then he swept out over the water and across the hook of Cape Cod, out of sight from the house.

He brought the chopper in very low, no more than fifty feet above the ground, and landed not far from Chief Schriver's car.

They took Johnny DePrisco out of the helicopter and used his handcuffs plus the ones on the Corone hardmen to attach all three of them to a steel-cable guardrail.

Bolan's impulse was to warn the small-town policeman that he had three dangerous men in custody, but on watching the Corone men limp painfully, their legs bleeding from dozens of little flesh wounds, he decided Jack Schriver knew his business.

Beside the helicopter and in view of a few gaping tourists who were stopped by the chief's roadblock, Bolan and Coppolo changed into combat clothes and hooked combat weapons onto their belts. Bolan fastened a flak jacket around his upper body, then pulled on desert-tan combat fatigues and heavy combat boots. The Desert Eagle, with the six-inch .44 Magnum barrel screwed in, hung in a quick-draw holster on his hip. He carried a knife and extra ammo in pouches hung from a web belt.

Coppolo dressed the same and carried the same equipment, except that he stuck with his Browning Hi-Power 9 mm.

Both men carried Heckler & Koch G-11 caseless assault rifles. A very special weapon, the G-11 doesn't fire cartridges in the traditional sense. Its bullets are set into solid blocks of propellant, so when the G-11 fires a round, there is no empty shell-casing to expel. It can fire two thousand rounds per minute. The 4.7 mm slugs travel at such velocity that they can penetrate steel helmets, body armor, or the bodies of light vehicles. The mechanism of the rifle is contained within a seamless plastic casing, so that water, mud or sand are effectively sealed out. It's an ideal weapon for fighting among sand dunes or along a beach.

The aerial recon had given Bolan a thorough knowledge of the terrain around the Plumeri house. Coppolo and Kruger had studied it, too, though not with Bolan's practiced eye.

"How the hell are we gonna do it?" Kruger asked. "I mean, you have the guns to blast them out of there, but Gina's in that house. How—"

"I've been thinking about that," Bolan said.

"Classic hostage situation," Chief Schriver added.

"Not really," Bolan said. "In this one you might make a concession."

"What do they want?" the chief asked.

"A life for a life," Coppolo informed him.

"Joe," Bolan snapped, meaning to cut him off.

Coppolo continued. "They want to trade Gina's life for his."

Chief Schriver shook his head. "You can't make a deal like that," he said. "Guys who take hostages... Weak, cowardly— You can't make deals with them. You give them something they demand, they demand something more. Get back this hostage, they take another one."

"Does that mean we give up on saving Gina?" Kruger asked bitterly.

"No," Bolan said firmly. "Let's get in close and take a look."

"THE CADILLAC'S drivable?" Rossi asked O'Brien.

The gunner nodded. With the help of Appiano, he had just dragged the body of Sandy Mac into the house, where it lay on the living-room floor beside the nearly decapitated corpse of Angela Corone.

"And the Chevy wagon? It's okay? Got gas in it?"

"You got here in it," O'Brien reminded him.

"Right. Okay. You and Appiano take the Cadillac. Get out of here as fast as you can. We'll unchain Gina

Claw, torch the house and be right with you. Now listen. When you get to Barnstable, there's an Irish restaurant right across the road from the big airport. We'll meet you and talk about where we go from there."

O'Brien hesitated for a moment, fixing a skeptical eye on Rossi. He didn't trust guys like this, businessman types, particularly this one, with his tanned face and square jaw. The hardware in his holster didn't make him what O'Brien looked for in a made man.

Even so, he was *capo di capi*, and Plumeri had worked for him. O'Brien had taken orders from Plumeri, and so had indirectly taken them from Rossi, for a long time. This wasn't the time to think about doing anything different.

"I'll drive," O'Brien offered.

Appiano got in on the other side. As he settled himself in the passenger's seat of the Cadillac, wrinkling his nose over the wet blotches of McMahon's blood on the seat and floor, he checked his Uzi. It was ready.

O'Brien wrestled the big Cadillac around in the sand. He hit the accelerator and forced it forward, gaining speed.

Salina stood beside Rossi on the porch, watching the lurching car. "Smart," she said. "If they get out, we can get out."

BOLAN AND COPPOLO WERE walking toward the house and the beach, Bolan on the north side of the road, the Justice agent on the south. Each was off the track in the sand, a little up the dunes. They had passed the

Buick abandoned by the two Corone men and had walked maybe half the distance to the house when the Cadillac roared into sight.

Bolan raised the assault rifle, pressed the optical sight to his eye, aimed at the hood of the Cadillac and loosed a burst. Fifty 4.7 mm slugs ripped through the sheet metal and tore everything off the left side and top of the engine—carburetor, air cleaner, fuel line, wires. They shattered three spark plugs. The big car still rolled forward, growling as it died. A second, shorter burst shredded the left front tire.

Appiano was out before the car stopped. Dropping behind the engine to use it as a shield, he jerked up the Uzi and fired a burst toward Bolan. Then he risked standing for two seconds as he fired a second burst.

Joe Coppolo had never before experienced the power of the H&K G-11. He had Appiano in his sights and pulled the trigger. He was astonished at how a short burst—what he'd *thought* was a short burst— ripped a man's body apart. He was in fact horrified to see bits of the man's flesh sprayed over the Cadillac.

O'Brien threw himself over the seat, into the back. He grabbed his own Uzi, blew out the right rear window with a short burst, and rose on his knees to fire a longer burst at Coppolo.

The agent threw himself onto the sand and rolled down the dune, barely escaping the force of O'Brien's fire, which chopped up sand only inches from his scrambling legs.

Bolan ran down the slope from the other side, G-11 at his hip, firing short bursts. High-velocity slugs whipped through the windshield of the Cadillac, fill-ing the whole interior of the car with a storm of glass. O'Brien was scored with shallow, bloody cuts, including ones across his forehead and eyelids. He screamed, rolled over and fired the Uzi blindly toward Bolan. Bolan cut him apart with one short burst.

"NOW WE KNOW," Rossi said to Salina.

Malatesta and Uccello came up from the cellar, where they had been piling up trash and wood to start a fire. They had found a small can of gasoline—fuel for the outboard motor on a small boat Plumeri had kept in the little garage—and they were ready to pour the gasoline on their heap of kindling.

Malatesta understood what he had heard. "It's in the fan," he said quietly.

"Bolan," Salina said ominously. "Did you hear those bursts? No ordinary guns."

"There's a little boat in the garage," Uccello announced. The tall, bald, almost scholarly-looking man was checking his Beretta as he spoke. "I mean it's a maybe."

"We've still got the advantage here," Rossi said. "Chained up in the bedroom. Say we sit three in the front seat of the Chevy, her between us."

"No," Salina told him. "We walk out. I walk out, with her right ahead of me on a chain. Pistol to the back of her neck. Joe, you and Malatesta come along in the car behind me. If they do drop me, you'll drop her—that's what we yell at them." She looked at Rossi and Malatesta. "You use Uzis to chop up whatever they've got—cars, maybe that helicopter that was flying around a while ago."

"What about me?" Uccello asked.

"You get that boat running. Don't burn any gas trying to torch the house. We're going to need it. There's only one road off this end of the Cape, and they'll have it blocked sooner or later. We'll drive the Chevy south a mile or so, then cut into the first lane to the beach. You'll see us on the beach, and you come in and pick us up."

"Salina—" Rossi tried to interrupt.

"Shut up," she snapped. "What we need is an end run around their roadblock."

"Awful small boat," Uccello said doubtfully.

"Big enough for three," she said. "You and Malatesta walk from the beach. You aren't known. You look like tourists. You take my advice and bury your guns in the sand. Even if you have to show identification, nobody knows who Malatesta and Uccello are. Just a couple guys on a vacation."

"And where do we go in the boat?" Rossi asked.

"To where you can rent a car," Salina replied. "We'll be out on that water with a thousand boats, and who'll know which is us? About fifteen miles will get us away from the north hook. In an hour we can be down where there are three or four highways and ten thousand tourists. We can figure it out from there."

"The Cape's a trap," Rossi warned.

"This house is the trap," she said angrily. "Cape Cod's a big place. But every minute we stand here jawing is a minute lost. Everybody move. Give me the keys to Gina's padlocks."

BOLAN LAY ON HIS BELLY on the last dune before the open sand where the Chevrolet station wagon waited. Coppolo lay on another dune twenty yards away and slightly farther from the house.

"Kruger," Bolan said quietly into his handie-talkie. "What would you guess is the weight of the chopper?"

"Don't have to guess," Kruger replied, his voice a little distorted. "It weighs 2150 pounds empty. We're carrying about two hundred seventy-five pounds of fuel at this point, five pounds of oil, say forty pounds of baggage."

"Plus one hundred sixty pounds of pilot," Bolan said. "Figure twenty-six hundred pounds. Okay. Let's try something to distract them."

UCCELLO TROTTED from the house to the garage, carrying the five-gallon can of gasoline. He had no confidence in the woman's judgment or her plan, and was surprised to see Rossi and Malatesta taking orders from her. But he had no choice as far as he could see. Walk out of here with the Indian girl ahead of them as protection? How did they know the cops out there cared anything about the Indian girl? Launch this boat and run south to a rendezvous on some beach without even knowing where? Then he and Malatesta were to *walk* off Cape Cod? And Rossi and the two women were going to cover fifteen or twenty miles in this little boat? The whole thing was crazy.

But she had two tough arguments—first, Malatesta had told him she'd just as soon kill a man as look at him. Second, nobody had any better ideas.

Just as he opened the garage and again saw the little open boat on its cart, he was startled by a roaring, rustling sound overhead and looked up to see the helicopter. It swept over the top of a dune, barely twenty feet above the low crest, its rotor wash blowing up a blinding storm of sand and dust.

Emilio Uccello knew what came from a chopper—machine-gun fire. He'd seen plenty of that in Vietnam. Plenty. He threw himself inside the garage—maybe out of sight. He hoped he was out of sight.

Malatesta ran out with an Uzi and swung the muzzle up to fire a good long burst at whatever arrogant bastard had brought that chopper in so close. A burst from a different direction cut his legs out from under him. He fell, writhing, watching the blood gush rhythmically. His light began to dim, and he knew he had no more than a minute before it went out.

With his last sight he stared dully at the helicopter. God, it seemed big now! It hovered directly above the roof of the house and it was settling, its skids touching the ridge of the roof.

Uccello had knocked a hole in the back wall of the garage, and he crawled out and began to inch his way on his belly in the sand, toward the beach. The noise of the rotor swinging persistently above him was terrifying.

He heard a crunch and looked up. The chopper was settling down on the roof of the house, crushing it beneath more weight than the old beams and rafters could possibly take.

SALINA KNELT in the bathroom and opened the padlock that secured the chain from Gina's ankle to the vent pipe. She heard the chopper, felt the house shudder under the beat of the rotor and ignored all of it. Rossi was acting the man at last and was running from window to window, loosing bursts from two Uzis, keeping whoever was out there at bay until they could show their hostage and demand a ceasefire.

"Okay, sis," Salina began. "We—"

The house shuddered and filled with the sickening sounds of snapping, splintering lumber. Plaster fell from the bedroom ceiling, some of it directly on Salina's head. She staggered.

Gina threw her chain over Salina's head and jerked it into her throat with all her strength. She lunged against the woman, knocking her against the wall. With both hands, straining every muscle, Gina held the chain tight and pulled it tighter.

This was the woman who had killed Joan, and she was choking and thrashing. The two of them fell. Gina jerked and jerked again, harder, and felt the cartilage tear.

And she felt the life begin to ebb out of Salina Beaudreau. The woman gagged and choked, and the power went out of her arms and legs. Unrelenting, Gina kept the pressure on the chain.

The woman's body relaxed; her urine flowed.

Gina didn't let go. When Joe Rossi stepped into the doorway, Gina still sat with the chain pulled tight. Salina Beaudreau's head lolled to her right. Her body slumped loosely.

"You bitch..." Rossi muttered.

BOLAN HAD DROPPED the G-11. He couldn't fire into the house with Gina still in there. Kruger had lifted the helicopter off the roof a few feet.

"Joe?"

Coppolo's voice came back on the handie-talkie. "Yo."

"Run around to the beach side. Chop the porch up with a couple bursts. Not into the house, though. See if we can make them think we're coming in that way. Let me know when you're ready to fire."

Coppolo raced behind the dunes. As he came to a crest where he could see the seaside porch of the house, he saw a man on the beach, frantically digging. He ignored him. Uccello saw him, quickly covered the hole in which he had buried his pistol, and walked north along the beach as casually as he could.

"Mack?"

"Yeah?"

"Ready."

"Let 'er rip," Bolan directed, already on his feet and sprinting for the house.

Bursts from the Justice agent's G-11 sent showers of splinters into the air. The porch roof, supports shattered, fell with a crash to the porch floor.

Bolan covered the fifty yards of open sand in seconds, jumped on the back porch and kicked the door in.

Gina shrieked. Bolan ran to where he heard her voice, to the door of the bedroom.

Joe Rossi was beating her with the chain. He had already hit her across the face and now was poised to strike again.

Bolan didn't take time to aim carefully, and the .44 Magnum slug from the Desert Eagle caught the godfather of the Rossi Family low in the back. Rossi screamed as he clutched at the exploded lower half of his trunk. He had time enough to know he was dying—and why—before he fell to the floor. Ten seconds later he was dead.

EPILOGUE

Mack Bolan looked back at the City of New York as the airplane lifted off. In the past three weeks he and some other brave people had cut some heads off the many-headed monster that was the Mafia. But how long would it take the monster to grow twice as many?

Carmine Samenza, though reluctant to become a godfather, was in the process of seizing the Corone Family assets.

Alfredo Segesta had decided to take over the businesses of the Lentini Family.

They were dividing up what was left of the Barbosa businesses.

As for the Rossi Family, something very strange was happening. Eva Mueller had friends on the Commission—not only that, she had a husband who appeared as soon as the word came down from Cape Cod that Joe Rossi was dead. He was a Sicilian, a young man with firm ideas about how Family businesses should be run. It looked as if Eva and her husband might take control of what was left of the Rossi Family businesses.

They would settle generously with Roxy Rossi and her children—provided Roxy and the kids quietly accepted what was offered.

The mayor of New York said he was satisfied that building inspectors were doing their jobs properly again, and the NLRB had announced an investigation into corruption of New York construction unions.

And so life went on.

"What good does it all do?" Gina Claw asked Bolan in the airport departure lounge, where she and Eric had gone to see him off. "Do we ever win one?"

"You bet," Bolan had said. "But you can't expect to win and then the fight's over. It doesn't work that way. It never has, and I don't suppose it ever will. The animals are always out there, and you have to fight back, all the time."

"All the time," Eric had repeated.

The warrior turned his eyes away from the window and began to scan a briefing book that had been sent up from Washington. A new danger, a new fight.

All the time.

Illegal nuclear testing in Antarctica sends Phoenix Force Down Under when a maniacal plot threatens global destruction.

SUPER PHOENIX FORCE #3

COLD DEAD

GAR WILSON

The two superpowers suspect one another of illegal nuclear testing in Antarctica when the bodies of two murdered scientists show high levels of radiation in their systems.

It's a crisis situation that leads Phoenix Force to New Zealand, where a madman's growing arsenal of nuclear weapons is destined for sale on the international black market....

Don't miss the riveting confrontation in COLD DEAD when it explodes onto the shelves at your favorite retail outlet in April, or reserve your copy for March shipping by sending your name, address, zip or postal code along with a check or money order for $4.70 (includes 75¢ postage and handling) payable to Gold Eagle Books:

In the U.S.
901 Fuhrmann Blvd.
Box 1325
Buffalo, NY 14269-1325

In Canada
P.O. Box 609
Fort Erie, Ontario
L2A 5X3

Please specify book title with your order.

GOLD EAGLE®

SPF3-1

by GAR WILSON

The battle-hardened five-man commando unit known as Phoenix Force continues its onslaught against the hard realities of global terrorism in an endless crusade for freedom, justice and the rights of the individual. Schooled in guerrilla warfare, equipped with the latest in lethal weapons, Phoenix Force's adventures have made them a legend in their own time. Phoenix Force is the free world's foreign legion!

''Gar Wilson is excellent! Raw action attacks the reader on every page.''
—Don Pendleton

Phoenix Force titles are available wherever paperbacks are sold.

PF-1R

GOLD
EAGLE

PHOENIX FORCE

DON PENDLETON's

MACK BOLAN.

The line between good and evil is a tightrope no man should walk. Unless that man is the Executioner.

TIGHTROPE	$3.95	☐

When top officials of international Intelligence agencies are
murdered, Mack Bolan pits his skill against an alliance of
renegade agents and uncovers a deadly scheme to murder the
U.S. President.

MOVING TARGET	$3.95	☐

America's most powerful corporations are reaping huge profits
by dealing in arms with anyone who can pay the price. Dogged
by assassins, Mack Bolan becomes caught in a power struggle
that might be his last.

FLESH & BLOOD	$3.95	☐

When Asian communities are victimized by predators among
their own—thriving gangs of smugglers, extortionists and
pimps—they turn to Mack Bolan for help.

Total Amount	$ _____
Plus 75¢ Postage	_____.75
Payment enclosed	$ _____

Please send a check or money order payable to Gold Eagle Books.

In the U.S.	In Canada
Gold Eagle Books	Gold Eagle Books
901 Fuhrmann Blvd.	P.O. Box 609
Box 1325	Fort Erie, Ontario
Buffalo, NY 14269-1325	L2A 5X3

Please Print

Name: _____

Address: _____

City: _____

State/Prov: _____

Zip/Postal Code: _____

SMB-3R